The world can't get enough of Miss Seeton

"A **most beguiling** protagonist!"
New York Times

"Miss Seeton gets into wild drama with fine touches of farce . . . This is a **lovely mixture of the funny and the exciting**."
San Francisco Chronicle

"This is not so much black comedy as black-currant comedy . . . **You can't stop reading. Or laughing**."
The Sun

"**Depth of description and lively characters** bring this English village to life."
Publishers Weekly

"Fun to be had with a **full cast of endearingly zany villagers** . . . and the ever gently intuitive Miss Seeton."
Kirkus Reviews

"Miss Seeton is the **most delightfully satisfactory character since Miss Marple**."
Ogden Nash

"**She's a joy!**"
Cleveland Plain Dealer

Hands Up, Miss Seeton

A MISS SEETON MYSTERY

Hamilton Crane

Farrago

This edition published in 2018 by Farrago,
an imprint of Prelude Books Ltd
13 Carrington Road, Richmond, TW10 5AA, United Kingdom

www.farragobooks.com

By arrangement with the Beneficiaries of the Literary
Estate of Heron Carvic

First published by Berkley in 1992

Copyright © Sarah J. Mason 1992

ISBN: 978-1-78842-082-2

Have you read them all?

Treat yourself again to the first Miss Seeton novels—

Picture Miss Seeton
A night at the opera strikes a chord of danger when
Miss Seeton witnesses a murder . . . and paints a portrait
of the killer.

Miss Seeton Draws the Line
Miss Seeton is enlisted by Scotland Yard when her paintings
of a little girl turn the young subject into a model for murder.

Witch Miss Seeton
Double, double, toil and trouble sweep through the village
when Miss Seeton goes undercover . . . to investigate a local
witches' coven!

Turn to the end of this book for a full list of the series,
plus—on the last page—**exclusive access to
the Miss Seeton short story** that started it all.

Chapter 1

"AND NOW," CAME the announcer's voice from the wireless, "it is exactly five minutes to nine, so we'll hand you over to Felton Butler at the London Weather Centre."

Miss Seeton pricked up her ears. Martha Bloomer, busy at the sink, stopped clattering the dishes and paid close attention.

"Good morning," said the meteorologist to his nation-wide audience. Miss Seeton, as she often found herself doing, murmured her own greeting in reply.

"And it *is* a good morning, for most of the country," the crisp accents of Felton Butler assured his listeners as, with an indulgent smile, Martha spared her employer's blushes by turning back to the sink. "Sunny and warm," went on the wireless, "with clear skies and steadily rising temperatures— that's the overall picture, although in the far north they're seeing rather more cloudy conditions, and later on in the day the west will have showers, with stronger winds, which are likely to spread eastwards during the early part of the evening . . ."

Miss Seeton listened carefully to the remainder of the forecast, which discussed the regional variations likely to be experienced throughout the British Isles. The London and South-East areas seemed, according to Felton Butler—and he always sounded so very confident in what he was saying that he inspired confidence in others—to be set to enjoy a fine summer day with a gentle breeze.

"Which will render my little excursion to London so much more pleasant," remarked Miss Seeton, switching off before the wireless could give her the Headline News. Miss Seeton did not want her day's enjoyment dimmed by any thoughts of mayhem or misery, when there was, after all, very little (if anything, indeed) that she could do about them. "Have you noticed, Martha dear, how often Mr. Butler is accurate in his weather predictions? More accurate than most of his colleagues, I should say, and though I am not so foolish as to suppose he works it all out by himself, he does seem to be far more fortunate in what he is given to read by whoever in fact does. Work it out, that is. Not that one can ever be entirely sure, of course, in England, and I shall take it with me, none the less—my umbrella, I mean, though maybe, on reflection, not my best one. One can never be too careful in the tourist season—such crowds—and I would hate it to be broken, or damaged in any way."

"I should think not," said Martha, "upsetting the chief superintendent as it would, him having given it to you, and telling you to keep it for best. You take your second-best, dear, and watch out for them crowds, like you say."

Martha, however, was not thinking so much of damage to the umbrella as the likelihood of its theft. Very few (if any) English gentlewomen protected themselves against the vagaries of the English climate with a brolly whose handle was pure gold—hollow, as Miss Seeton was always careful to point out, because of the weight, but twenty-four carat hallmarked gold nonetheless. Miss Seeton was innocently proud of her prize possession, and innocence, in the more worldly wise opinion of Martha Bloomer, wasn't always a good thing. Yet she hated to disturb Miss Emily's happiness with undue alarms and was therefore careful how she phrased her warning. "Cluttered and crowded, London's sure to be," she agreed, "on a fine day like this, and no place for valuables with visitors about, mark my words."

"And in Plummergen as well, I have little doubt," Miss Seeton reminded her as she finished sweeping crumbs from the table with her neat brass-handled brush, then went to the door to shake out the cloth for the birds. "Visitors, I mean. How pleased everybody seems to be, even though we came only second in the Best Kept Village competition—Mr. Stillman tells me the post office has seen a most gratifying increase in business—or do I mean turnover?" Miss Seeton frowned, her thoughts drifting to pastry. "I suppose the apples will soon be ready for picking . . ."

"Never you mind the apples being ready, it's you that's got to be ready, if you're not to miss your bus," Martha scolded her employer gently, seizing the tablecloth from her dreaming hands and briskly folding it into a rectangle. "Done all your yoga for this morning, have you?" Miss Seeton gave her a grateful smile and nodded. Dear Martha, always so concerned for one's welfare. "Checked the time of the train for the cheap day return ticket?" Miss Seeton's smile grew wider, and she nodded again. "Shopping list?" enquired Mrs. Bloomer, unable to believe that anyone would voluntarily plan a day out in London without visiting Oxford Street or Kensington. Miss Seeton shook her head, still smiling.

"All I intend to do is visit the galleries and take tea in the Corner House," she said. "Perhaps a little visit to Harrods, for art supplies—though I cannot recall there is anything in particular that I need, and then, of course, I would have to carry whatever I purchased home on the train, and before that the Underground, which is always so crowded, and although a taxi would not be ruinously expensive, there is always the trouble of hailing it when one is burdened by awkward bundles. No," mused Miss Seeton, "today I have no real need of a shopping list . . ."

"Time to be on your way," said Martha with a look at the kitchen clock and a gentle push in the small of her employer's back. "Jack Crabbe won't hold his bus for anyone, remember, so you'd best get a move on—but don't you fret about nothing. By tonight this place'll be clean and tidy as you wish, and supper laid, if a cold spread'll be enough, not knowing what time you've planned to get back. Don't you dally any longer, now." And Martha continued to direct Miss Seeton towards the hall table, on which her handbag and hat lay waiting, and the front door beyond. Fastened to the wall beside the table was a row of clips, in each of which an umbrella neatly nestled. Once Miss Seeton had adjusted her distinctive headpiece, it was the work of a moment only to select one of her second-best brollies and hang it by its sensible crook handle over one arm. With her handbag over the other arm, she was ready to depart.

"I can hardly believe I need a hat today," she murmured, gazing up at the cloudless sky. "Mr. Butler sounded so very sure that the weather would stay fine . . ."

"He could be right—but even if he's wrong, you'll be near shelter of one sort or another most of the time, won't you, with shops"—Martha was still unconvinced—"and these blessed galleries of yours, if go to them you must. But you have a lovely day out, dear, doing whatever you feel like, and don't come back until you're good and ready."

She watched the brisk little tweeded figure trot happily down the front path of Sweetbriars and cleared her throat pointedly as Miss Seeton paused by the gate to admire the new fence which Daniel Eggleden, blacksmith to Miss Seeton's Kentish village of Plummergen, had worked in traditional arrowhead pattern to replace the wooden palings burned to ashes last month by an arsonist who had hoped to dispose of the fence, the house, and their owner all together in one nocturnal attack. Miss Seeton's guardian angel having been on night duty at the time, the arsonist was thwarted, while Miss Seeton escaped with nothing worse than a headache. She had planned to replace the palings in any case, as her contribution to the Best Kept Village competition, and first thing next morning popped across The Street, as Plummergen's main thoroughfare is known, to slip a note through the door of the smithy. Dan Eggleden was a quick, reliable, and skilful worker, and Miss Seeton was delighted with the result of his labours. The gate swung merrily on its hinges, and its pattern complemented so well the entire fence—

"You hurry up, Miss Emily, or you'll miss the bus," came the warning voice of Martha Bloomer, and Miss Seeton gave a little guilty start. She turned back once to wave goodbye to the kind friend who so sternly kept her under control, then sighed briefly with pleasure, patted the garden gate shut behind her, and hurried diagonally across The Street in the direction of Crabbe's Garage.

The geography of Plummergen is simple. The Street runs in a gentle curve almost due north and south, with few side roads to distract from its grass-verged width. At the south end it narrows sharply into a lane, which is carried by a bridge over the Royal Military Canal. Down one side of the lane is a row of cottages: in one of these live Martha Bloomer and her husband, Stan, both of whom work for Miss Seeton to a greater or lesser extent: Martha twice a week as cleaner-cum-general-factotum; Stan, in moments spared from his official employment as farm labourer, in Miss Seeton's garden. The wall of this garden runs down the side of the lane opposite the cottages, while Sweetbriars itself faces northwards up The Street. There is a side door set in that mellow brick wall, a door to which Martha and Stan hold a spare key—a door Miss Seeton does not always remember to lock. For the sake of the chickens and their eggs, she does her best not to forget but, as regards her personal security sees no real need . . .

For Miss Seeton, despite all evidence to the contrary—evidence which she appears unable to assimilate—remains convinced that there is nothing remarkable about her. Chief Superintendent Delphick of Scotland Yard, for one, stoutly disagrees with this conviction, yet Miss Seeton maintains that she is no more than one among many such, a retired art teacher, a spinster gentlewoman living peacefully in the depths of the English countryside, where nothing untoward ever happens. Why, Miss Seeton might well argue, should such a person require locks, and bolts, and burglar alarms?

Chief Superintendent Delphick knew the answer to this so well that he had some time back insisted on the installation of the latest alarm system in Sweetbriars, for his own if not Miss Seeton's peace of mind. Yet of such little concern to Miss Seeton was this system that, when it was recently shorted by a bolt of lightning, she took no steps to have it put right, thinking it to be more bother than it was worth. The quiet, conventional life of Plummergen was hardly, to Miss Seeton's mind, the equal for criminal occurrences of such places as, well, Chicago, or even (with a sigh) London.

But to London, this morning, Miss Seeton planned to go. Her little trip was the treat with which she had rewarded herself in celebration of the end of the school term, for, although officially retired, she had been helping out as a supply teacher at the village school during the absence of Miss Maynard, who was at her sick mother's bedside. Mrs. Maynard's operation had not been the success for which everyone had hoped, and her convalescence was taking longer than expected. Miss Seeton had been teaching now for several weeks, and, although fond of the children, found them rather more tiring than in her Hampstead days. She sighed again. Her age, she supposed, although on the whole she enjoyed remarkably good health. The yoga exercises which she had taken up some years ago, for the benefit of her knees, were every bit as good as that inspirational book, *Yoga and Younger Every Day*, had originally claimed . . .

Having come thus far in her musings, Miss Seeton arrived at Crabbe's Garage, which is situated on the eastern side of The Street and about halfway up it, just past Mr. Stillman's post office. From Crabbe's Garage, twice a week, a bus runs into Brettenden, the nearest town, with a main line railway station running into London's Charing Cross. Miss Seeton was in good time to catch today's bus and settled herself in her seat with a pleased smile and a murmured greeting to the driver, young Jack Crabbe, and to her fellow passengers. Most of them, she guessed, would be travelling no farther than Brettenden, which was normally an excellent shopping centre supplying almost every want—but there were times, Miss Seeton acknowledged, when her beloved adopted county could not supply her wants, and today was one. She knew herself to be only a competent artist, but this did not stop her admiring true genius in others: she longed to view great paintings and to enjoy the mental escape they would afford her, for a little while. And perhaps (with a secret smile) she might, after all, visit some of the shops for which London was renowned. She would hunt out a little gift for Martha, who was so good to her—and for Stan as well—and possibly something for poor Mrs. Maynard, not that Miss Seeton had ever met her, but her daughter always spoke of her in such terms that Miss Seeton felt she knew her . . .

A simple programme, Miss Seeton thought. Nothing too strenuous or exciting, nothing to do more than gently ripple the quiet tenor of her normal days . . .

Miss Seeton would have been greatly astonished if it had been explained to her that, before many hours had passed, she would find herself at New Scotland Yard.

Under arrest.

Chapter 2

MISS SEETON'S TRAIN arrived at Charing Cross station only two minutes later than it was officially due, which she saw as a most praiseworthy attempt at keeping to the timetable. So complicated, with all those connections, and printed in such small figures, with arrows crossing and recrossing the columns—it was, she thought, amazing that any train ever reached anywhere on time. As she headed along the platform towards the ticket barrier, she noticed, climbing down from his cab, the driver. She smiled at him.

"Good morning," she called. "Such a very pleasant trip, thank you, and not the least bit bumpy—almost soothing, quite musical, in fact. Diddly dum," said Miss Seeton, and the driver, who had been about to return her smile, looked startled. "Diddly dee," she went on, "diddly dum, diddly dee," and with her umbrella beat out the rhythm of imaginary wheels passing over the joins in imaginary rails. "*Scherzando*," said Miss Seeton, who was fond of music while knowing little about it. "Or do I mean *rubato*?"

"Espresso, most like," suggested the driver with a weak grin and a nod in the direction of the coffee bar. "Up for the day, are you, ducks? Enjoy yourself, then," and was gone before she could unsettle him still further.

Miss Seeton had every intention of enjoying herself. It had been her original plan to spend all day at one gallery or another, studying the pictures, until it was time to come home. But Martha, with her talk of shops, had jogged Miss Seeton's conscience, which was always tender. Memories of her day out in Town would be twice as sweet if they came now to include the pleasure of buying, and later giving, little tokens of affection and gratitude. She owed Martha and Stan so much, and they had made her so welcome—after half-a-dozen years Miss Seeton had not ceased to marvel at this. Martha, that expatriate cockney, would surely appreciate the meaning of the green-and-gold bag in which her present, gift-wrapped as Miss Seeton would insist, was handed to her, fresh from the celebrated Knightsbridge store.

By missing out her intended trip to the Marlborough Fine Art Galleries, and continuing down Piccadilly from the Royal Academy to Green Park Tube, Miss Seeton felt sure she could squeeze in an hour or so wandering around Harrods, hunting for presents. Better to miss out one place completely than to rush round the others, spoiling her enjoyment. She would take just as much time as she had originally planned at the National Gallery and the National Portrait Gallery, and come back another day for the Marlborough pictures.

"Feed the pigeons, miss? Shilling a bag." Miss Seeton, functioning on automatic pilot, now emerged from her happy daydream to find herself safely over the Strand and in the middle of Trafalgar Square, heading north. Through the mass of circling birds, over the tops of the Landseer lions' heads, she could see the beckoning portals of the National Gallery. "Go on, duck, make an old man happy," insisted the little man in the flat tweed cap, holding out a paper bag. "Make the pigeons happy, too. A bob's worth of happiness, guaranteed, and cheap at the price. Would I lie to you?"

"I'm sure you would not," Miss Seeton replied with one of her kindest smiles. Really, the pigeons in their wheeling flight did look so charming—not exactly graceful, but vigorous, streamlined, a pleasure to watch—yet exhausting to watch, as well. What a great deal of energy they must expend in their perpetual motion! "A shilling, you say? Five new pence? Then I will take," decided Miss Seeton, "two bags, please." And she handed over four sixpences, as she still could not help thinking of them (two-and-a-half new pence now, she reflected rather sadly) and received in exchange two of the paper bags.

The little man tipped his cap, winked once in farewell, and turned his attentions to a small crowd of bystanders who wore cameras round their necks and were obviously all set to take one another's photographs. The tourist season was well under way. "Feed the pigeons, ladies and gents? Bob a bag, to you that's five new pence . . ."

Miss Seeton smiled and moved away. She did not wish to spoil his—pitch, was it? Strange, when there was no blade of grass anywhere in sight. Football pitch, cricket field, tennis court—all of them green, not grey with concrete and stone. But why *pitch* in any case? Why not, for instance, *court*? Why would one not say that the little man was courting his customers? It would make just as much sense as . . .

"Barking," said Miss Seeton, pleased at recollecting the correct term for crying one's wares. A nearby mother with three small children eyed her warily, then beckoned them all away from this madwoman who evidently supposed that pigeons made the same noise as dogs.

Oblivious to stares, Miss Seeton broadcast pigeon food with a lavish hand, trying to coax the birds ever nearer to her neatly shod feet. The sun cast her shadow sharp against the great flagstones, and as the pigeons darted in and out of darkness, their feathers glistened, and were dulled, then glistened again. Bright black eyes blinked up at her, and beaks pecked busily as little clawed feet scuttered across the hard ground. The ground, Miss Seeton noticed, which was speckled with white . . .

"Oh, dear." Another white speckle had deposited itself with a splat rather close to Miss Seeton's left foot. "How very, well, messy, although of course the birds could not be expected to understand—but there is no food left now," she told them, emptying the paper bags briskly in front of her. She frowned up at the crowds of birds overhead, outlined against the summer-blue sky, and with a skilful eye estimated the distance to the safety of the National Gallery. She shook her head thoughtfully. Then she smiled.

Oblivious once more to stares, Miss Seeton, her umbrella open above her cockscomb hat, trotted away from the pigeons across the broad flagged expanse of Trafalgar Square. There was no hint of a cloud in the sky. It was assumed by charitable persons that she was suffering from heatstroke and using the brolly as a parasol. The pigeons, realising they were beaten, turned their attentions elsewhere.

After her intense exposure to artistic genius in the halls of the National Gallery, Miss Seeton grew conscious of a need for some fresh air. When she emerged through the main door to hover on the steps, she noticed that the sky wore a slightly hazy aspect, and the shadows cast by the sun were perhaps not quite as sharp as before. Her head felt very slightly woozy.

Might it be that, despite Felton Butler's forecast, there was thunder in the air?

As an hour later she came out of the National Portrait Gallery and set off for Orange Street, she was sure of it. There were dark, grey, looming clouds in the sky, clouds which did not drift in a breeze but were whipped along by speedy winds. Anxious tourist faces frowned and gazed about them in search, Miss Seeton thought, of shops selling raincoats or (she nodded in approval) umbrellas. She gripped her own umbrella handle in a firm clasp, tucked her bag under her arm, and headed in the direction of the Haymarket.

As she turned the corner out of Orange Street, the winds arrived at ground level. And with them came the rain, sharp spears of sudden wetness flung first from one direction, then the other. Miss Seeton struggled to put up her brolly, dropping her handbag and groping for it through the blinding lashes of the storm, feeling moisture soak straight through her outer garments in a most uncomfortable way. Her shoes splashed into the puddles which formed almost at once on the pavement. She dropped her handbag again as she continued to struggle with her umbrella and uttered a little cry of vexation which was snatched away by the wind and drowned in a tumult of raindrops.

Her umbrella safely up, and her handbag retrieved for the second time, Miss Seeton found herself being forced in staggering steps by the wind along Haymarket, and paused on the corner of Panton Street to catch her breath before heading for the safety of Piccadilly Circus and the Underground. Gasping, she realised she must leave Burlington House for another day, and instead go straight to Harrods, by Tube. The station could only be a matter of yards away now . . .

Then, without warning, the fickle wind came racing round the corner of the street, fast and strong and vicious. With a gusty roar it wrenched Miss Seeton's umbrella completely inside-out, almost tearing it from her hands.

She barely had time to bless her own foresight in always insisting upon a crook handle—so much easier to hold on to than a strap, or one of those knobs that dug so cruelly into the palms of one's hands—before she was buffeted by the storm right across Panton Street. There came a rumble of thunder overhead: she had been too busy to notice the flash of lightning which must have preceded it.

"Oh, dear," gasped Miss Seeton, peering wistfully through the lashing rain in the direction of Piccadilly Circus. She could hardly, she knew, get much wetter, but it was so very unpleasant to have the breath driven from one's body in such a very blusterous fashion, and there was her umbrella to set to rights, as well. She must take shelter until the storm had passed and she could gather her scattered wits.

She glanced at the building against whose wall the wind had blown her, and which afforded her a very little shelter. Across the top of the door, in discreet lettering outlined in dull gold, were the words *Van Meegeren Gallery*. With a sigh of relief, Miss Seeton smiled. She would recover herself in congenial surroundings, after all. She shook rain from her umbrella as best she could, and in the doorway paused to wrestle with the spokes—how fortunate that the fabric was not torn—before, having turned the umbrella the right way round, she was able to furl it safely and hook it in its accustomed place over her arm.

The Van Meegeren Gallery was a new discovery for Miss Seeton. She could not remember what had been on the site previously, and the whole ambience was so subdued that the place could indeed have been there for years without her noticing it. It was lucky, thought Miss Seeton, that in her hour of need—if this was not too dramatic a phrase for her little mishap—she had happened upon so congenial a refuge.

And so amusing, too. Having accepted a catalogue from the aesthetic young man at the entrance, Miss Seeton moved from picture to picture, nodding to herself and from time to time frowning, as her progress along the carpeted floor was marked by large drips of water; from time to time smiling, as particular paintings caught her eye. The yellow stickers in the top left-hand corner of many seemed to make it all the more amusing, and by the time she had made her way right round the entire display, she was chuckling to herself and had entirely forgotten her dampness and discomfort. Indeed, so thick were the carpets in the Van Meegeren Gallery that her shoes no longer squelched as she made her way out, and the subtleness of the air-conditioning had dried her clothes without her noticing.

"Sunshine!" exclaimed Miss Seeton with pleasure as she emerged from the heavy double doors of the gallery into the Haymarket once more. The wind had dropped, the clouds had disappeared, and little puffs of steam rose from the drying pavements in lazy greeting to the tourists, who were out in force again. Miss Seeton stood and admired the bustle of a summery London day, smiling with pleasure.

"Oh, dear. Oh, no! How dreadful!" Her smile turned to a look of horror as she suddenly saw a man, a businessman, if his smart suit did not mislead, stagger amidst the bustle, almost as if someone had deliberately bumped into him. Miss Seeton caught her breath. Bumped into—or, or (she could barely bring herself to put the dreadful thought into words) stabbed? There was a sudden, horrifying red stain spreading across the man's pinstripe back . . .

And Miss Seeton, wildly waving her umbrella to clear a path before her, with an instinctive cry of warning rushed through the sight-seeing crowds to the rescue.

Chapter 3

"Excuse me—that poor man, I really must . . ." Miss Seeton, panting, pushed her way across the pavement to where the man with bloodstains down his back was talking with (she was thankful to see) another man, younger, who looked, to her relief, as if he knew exactly what he was doing. Now she would not have to render first aid—her knowledge was so shaky, and limited to basic girlish requirements from school—by herself until the ambulance came. Had someone, she wondered as she reached the pair, summoned the ambulance? Probably not, as yet—everything had happened rather fast. Perhaps, as this other gentleman seemed so sure of himself, and appeared well able to take care of the poor man with the reddening jacket, dialling nine-nine-nine could be her own contribution to the emergency . . .

"Oh, dear, are you all right?" Even as she spoke, she knew how flustered and foolish she sounded: it didn't need the surprised looks on the two male faces turned towards her to remind her that anyone with a massive bloodstain on his back could hardly be all right.

"I mean," she said, gripping her umbrella tightly with both hands, as if for moral support, "that is to say, should I call an ambulance?"

"I don't need an ambulance," said the bloodstained man at once. "I've been trying to tell him"—with a jerk of his head towards the other man, who held him firmly by the arm—"there's nothing wrong with me, but—"

"But," broke in the other man loudly, "you've been in the wars right enough, chum, believe me. This lady," and he shot a far from friendly look at Miss Seeton, though he was careful not to let the first man see it, "she'll tell you, if you ask her—a nasty accident you've had round the back, make no mistake. You slip your jacket off and take a look, then you'll see why we were so worried about you."

"I feel perfectly well, thank you. There is no need for you to start stripping me naked"—he scowled and tried to pull his arm from the other man's grasp—"in the middle of the street, for heaven's sake."

"Delayed shock," the young man explained, ostensibly to Miss Seeton but with a wary eye on the first man's re-action to this idea. "Often gets people like that—ask any copper and they'll say the same—folks come shooting through the windscreen with their faces all over blood, but just you try telling 'em they've forgot to wear their seat belts!"

"I haven't," snapped the first man, "been in a car crash—I'm not foolhardy enough to drive in London."

"Lost his memory," said the young man to Miss Seeton. "Come on, chum, let's take a look." He began to drag at the lapel and sleeve of the arm he was still holding.

"Kindly stop that at once!" The first man tried to shake him off. "I insist that you leave me alone!"

"Oh, but really," broke in Miss Seeton, "there is such a very great deal of"—she gulped—"blood down the back of your jacket—I'm sure this kind gentleman is trying to do his best for you—and let me help you, too." She tucked her umbrella under her arm so that with both hands she could support the bloodstained man, who by now was struggling with the other man most energetically. The frenzy, thought Miss Seeton, of incipient delirium, and she seized the man even more firmly. "Do take care!" she cried to the young man, as with a strong pull he managed to slip the first man's jacket down over one shoulder. "Please—you'll hurt him—"

"Ugh!" The end of Miss Seeton's umbrella caught the first man in the midriff. At once all the fight went out of him as he sagged, winded, to the ground. There came a sound of tearing as the other man failed to release his grip on the jacket.

"Oof!" The handle of Miss Seeton's umbrella caught the young man in a delicate place as she bent with anxious haste to assist the writhing figure of the first man, who groaned and gasped on the pavement. He could not, in all honesty, now deny that there was something wrong with him: his eyes bulged, his mouth gaped, and his face was turning purple.

"You poor man, let me—oh dear, do try to keep still, you will hurt yourself even more badly . . ." Miss Seeton had no thought now in her head beyond the man, plum-faced and breathless, on the pavement. He, in his misery, had no thought of anything except the pain in his diaphragm as he struggled for air while, at the same time, fighting off the well-meaning ministrations of Miss Seeton.

Neither of them noticed the departure, slightly hobbling but speedy, of the young man. The interested little crowd of spectators which had gathered to watch the excitement let him pass without hindrance. One or two wags made such comments as, "Nearly scuppered your chances, didn't she?" or, "What price the bachelor life now, mate!" as the man, hands clasped protectively above his groin, with tears of pain in his eyes, disappeared in the direction of Piccadilly Circus. He shook off all offers of help, looking embarrassed at what had happened; and was soon forgotten.

The little tableau was almost at an end. As the man on the pavement regained his breath and his powers of speech, he began clambering to his feet. Miss Seeton tried to help him but was curtly brushed aside. "Anybody," snarled the man, still gasping, "but you!"

But now that no one seemed to be dead, or dying, and the excitement was over, there was nobody left to help him up except Miss Seeton, who alone of all the earlier crowd about him remained at hand. "Are you quite sure?" she said as he made a second attempt to rise, ignoring the umbrella which she held out to him for support, begging him to make use of it as a walking stick. Miss Seeton decided that her hearing—which was, she had previously thought, in rather good condition for her age—must be fading at last. Surely this gentleman, so smartly dressed, could never really have said what she thought she heard him say as he pushed her umbrella aside? Unless it was, of course . . .

"Delayed shock," she decided, nodding to herself. There was an expression of baffled fury on the man's face.

"I am not in shock. I have not been in an accident. Your good intentions are not appreciated one iota, my good woman. Let me assure you that I am perfectly capable . . ."

He had, as he spoke, been trying to tidy his appearance, straightening his tie and his jacket. But his voice trailed off into silence as he heard the ominous sounds of parting threads. He glared at Miss Seeton, still hovering anxiously close by, and with great care slipped off his jacket to examine the collar and back.

Miss Seeton, on seeing again that spreading red stain which had so horrified her, closed her eyes with a shudder. The man let out a cry of dismay—and then Miss Seeton could have sworn she heard him sniff. Warily she opened her eyes and risked a peep.

She opened her eyes wide. The man, his head bent close to the grey-and-scarlet jacket in his hands, was sniffing at the scarlet patches and beginning to swear. "Tomato ketchup—tomato bloody ketchup!" He raised his head and stared at Miss Seeton, who blinked at him, bemused. He thrust the jacket under her startled nose. "Go on, see for yourself! Tomato ketchup, and why anyone should play such a—"

He broke off once more, snatched back the jacket, and in one frantic movement thrust his hand into the inner pocket. "Gone!" He felt again, then checked the outside pockets and returned to the inner pocket for a third time. "Stolen—my wallet—falling for a trick like that—and you," he cried, rounding on Miss Seeton, "were helping him, weren't you!"

"Indeed I was not," began Miss Seeton, hurt that her attempts to play the Good Samaritan had been misunderstood, but realising that shock made people have strange fancies. "I was only trying to—"

"I know perfectly well what you were trying to do," said the man, taking two purposeful steps towards her. "And with me being a regular mug, and the pair of you having your act worked out nicely, you almost got away with it—but *you* didn't quite make it, did you?" He shot out a hand and took Miss Seeton by the arm. He shook her briskly. Her squeak of protest was drowned out by his next words.

"You thought you'd put one over on me, didn't you? Well, maybe you did, but that was the last time! I'm going to make sure you never have the chance to work your damned double act on any other unsuspecting beggar like me. I'm making," he said in a very firm voice, "a citizen's arrest. You just come along with me to the nearest police station—and don't you dare try to say one word, or I'll wrap your blasted brolly round your neck!"

He continued to grip Miss Seeton by the arm as he strode off up the Haymarket, and she was so startled by this turn of events, so breathless at trying to keep up with his fast, angry steps, that she could say nothing in her defence. She pattered along, panting, slightly in front of him, feeling him push her every time her feet faltered. Not one person in all the milling crowds seemed to notice what was happening: there were too many people for that. Miss Seeton felt very upset. She had meant so well—that man, the young man with the tomato ketchup, had quite confused her with the way he acted his part—no wonder this poor man (she winced as she stumbled, and his grasp tightened in case she tried to make a break for it) was angry and felt she was somehow to blame— which she supposed, when one thought about it calmly and sensibly (only she felt far from calm and sensible now), she was. She would have apologised again and tried to explain, but she was so out of breath . . .

The man forced her towards Jermyn Street, and she gave a little nervous squeak as the lights changed when they were barely halfway across the Haymarket; she subsided at once as the man growled something—surely she was mistaken in what she heard?—deep in his throat. In silence they crossed Regent Street and turned back up into Piccadilly. The man kept scanning the passing faces, looking for a policeman's helmet to come bobbing above the heads of the crowd, but he saw nothing. He kept on walking, forcing Miss Seeton ahead of him, and they came, at last, to Bottle Street.

Bottle Street, a cul-de-sac, showed a blue lamp halfway down, over an official-looking doorway. Miss Seeton gulped at the sight and blinked twice in case her eyes had been playing her false. But they had not.

"Police," said the man, in case she had not clearly read the letters on the dark blue glass. He shook her once more, then pushed her up the steps and through the doorway. "Now we'll see what you've got to say for yourself!"

But Miss Seeton, to her dismay, found that the events of the morning had rendered her speechless. She could only try shaking her head, which made no sense at all without words, and words were what she was unable to produce. The man, his grip on her relaxing only slightly, marched her across to the desk and cleared his throat.

The sergeant looked up from the neat copperplate he was inscribing in a leather-bound ledger and nodded. "Yes, sir— and madam," with a smile to Miss Seeton, who could only stare at him. "What can I do for you?" He blotted what he had been writing, screwed the cap back on his fountain pen, and came over to the counter. He eyed his visitors with an expert air. Somebody's auntie, up for the day and lost her purse, and not liking to bother anyone about it really, and nephew being a bit cross with the poor old duck for causing a fuss, but trying to overcome his embarrassment by just asking whether the police might be able to help, because he pays his taxes with the best of 'em . . .

"You can arrest this woman," the "nephew" said, breaking into the sergeant's thoughts with startling clarity. The sergeant's jaw dropped. "And don't call her 'madam'—she's no more a lady than I am! This woman is a common thief!"

And while the station sergeant continued to gape, poor Miss Seeton could only stand, dumbstruck, shaking her head in attempted denial over and over again.

Chapter 4

AT HIS DESK in the office of Chief Superintendent Delphick, in New Scotland Yard, sat Detective Sergeant Bob Ranger. Every few minutes he raised his head from his work to look across at the wall clock above the filing cabinet, evidently increasingly surprised at the passage of time. Not like his chief to be late when there was a big case going on—though possibly, Bob reflected with a grin, it had dawned on the Oracle that if he made sure to arrive after his sergeant, it would mean Bob would be lumbered with breaking the back of the paperwork. You didn't reach chief super's rank without picking up a few tips on the way.

It was a beautiful day, too, though that didn't mean the Oracle would be skiving off anywhere. Conscientious as they came, that was Chief Superintendent Delphick—but he might, Bob supposed, just this once have got a touch of late spring fever—very late, seeing this was the beginning of July. And what a July! Through the half-open window the sound of cooing, from the pigeons that roosted on the sill, drifted in on the gentle breeze which blew fleecy white clouds across the sun-sparkling sky. He couldn't remember the last time it had rained. Far below, the mighty roar of

London's traffic was a muted background to birdsong and the occasional rustle as Bob turned over another sheet of paper.

He came to the end of his selection of reports, slammed the last folder shut, and looked at the clock again. He'd come in earlier than usual, of course, but even so it was on the late side for the Oracle to arrive. Should he ring him at home, in case there was trouble? Or maybe the clock was wrong. Bob checked his watch. It wasn't.

Pushing back his chair, Bob rose from his desk, took up the pile of reports on which he'd been working, and was just carrying them across to set them squarely in the middle of Delphick's blotter when he heard the sound of footsteps— fast, ill-tempered footsteps with a familiar ring to them—approaching down the corridor. He barely had time to select one report in particular, removing it from its folder to lay it, unmissably, on top of the pile on Delphick's desk, when the door was flung open with a shuddering crash, and the clock came leaping from the wall, bounced off the filing cabinet, and exploded in several directions at once.

"Good morning, sir," said Bob as the mainspring whizzed past his ear and fell tinkling into the visitors' ashtray.

"Thus far, I am unable to agree with you," retorted his superior, trampling through the shards of broken glass towards the window. "And we'll have this shut, if you don't mind." With the Oracle in this mood, Bob would never dare to say he minded, and he watched in silence as the chief superintendent slammed down the sash with such force that the glass shivered in the panes. A braver man than Sergeant Ranger might have warned of seven years' bad luck, but that, mused Bob as he twiddled the mainspring round a thoughtful finger, wasn't windows but mirrors, anyway.

"I don't want to hear another damned pigeon billing and cooing for the next month, Bob, understand? Or," Delphick threatened, throwing himself down at his desk and twirling crossly round on the chair, "budgerigars, or canaries, or any of our feathered friends—not one mention, if you value my sanity." Bob blinked, and nodded, and ventured on a grin which Delphick acknowledged with a scowl. "Birds," muttered the chief superintendent, bringing his teetotum movement to a sudden end with a vicious stamp of his foot. "Right now I loathe every blessed one of the things."

"Oh," said Bob, dropping two cogs and a small flywheel thoughtfully into his metal wastepaper basket, which echoed with little piercing clangs. With the minute hand he made tracings on his blotting pad. Delphick caught his eye.

"Yes, I do. And I loathe even more being humoured with such obvious tact as you are displaying, Sergeant Ranger."

"As you wish, sir." Bob sent the minute hand clanging after its fellow *disjecta membra* and started a pointed hunt on the floor for the second hand. Delphick watched him in a thoughtful silence for a moment, then:

"I'm in a rotten mood this morning, Bob. Sorry. Aren't you going to ask me what's wrong?"

"I wouldn't dare, sir." Bob accepted the olive branch cheerfully. "I'm far too scared of experiencing even more, er, devastating results of your emotion." He produced the second hand from beneath a chair and waved it with a grin under Delphick's nose. The Oracle, after a moment, grinned right back at him, and they both began to laugh.

"Sorry again, Bob, but I really have been having a time of it. No excuse for losing my temper with you, I know, and I do apologise—though I cannot believe that anybody your size would ever be remotely worried by any little displays of emotion, as you so kindly put it, in which I may choose to indulge. I'm sure" —and he viewed his subordinate with a calculating eye— "that it's more than seventeen stone now, Sergeant Ranger. Anne's cooking has given you rather a tummy—four or five pounds heavier at least, I'd say."

Bob sucked in his stomach and looked pained. "I don't think so, sir. Well"—as Delphick looked at him quizzically—"perhaps a couple of pounds, but no more, surely."

"As you please," Delphick said, grinning wickedly as Bob eased an anxious finger round the waistband of his trousers and frowned. "And if you've been eating pigeon pie, then I forgive you—actively encourage you, indeed." He cast a darkling look in the direction of the closed window, whose panes of glass had only just finished vibrating.

"It was a pigeon that delayed you, sir," deduced Ranger, the detective. "What happened?"

"Flew into one of our upstairs windows and knocked itself out on the glass, the damfool thing—dazzled by the reflection of the sun, I suppose. Lucky not to break its neck, the way it came walloping along. And I was not at all pleased, let me tell you, when my softhearted spouse said that it ought to be taken to the vet—and even hunted out a cardboard box to put the wretched fowl in, dammit."

There was a pause, during which Delphick ground his teeth, and Bob pondered the little he knew of his superior's lady. Sergeants and chief superintendents not sharing the same social circle, they had met on few occasions, the last having been Bob's wedding to Anne Knight. The day when Superintendent Brinton and his wife had collected her from Ashford railway station, because . . .

"Mrs. Delphick doesn't drive, does she, sir?"

"She does not, as you seem to find very comical, from the way you're grinning. I am prepared to forgive you for this *lèse-majesté* on one condition: find me," begged the Oracle, "if there's one to be had in this place, a decent cup of coffee. I need it, believe me."

"Sounds as if you do," agreed Bob, adding, "I'd started to wonder where you were, sir, and what had happened—not that I imagined anything like that, of course—and then the clock might have gone wrong, as well, so—"

"It has now," his superior interrupted him with a shake of the head and a rueful smile. "The power of a righteous wrath, I suppose. Can we indent for another without having to explain exactly how this one met its, ah, untimely end?"

Bob grinned his appreciation of the little joke, pleased that the Oracle was his usual self once more. "I'll think of something, sir. You know paperwork is what I enjoy more than anything." The look on his face gave the lie to his solemn assurance, however, and Delphick started laughing again, his tantrum forgotten. "Oh, yes," said Bob as he headed for the door: "Talking of paperwork, sir, on your desk—the first report—another drug incident, and no idea where the stuff's coming from, same as usual."

"Back to work," Delphick said, becoming serious at once. "I'd give a lot to know how they manage it . . ."

But Bob had already vanished coffeewards. The morning could now continue as normal; which it duly did, until the sudden storm which chased Miss Seeton into the Van Meegeren Gallery threw heavy spears of rain against the windows of Delphick's office high up on the umpteenth floor of New Scotland Yard. Whereupon he and Sergeant Ranger learned that it is inadvisable for anyone, no matter how sorely provoked, to slam windows out of temper. In came the rain through cracks which, in the sunlight's dazzle, had not been visible before; and, as the wind howled, the thunder rumbled, and the room began to fill with a fine mist, Delphick cursed again the habits of pigeons with no directional sense, and the tenderheartedness of his wife.

At Bottle Street police station Arthur Havelock Thundridge had given his statement and was now demanding action.

"My jacket," he insisted, "has been ruined—no amount of dry cleaning will take that stain out. I look exactly as if I've been stabbed in the back—just as that woman and her accomplice kept pretending while they robbed me. My wallet, stolen! All my money, my credit cards, even the keys to my briefcase—I suppose I should be thankful for the small mercy that I wasn't carrying it with me—but now they'll have my name and address. There will be nothing to stop them keeping watch and snatching the case when I'm not expecting them."

"That hasn't exactly been their style, so far, sir," he was told, in a soothing voice. "Their regular trick is—"

"Regular?" repeated Arthur Havelock Thundridge, shocked. "Do you mean to tell me this is not the first time that this—this daylight robbery has occurred?"

"Well, sir, no, it isn't." The uniformed officer who'd been detailed to take Mr. Thundridge's statement looked glum. "As a matter of fact, you're the seventeenth this month, not to mention—"

"Seventeenth? But that's outrageous! Has nobody done anything to put a stop to this—this racket?"

The policeman looked uncomfortable. "Well, sir, we've been doing our best, but it isn't easy. They have, as you might say, been working almost to professional standards, whoever they are—"

"You *know* who they are. At least, you know who one of them is—that woman I brought in. When you question her, which I hope someone is doing this very minute, she'll tell you everything you want about the others, I'm sure. Probably take you right to their hideout, if you aren't too soft with her—don't be fooled by that fluffy, helpless manner. Nobody can really be like that—it's an act, and a damned good one. She fooled me, after all," said Mr. Thundridge, frowning. "Why, the woman's quite clever enough to be the brains behind the whole enterprise—and if that's the case, I trust there will be due recognition, when the time comes, of the part I played in bringing her and, through her, the rest of the criminal gang to justice."

"As to that, sir, we are indeed grateful for the help you've given us—"

"No more than my duty as a citizen," replied Mr. Thundridge, preening himself. "Quite apart from the fact that I have been a victim of this—this extortion, I hope that my actions would have been the same had I witnessed another in similar circumstances."

"Exactly so, sir. And, bearing in mind the duties of good citizenship"—he began to speak faster now, trying to get the rest of the sentence out before Mr. Thundridge interrupted him again—"it would be very much appreciated if you could spare the time to come across to Scotland Yard and have a word with the officer who's coordinating enquiries. Look at a few photographs, that sort of thing." He regarded Arthur Havelock with an experienced eye. Mr. Thundridge, as expected, had nothing more to say for himself; he seemed to be highly gratified by the suggestion. Once more the name of Scotland Yard had worked its familiar magic.

Chapter 5

IN ANOTHER ROOM of Bottle Street police station, struggling politely to drink a cup of constabulary tea, Miss Seeton sat and puzzled over the events of the morning.

She had been enjoying everything so much—apart from the storm in which she had become so damp, though the unexpected visit to the Van Meegeren Gallery soon made her comfortable again—until the poor man in front of her had been . . . Miss Seeton frowned as she took another sip of tea. Who was it who had once spoken of "burnt molasses" and "stewed treacle" in this context? She very much feared that her recent series of adventures had affected her memory . . .

"No," she murmured at last. The young woman officer who had accompanied Miss Seeton to the interview room leaned forward across the table to catch her words. "He was not stabbed—he said so."

Official instructions had been not to press the old duck for a statement until she was ready to give one—obviously never expected to get caught, so it was bound to be a shock at her age. She was to be treated with care—and, thought Woman Police Constable Ware, you couldn't help feeling a bit sorry for her, looking so upset, though of course it was all part of the act: whoever would have thought of this little old lady being a crook in disguise? But then, that was what made a successful crook, wasn't it, and here was one of the best, a real pro. She'd hardly spoken a word since she'd been brought in, mostly stared and gulped a lot as if she couldn't believe what was going on, pretending not to want any tea and taking her time over drinking it, trying to put off the moment when, like it or not, she'd start to spill the beans. And once she could be persuaded to talk, they'd soon have the rest of her pals in the bag. The Yard would be very interested to see her, no mistake about that; if she thought she'd be able to get away with saying nothing over there, she'd got another think coming. Odd, though, that she hadn't even asked for a solicitor—it was usually the first thing they said, once they knew the game was up.

"He wasn't stabbed," prompted WPc Ware. Miss Seeton gave her an apologetic smile (such a foolish, if understandable, error to have made—that vivid scarlet splash), which WPc Ware interpreted as the first glimmerings of repentance, the first hint of a confession to come. "Yes?" prompted WPc Ware, then held her breath. Had she pushed the old duck too far, too fast?

Miss Seeton was grateful to this young woman—so well meant, the offer of tea, even if it was far too strong for her taste—for allowing her the release of talking through the shocking experience of the morning. Catharsis, wasn't that the term? If she could only remember clearly what had happened, she was sure it would be of great benefit to her agitated mental state, rather in the way that, if she had been at home, some of her yoga breathing exercises would have helped to settle her thoughts. But she was still too shaken even to contemplate any of the exercises. Every time she tried closing her eyes, she had seen again that—horrid—sight . . .

"It really did look like blood, you know—so startling, and everyone passing by in ignorance of the poor man's suffering—not that he was, of course, and indeed, that was what he said, but then the other man"—and she frowned—"said it was the shock, and he sounded so sure of himself—anybody might have believed him, you see."

Which was what they'd relied on, thought WPc Ware, trying not to let her excitement show. If she could come up with a signed confession, it wouldn't do her promotion chances any harm at all—they'd been after this Tomato Ketchup Gang for two or three months now, and until they were caught, the tourists were at risk every minute.

"Anybody might have believed him," repeated WPc Ware, in an attempt to coax something further from the old dear—she corrected herself, from the *suspect*—before the case was taken from her and handed over to the Yard. Though anything less like a suspect in the well organised and widespread ketchup racket it was difficult to imagine. She looked more like someone's favourite maiden aunt than a criminal mastermind, and it was just as difficult to see that umbrella of hers as the lethal weapon the man who'd brought her along to Bottle Street had insisted it was.

"Confiscate it" had been the advice of Arthur Havelock Thundridge before the taking of statements began. "If I'd really been stabbed, that damned brolly would have to be the first choice for the murder weapon, believe me. Why, she was here, there, and everywhere with the thing—winded me, tripped us all up, and even pretended to nobble her partner in the unmentionables, to give him the chance to make his escape. You've got to hand it to her, the woman's an artist—but I don't appreciate her practising her artistry on me, or on anyone else, for that matter. Don't let her take the thing into the interview room with her, or she'll use it to brain someone and chisel her way out through the walls, or pick the lock on the door of her cell, mark my words."

"We won't be putting anyone in the cells just yet, sir," he was told as Miss Seeton was being led away. She had not long remained dumbstruck after the startling accusations of Arthur Havelock had been levelled against her but, still breathless after her whirlwind journey through the byways of Piccadilly, found that her attempts at denial came out even more confused than she might, in the circumstances, have expected. She realized that she must collect her thoughts before trying to say anything else, for it was no surprise that the poor man was too distressed and angry to be able to listen to her, while she knew herself to be more than a little shaken by what had happened. A cooling-off period, wasn't that the phrase?

"Cooling off," murmured Miss Seeton. "So very apt," and made a face as she tried another sip of rich tannin. WPc Ware looked at her. Was the old duck trying to take over the interview by asking for a second cup, when it had been her own choice not to drink the first? She was a skilled operator, all right. But WPc Ware wasn't falling for that ploy: suspects weren't supposed to take control of official proceedings, and certainly not this one. She was far too confident, anyone could see that, as calm as they came: the way she was smiling now, thinking she'd scored a point . . .

"Bow Street," said Miss Seeton, rejoicing that her memory wasn't at fault, as she'd been afraid it might be. For she had remembered, as she struggled with the tea, just where it was she'd had her first encounter with such a dark, unpalatable brew: in Bow Street police station, where she had gone to give her statement after witnessing the murder of that poor prostitute, Marie Prevost . . .

"Bow Street?" WPc Ware regarded her sternly. "Scotland Yard it'll have to be this time."

Miss Seeton nodded, still smiling. "Chief Superintendent Delphick," she said happily, "although, of course, he was only a superintendent when I first met him . . . so many years ago now, but it seems almost like yesterday," and she sipped once more at the tea, sighed, and set the cup firmly back on its saucer. She recalled every detail of that first meeting with dear Mr. Delphick: how he'd recognised her dislike of the sweetened tar that nice young policeman had offered her, and how he'd persuaded him to water it down to an acceptable strength—but it would, reflected Miss Seeton, be too much of an imposition now, although she really could not—even for the sake of politeness—manage to swallow any more.

"Chief Superintendent Delphick? You mean the Oracle?" WPc Ware was, despite herself, impressed: she'd landed one of the big-time ones here, and no mistake. Delphick didn't have much to do with the small fry: and if this little duck had known him when he was just a superintendent, she must be one of the longest-serving, biggest big-timers around. WPc Ware looked in amazement at her prisoner—she begged her mental pardon, *suspect*—and found herself saying: "Would you like another cup of tea, dear?"

Miss Seeton sighed, recollected herself, and politely shook her head. "So very kind," she murmured, "but I think not." She glanced at her wristwatch. She felt a great deal better now, and once she had commiserated with the man who had lost his wallet, and apologised for not having been able to help him more usefully, she really ought to be on her way if she was going to catch Harrods before the rush hour began and travel on the Tube became impossible. "The station," enquired Miss Seeton. "Is it very far away?" She had lost her bearings during that breathless dash through the side streets, but one could always rely upon the police for helpful and accurate directions.

WPc Ware noted the professional's avoidance of the words *Scotland Yard* and was even more impressed, though she tried not to let it show. "Don't you worry about that," she said, sorry now that her part in the affair was almost over. The old dear had dropped the hint she'd confess in full once she was at the Yard: probably thought it beneath her to talk to a uniformed constable, if she was used to hobnobbing with the likes of Chief Superintendent Delphick. The underworld, as well as the legitimate citizens, took pride in keeping to certain standards of behaviour.

"You'll get to, er, the station all right, don't worry," said WPc Ware. "We'll see to that."

"How very kind," said Miss Seeton, "but I would not wish to cause anyone any more trouble, and the traffic, you know, so heavy, as well as wasting petrol. I am perfectly able to walk—it cannot, surely, be far, and I believe the chief superintendent would say the same. He knows all," explained Miss Seeton earnestly, "about my knees," and, thinking with pride of her yoga-inspired fitness, smiled at WPc Ware in a way that made the young woman suddenly very nervous. What strange password was being used, what coded message was she supposed to be understanding and acting upon? Delphick, the Oracle, knew about this old lady's *knees*, for heaven's sake?

Rhyming slang? She thought frantically. Knees and toes—hose, nose, rose? Elbows, bungalows, overflows? Nothing seemed to make any sense. Knees and boomps-a-daisy? Lazy? Hazy? "Crazy," said WPc Ware with conviction. Miss Seeton blinked and looked startled. Her smile faltered.

WPc Ware, frowning at her lapse, said firmly: "Crazy for you to worry about getting to—the station." She couldn't help stuttering a little: she felt an absolute beginner when she compared this old lady's calm manner to her own fluster, faced with such an unusual situation. "We'll take you right the way there, make no mistake—after all, it's our job."

And Miss Seeton, smiling again, was reassured by the certainty of her tone, thanked her, and bothered her with no more questions beyond wishing to know when they would be leaving, because she had rather a busy day ahead of her . . .

Whereupon WPc Ware murmured, just too low for the suspect to be able to hear: "You have indeed, my dear. You have indeed."

Miss Seeton seemed so willing to come quietly that they were all thrown into a panic when she asked, very politely, for her umbrella to be given back to her before she left the police station. After all, she explained, it was unlikely that she would be returning to Bottle Street, and, while it had been most thoughtful of them to take care of it for her while she collected her thoughts, she now felt fighting fit again. She beamed a grateful smile round at the watching group of officers and wondered fleetingly why they were all giving one another such pointed looks. She could not know that her casual use of the phrase *fighting fit* reminded them of the warnings uttered by Arthur Havelock Thundridge . . .

On the other hand, she hadn't yet been charged: she was still, technically, only a suspect, helping with enquiries. And if they refused to hand over her rightful property while she was legally as innocent as any genuine sweet little old lady, never mind that it was hardly routine to allow a suspect to travel in an official vehicle armed to the teeth: a good lawyer would make mincemeat of the case when it came to court. And if she really was the brains behind the Tomato Ketchup Gang, she'd brief the best lawyer in Town . . .

"My umbrella, please?" prompted Miss Seeton as the desk sergeant stared in perplexity at the driver, and the driver stared at the detective who had taken Mr. Thundridge's statement, and who was to accompany the party of Arthur Havelock, Miss Seeton, and WPc Ware to Scotland Yard. And it was Detective Sergeant Wadesmill who found the solution.

"I'll be sitting in the back, with you and Policewoman Ware," he said, "so it will be a bit of a tight squeeze, but Mr. Thundridge'll be in the front, and he can look after it for you." He glanced enquiringly at Arthur Havelock, who replied at once that he would be only too glad to take care of the umbrella. It could not, he assured his listeners grimly, be entrusted to safer hands. Miss Seeton smiled her thanks, adding:

"Does this mean you will be coming all the way to the station as well? That will be very pleasant, as well as a sensible plan, because of course, with so many of us, it is wise, would you not agree, for us all to share the same car rather than to walk, being so much less wasteful of petrol—and then there is always the risk of losing one another in the crowds, as well."

"There certainly is," remarked Wadesmill, slipping his hand protectively about her upper arm. "Let's be getting along, shall we?" And WPc Ware fell in as escort on Miss Seeton's other side. Anyone who was cheeky enough to drop a hint that she'd try to make a bolt for it needed watching every inch of the way.

Miss Seeton headed automatically for the front of the car, then recollected herself, murmured apologetically to Mr. Thundridge that she generally rode beside the driver, and settled herself in the backseat between Wadesmill and WPc Ware. These two officers regarded each other with knowing looks. She was a cool customer, all right—tried to slip from their grasp (hadn't they felt her tensing for flight between them just now, outside the car?) and, when she knew she couldn't make it, turning it off with a casual remark. One for the records, she was, one to remember.

WPc Ware had something else to remember, as well: something she wished she'd thought to consult her colleagues over, except that she'd felt uncomfortable at even thinking of someone like Chief Superintendent Delphick and, and—her mind could hardly put the idea into words—and . . . whatever the old lady had been hinting at. Hinting at Delphick's full knowledge of her activities—hinting, more than hinting, at his compliance. Coded messages, knowing smiles, that air of utter innocence—WPc Ware felt all the horror of a police officer who stumbles upon evidence of . . . of . . .

Of corruption. As she forced herself to think that dreadful word, WPc Ware felt herself go cold, her face flush, and her hands shake. She knew little of Delphick beyond his nickname of the Oracle, but he was her superior, someone she was supposed to look up to, supposed to take as her example. And yet, beside her in the police car, sat evidence that the example might be flawed . . .

And the only thing to do, she reasoned to herself, was for her to insist, on one pretext or another, upon Delphick and the suspect coming face to face as soon as possible, at the Yard, in front of witnesses. Because the element of surprise must surely reveal the truth—and, if there still remained any doubt, the Yard's more skilful interrogators would soon learn every one of the old lady's secrets. So far she'd been treated with kid gloves, hardly questioned at all, keeping her own counsel about everything to do with the case. But the time for kid gloves was passing, and the truth about Delphick must be made known.

Chapter 6

DELPHICK AND BOB were making plans to snatch, at last, their well-earned lunch. The Oracle had insisted on working right through the morning, as compensation for the time he'd lost over his troublesome pigeon; he told Bob to pop along to the canteen without him, but the sergeant, brooding over certain of his superior's remarks concerning his incipient tummy, in lofty tones of self-denial said that he was happy to wait as long as the chief superintendent wished.

But now the time had come. The Oracle closed the file, thrust it into his desk drawer, and pushed back his chair, stretching. "I don't know about you, Bob, but I could do with a bite to eat. Reading too much paperwork always has a stimulating effect on my appetite, I find. Don't you?"

"I'd say it was rather depressing, really, sir. There's a heap of reports over a foot high still to go—we've read dozens of them already—no doubt there'll be more tomorrow. And we're no nearer knowing how the drugs are brought into the country, or how the distribution system works, than we were when we started. For all the good it's done," grumbled Bob, in whom hunger striving with vanity had produced acute pessimism, "we might just as well not have bothered coming in today. Oh, I know that's an exaggeration"—as his chief quirked an eyebrow at him—"but that's how it feels to me, sir. It'll take a slice of incredible luck to break this case, if you ask me."

"Come to the canteen and have a slice of incredible meat pie, instead. Build up your strength and cheer up your view of life at one and the same time. You're not normally so gloomy, Bob—think positive. And we'll start," Delphick said firmly as the telephone rang, "by not answering that until it's rung at least seven times. Willpower, Sergeant Ranger, plus deduction. If it's important, they'll keep on; if it isn't, they'll hang up or try someone else . . ."

On the eighth ring, with a rueful look, Delphick picked up the receiver. "And this had better be important," he muttered before announcing: "Delphick here . . . I can't say that I'm glad you caught me. My sergeant and I were just leaving for a spot of lunch . . . A word with both of us? What seems to be the problem?" And Delphick motioned to Bob to listen on the extension. "Carry on, Sergeant," he instructed, and the telephone continued its apologetic explanation.

"It's like this, you see, sir. There's been another of those tomato ketchup robberies. Chap had his wallet pinched in the Haymarket, a really professional job, as good as any of the others, but this time was a bit different. It wasn't just chummie on his own, you see, sir, and the accomplice was a bit on the slow side getting away, so the punter was able to collar her and take her along to Bottle Street station on suspicion."

As the desk sergeant drew breath, Delphick said: "That's all very interesting, and I'm glad they've turned up a lead on the ketchup crowd after so long, but I'm not handling the case, Sergeant. You want Inspector Youngsbury."

"Well, I'm not sure that I do, sir, not just yet." The telephone sounded even more apologetic. "The suspect, sir—I told you it was a woman, didn't I?"

"You did. It's not so unusual, nowadays—women's lib and so on. Are you expecting me to lecture her on the error of her ways, and my sergeant to find her a mailbag to sew?"

Embarrassed throat-clearing sounds came from the telephone. Delphick looked across at Bob, shrugged, and briskly instructed the desk sergeant to come right out with whatever he was trying to say, because he had two detectives dying of slow starvation while they listened to him splutter.

"I'm sorry, sir," said the desk sergeant, speaking now in low tones. "But Bottle Street says she's been behaving very strangely, sir—claims she knows you and you know her, and you'd insist on them giving her her umbrella back—"

"Her umbrella!" burst in unison from Delphick and Ranger at such a volume that the handset clutched to the listening ears of the desk sergeant positively hummed. With the cries of his colleagues still echoing in his head, he was unable to make any sense of their subsequent remarks and could only keep repeating his pleas for them to speak one at a time, if they wouldn't mind, because he didn't think he could cope with it all otherwise.

Delphick pulled himself together first and told Bob to shut up and hang up, then to go down to the Back Hall (as Scotland Yard's entrance lobby is known) and extricate Miss Seeton from whatever predicament she seemed to have got herself into this time. "It has to be MissEss," he said, and Bob agreed, with a grin. "Whenever I hear the word *umbrella*, I reach, not for my revolver, but for my worry beads, or the aspirin, or a stiff whisky. Away with you, Sergeant, while I rustle up a decent cup of tea for your dear old Aunt Em.

And something stronger," he added reflectively, "for the two of us—never mind drinking on duty, for once. I have the feeling we're likely to need it."

The canteen cook, learning that the Battling Brolly was paying a call on the Oracle, excelled himself. A tray was sent up to Delphick's office bearing the only unchipped teapot in the place, three well-polished cups on sparkling saucers, and a plate containing not only a selection of biscuits, but several iced buns as well. Delphick assured the tray-bringer that MissEss would be duly appreciative of his efforts, but that it was unlikely she would have time, today, to visit the canteen. Yes, he would ask her if she would agree to autograph one of the paper napkins—and yes, she might be persuaded to doodle a little cartoon, perhaps of a constabulary cook in a chef's hat.

And why not? mused Delphick on being left alone again. If Assistant Commissioner Sir Hubert Everleigh could yearn to build a collection of Miss Seeton's sketches (in which he was regularly thwarted by the Oracular insistence that said sketches, being evidence, must instead be stored in a safe place), what harm could there be—Delphick felt a smirk flicker across his face—in humouring the whims of Scotland Yard's canteen cook? Sir Heavily might be no greater, or lesser, judge of artistic merit than the man who sent the forces of the Metropolitan Police well fed into the fray.

At which point in his musings, the Oracle noticed that steam had ceased to rise from the teapot spout, and cream was thickening on the surface of the milk in its jug. Where on earth had Bob got to with Miss Seeton? Even in her wildest moments—and, heaven knew, these were wild enough—she surely couldn't have so disrupted the hallowed regions of Scotland Yard that his sergeant was unable to find his way back to this office? Surely?

"Oh, yes, she could," Delphick said, grimly resigned to any fate which awaited him. "Yet I'd have expected them to ring me, if there were problems—unless she's managed to fuse the entire internal telephone system. Which I can't believe even she has had time to do—still, I'd better go and see . . ." And he left, failing to observe that, in all the original excitement, Bob had neglected to replace his handset properly on its cradle, so that incoming calls were completely blocked.

By the time Delphick arrived in the Back Hall, however, everyone had given up trying to telephone him, and Arthur Havelock Thundridge was apologising profusely to Miss Seeton while WPc Ware, blushing hotly, looked close to tears at the enormity of her mistake. Bob was in an explanatory huddle with Detective Sergeant Wadesmill, and Inspector Youngsbury, coordinator of the Ketchup investigations, was hovering by the desk, waiting for the commotion to die down so that he could take Arthur Havelock away to study mug shots and talk to the PhotoFit people.

"Of course, sir," he informed Delphick as the Oracle arrived at the desk to learn from the sergeant what had been going on, "Miss Seeton's your pigeon, isn't she? I wouldn't want to go poaching your star witness—retainer fee and all that on account of her drawings, sir, I understand perfectly—but I'd be grateful if you'd ask her if she wouldn't mind giving a description of the bloke who did the ketchup job, sir, and then, if you'd be kind enough to pass the information on to me . . ."

Delphick smothered a grin. Youngsbury was too clever a copper to come right out and admit his apprehensions about dealing with MissEss—and who wouldn't be a bit nervous, with her reputation for chaos preceding her wherever she went? The Misguided Missile, Sir Heavily had once called her, and this was every bit as fitting a soubriquet as the Battling Brolly, which was Fleet Street's headline-catching name for her.

She came trotting up to him now, all smiles, dragging a pink-cheeked young woman constable with her. "Why, this is indeed a pleasure, Chief Superintendent, and such a thoughtful surprise on your part, for your kind driver to bring me here to see you, and the dear sergeant." She nodded in the direction of Bob, her adopted nephew, still busily explaining things to Wadesmill, then turned back to Delphick, saying: "May I introduce Miss Ware? She has been so very kind and insisted on accompanying me in the car, when I assured her I could easily have walked to Green Park Tube station, and she was so clever, not telling me until we had arrived here that we were coming to see you, and when I learned that she had never met you, I felt it was the least I could do, to thank her for taking such good care of me."

"The very least, I agree." Delphick had understood the main gist of Miss Seeton's speech and reasoned that the rest of it could wait, if necessary, until later. He nodded politely to WPc Ware, who was even pinker than before. "You have my compliments, Miss Ware, on your handling of what I am sure was a rather, ahem, delicate situation." WPc Ware went bright scarlet, and her feet shuffled nervously on the polished floor. Delphick smiled. "On your return to Bottle Street, Miss Ware, you will be the envy of your colleagues, I'm sure. You will be able to tell them that you were in on the very first act of whatever remarkable case Miss Seeton has brought us—for, rest assured, Miss Ware, a remarkable case there is almost bound to be." Miss Seeton, shaking her head, uttered sounds of protesting denial, but Delphick took no notice. "A remarkable case," he repeated and, excusing himself briefly to Miss Seeton, led WPc Ware out of earshot.

"Sir," the wretched young woman began, but he raised a hand to stem the flow of apology he could sense was about to torrent from her shaking lips.

"You don't have to explain—indeed, if I know my Miss Seeton, you probably *couldn't* explain, because she's got you so confused you've no idea where to begin. Am I right?"

The twinkle in his eye emboldened her to risk a feeble chuckle. "That's about it, sir. Honestly, I had no idea it was MissEss we were dealing with—she never said her name, and we were told not to ask her too many questions because of her being, well, elderly, sir, and waiting for the Yard to take over—and then Mr. Thundridge was so convincing when he accused her of . . . of being one of the gang—"

"So long as she hasn't been charged with anything, it's all right. The paperwork for sorting out a wrongful arrest would put years on everyone's life in the normal course of events, and if the arrested person is Miss Seeton, the course of events, believe me, would be far from normal. One wave of her umbrella, and the files would go completely haywire."

WPc Ware was quick to assure him that no paperwork was involved, and Delphick thanked her gravely.

"I see your colleague beckoning to you," he added. "The explanations of my sergeant—who, for his sins, has chosen to adopt Miss Seeton as a favourite aunt—to your chap seem to have come to an end. Shall we join them?"

Ten minutes later, Mr. Thundridge was looking at mug shots with Inspector Youngsbury; Sergeant Wadesmill and WPc Ware were on their way back to Bottle Street wondering what their colleagues would say; and Miss Seeton herself—still with no realisation of the trouble she had inadvertently caused—was in Delphick's office, drinking tea which tasted just the way she liked it.

"And now, having duly fortified yourself," Delphick said as she politely refused a second iced bun, "do you think you might be ready to produce your usual statement? There are pencils and paper right here, and—is something wrong, Miss Seeton?" He had noticed the brief flicker of anxiety in her eyes, and the unhappy way her hands danced on her lap.

"I—I'm not sure, Mr. Delphick. Of course, I know it is my clear duty, and I will do my best to help, but this time I rather fear—the blood, you see, although now of course I know it wasn't. A very clever scheme, so mischievous and so quick—that nice little Miss Ware tells me they use yoghurt sometimes, as well—but this was so very, very red," Miss Seeton said with a gulp. "So vivid, you see. And when I try to compose my thoughts to think of what happened, all I can see is . . . it sounds foolish, now that one knows it was only tomato ketchup—everything I see is a mass of red, I'm afraid. Which will be, I'm sure," finished Miss Seeton in regretful accents, "of no help to you and your colleagues at all, will it? Though, naturally, I intend to try my best—only, I wished you to understand before I begin trying that . . . that I rather doubt if, this time, I will justify your faith in me and earn the generous retainer paid me by the police."

And to Delphick's secret surprise—for Miss Seeton had often in the past earnestly explained that her little drawings could not possibly be of any interest to the police, to be proved wrong by later events—this time she appeared to have been right. Though he and Bob left her tactfully alone while they repaired to the canteen for something more filling than biscuits and buns, on their return to the office they found Miss Seeton, looking unhappy, sitting at Delphick's desk with several sheets of paper in front of her. Of which all but one were covered by masses of scarlet, and crimson, and generally sanguine shades.

Delphick pounced on the one drawing which was different. It was a sketch of Trafalgar Square, with figures feeding the pigeons in the foreground, and the National Gallery outlined quickly in the distance. "Because I went there first of all, and enjoyed myself so much," Miss Seeton told him, when he asked her why. "I thought, you see, that if I could go back in time—not that one can in reality, of course, Mr. Dunne, such a very interesting book—not that I understood the mathematics, but some of the . . . the case histories, isn't that the term? were most illuminating—but it didn't work," lamented Miss Seeton. "I am so sorry."

Delphick also, in one of his more philosophical moments, had struggled with *An Experiment with Time* and could sympathise with her sentiments, although he knew well that it was not J. W. Dunne's theories she now regarded as having failed to work. "You mustn't worry," he told her, hiding his disappointment. "We can always show you a few mug shots instead, if you'd prefer. I'll give Inspector Youngsbury a ring, and he'll send along his files for you, if you wouldn't mind. Don't worry about it," he repeated as the look in her eyes grew even more unhappy. If he didn't nip her conscience in the bud, he knew she was capable of working herself into an anguish of guilt at having let her constabulary colleagues down. "Don't forget, there's always Mr. Thundridge's statement. I'm sure he got a far better view of the man than you did—and he won't be the last, I'm positive of that, to meet up with the tomato ketchup crowd. We'll have a fine selection of pictures to look at before long, just you ask Inspector Youngsbury . . ."

But, as she later said her goodbyes, Miss Seeton still looked downcast at having disappointed her kind friend Mr. Delphick, who had always been so good to her.

And she knew she wouldn't have the heart to go shopping now for the little presents she had promised herself to buy for Martha, and Stan, and poor Mrs. Maynard.

Chapter 7

NEXT MORNING, IN Plummergen's post office, all the talk was of yesterday's unexpected storm: how, for instance, one of the yews in the churchyard had lost a branch, narrowly missing the respected head of Miss Molly Treeves, the rector's sister, and scaring the life out of little Miss Armitage. Phyllis Armitage had been co-opted by Molly into the Graveyard Tidying Committee and had been picking her dainty way between the tombstones in Miss Treeves's wake when the rain came down and, with it, the heavy evergreen bough.

"A fit of hysterics she went into," recounted Mrs. Spice, with relish, "and Miss Treeves having to slap her round the face, not to mention carry her back soaked to death to the vicarage, before the doctor came."

"She may have missed getting concussion, but there's no telling but what she'll end up with galloping pewmonia," an eager doomster opined. "Sent her to Dr. Knight's nursing home, did they? Cost a pretty penny, if they have."

Mrs. Spice was reluctant to admit she didn't know, turning the conversation skilfully with: "Not that she was the only one taken unawares. Not a word of such a storm on the wireless, was there? And me with my washing out—"

"Well, and so had we all," grumbled Mrs. Scillicough, on whom the demands of her notorious triplets grew more burdensome every day. "Broke my washing line, that squall did, brought everything down in the mud and having to be done again. You can't trust the weather forecast like you used to, can you?"

There came a general chorus of agreement that indeed you couldn't before Mrs. Skinner said gleefully, "Too bad about your roses, Mrs. Henderson. Quite blown about by the wind, weren't they? Take a time to recover, I should think." Mrs. Skinner had once quarrelled with Mrs. Henderson over who was to arrange the flowers in church that week, and not all the tact of Molly Treeves ever achieved true reconciliation.

"I noticed your sweet peas weren't looking too healthy after that heavy rain," retorted Mrs. Henderson, and the two ladies glared at each other while everyone held their breath. Was there to be an out-and-out quarrel, one to enter Plummergen legend and start the sort of feuding on which the village thrived? Mr. Stillman, behind the post office counter, tried desperately to think of some remark to defuse the situation.

The bell over the door tinkled as another customer came in. Everyone turned to see who it might be—and breath was released in joyous sighs. Miss Seeton was always good for a riot of speculation: half of Plummergen harboured serious doubts about her, the other half supported her in her every enterprise. Squabbling together over Miss Seeton was, in village opinion, far more rewarding than any feeble dispute over floral decorations.

United, everyone replied to Miss Seeton's murmured good morning, then intimated that she might go before them, if she wished to complete her shopping quickly, as they were in no hurry. It did not occur to Miss Seeton to be surprised that an entire shopful of busy ladies could be so willing for her to jump the queue: she was most grateful to them for their kindness and, smiling round, said as much. "If you are all quite sure?" she added but took heart from further nods and beckoning gestures and trotted across to Emmeline Putts at the grocery counter.

"Half a pound of butter, please, Emmy, and a packet of Earl Grey tea . . . and may I buy birdseed here—not for my chickens, that is—or must I go somewhere else?"

"Birdseed's the other counter," Emmy confirmed, "but when I've got the rest of your order added up, I suppose I don't mind—what sort were you wanting?"

Miss Seeton blinked. "My usual brand, please. I rather fear I can't remember—oh, the birdseed. How foolish of me to . . . What did you say? I'm sorry, but really I'm not at all sure—"

"There's Flutter, or Chirrup—or Quill, of course, and 'Quill makes parrots perk up proper,' " Emmy chanted in a nasal television tone, living proof that good slogans pay dividends. "How about a packet of Quill?"

Miss Seeton frowned. "Perhaps if I might read the label—parrots, you see—no, I think not. At least . . . no, this looks more suited to my requirements, thank you." While she had been speaking, she was studying the packets which Emmy, sulkily, passed to her across the hardware and general counter. Emmy thought the picture on the Quill label was really pretty and wondered at Mr. Stillman stocking anything else; but she accepted the box of Chirrup from Miss Seeton's hand, then shook her head at the proffered coins.

"Got to add it to the rest, remember? Back over there," and she returned to the grocery counter, where she proceeded to tot everything up again before announcing the result in a smug voice, wrapping the odd assortment into a more or less neat brown parcel while Miss Seeton searched for the correct money.

"Well!" exclaimed Mrs. Spice as Miss Seeton hurried out of the door. "Birdseed—whatever next! Anyone with sense knows you don't go feeding wild birds once they've started nesting, and she's not bought herself a budgie to my knowledge, nor anything else in a cage."

"No more she has," said Mrs. Skinner, "unless it was done yesterday when she went up to London." Since Plummergen is regular in its travelling habits, any deviation from the norm is soon noticed. Everyone on Jack Crabbe's Brettenden bus the previous day had observed Miss Seeton amongst them, smartly dressed; they had watched her head in the direction of the railway station, and made the appropriate deductions with accustomed ease.

"Did anyone see her come back carrying a birdcage? Slip of a thing like her, she'd not have found it easy getting down The Street from the stop, would she?"

Mrs. Spice was thought to have made a good point, which could best be answered, once they arrived (as they could always be relied upon to arrive, scenting gossip as a dog scents a bone) by The Nuts. Miss Erica Nuttel and Mrs. Norah Blaine have lived in Lilikot for a dozen years or more: Lilikot, their plate-glass-windowed home in its prime position almost directly opposite the post office—and the garage, with its bus stop. Nobody leaves or enters or moves around Plummergen without the full knowledge of these ladies: they are as good as a newspaper and cost not a penny.

"The Nuts would know," was the general opinion. "About time they were here, isn't it?" And eager glances were cast at

Mr. Stillman's post office clock, and then through his own plate-glass windows in the direction of Lilikot. But there was no sign of anyone across the road, and, with mutterings of disappointment, everyone turned reluctantly back to the shopping they had abandoned in favour of a good gossip.

The doorbell tinkled again. Everyone looked round: Miss Erica Nuttel, vaguely followed by Mrs. Blaine, appeared, with a portentous look about her.

"Morning," Miss Nuttel greeted the shoppers generally, a gleam in her eye. "Come on, Bunny, no good trying to peer down the road now they know we've rumbled them." Mrs. Blaine stopped craning to see through the half-open door and shut it properly, with a sigh.

"It's too peculiar, though, Eric, you must agree. Such distinguished-looking people—even if"—with a sniff—"she was wearing rather too much scent for my liking—and then a brocade waistcoat is really rather too much at this hour of the day, isn't it? A pound of sugar—molasses, of course—please, Emmy, and two lemons. I am making one last batch of strawberry jam."

"Waxed paper," Miss Nuttel reminded her, then pulled herself up with a feigned start. "Jumped the queue, haven't we? Sorry—thinking of something else."

"Yes," chimed in Bunny, "we've been puzzling about them all the way up The Street. We went to the church to look at the tree that blew down yesterday," which solved the mystery of why nobody had seen them on Lilikot's path a few minutes ago. "Too dangerous, yews. I'm glad we don't have one."

"Poisonous berries, for one thing," said Miss Nuttel. "Leaves, too—might keep goats one day, and where should we be then?"

"Our own milk and cheese, too healthy for words!" cried Bunny, her blackcurrant eyes sparkling. Sparkling with the delight that comes from thwarting the expectations of one's audience by changing the subject and making them wait. It was a favourite Nutty conversational trick: but Plummergen, after thirteen years' knowledge of the ways of The Nuts, knows how to handle them. As the goat motif had been introduced to tantalise, so would it tantalise The Nuts, far more than their audience, if goats now became the major topic of conversation in preference to the briefly mentioned puzzle encountered by Miss Nuttel and Mrs. Blaine on their journey up The Street, that puzzle which was clearly the object of the entire exercise.

"Now, if it's goats you're wanting"—Mrs. Henderson set the ball rolling—"I'd be pleased to put you in touch with my son-in-law's cousin over Murreystone way, Miss Nuttel. Not such a bad youngster, for someone as can't help where he was born" —a reference to the age-old rivalry between Plummergen and its smaller neighbour. "He's got a few goats, I'm told—breeds 'em for pet food, mostly, but doubtless he'd be only too pleased to oblige, seeing as you're known to the family, in a manner of speaking."

Miss Nuttel was still trying to work out whether or not to feel insulted when someone else said, "Ah, but you need to take care with goats, and that's the truth. Treacherous, they can be, if you're not used to—"

Mrs. Spice broke in: "Pet food, ah, very profitable, and I'm sure he'd only sell to people as had pets needed feeding—am I right, Mrs. Henderson?" Before Mrs. Henderson had time to agree, Mrs. Spice hurried on, "Which is what makes it all a bit odd, to my way of thinking—for Miss Seeton to be in here, not ten minutes ago, buying birdseed, when everyone knows she's got neither budgie nor canary." She smirked round at the cluster of speculating shoppers. "A bit odd," she repeated, prompting someone to reply.

As everyone had expected, it was one of The Nuts who rushed into speech: after all, they had harboured grave doubts concerning Miss Seeton since her first days in the village and rarely refrained from voicing these doubts when the opportunity arose.

The voicer on this occasion was bright-eyed Bunny. "And that's not the only thing that's odd! Is it, Eric? We were coming back from the church—too sad, to see those gravestones smashed by that great branch—when we saw two of the most remarkable people just outside the George and Dragon. Didn't we, Eric? A man and a woman, and she was positively *drenched* in perfume, and her clothes were of the finest cut, anyone could see that." The look she cast in Miss Nuttel's direction suggested there might have been some dispute about this. "And *he* was too dashing for words, a most distinguished-looking man. Both of them, so well-turned-out, if a trifle on the *outré* side—you know, it would never surprise me," breathed Bunny in delight, "if they weren't royalty, of sorts. After all . . ."

There came a chorus of sighing agreement, as everyone thought of the minor Russian royalty leasing one of Plummergen's larger houses, a high-walled haven of peace and solitude, for six months. Solitude which meant that any visitors would tactfully make their stay elsewhere . . .

"More reporters, probably," remarked Miss Nuttel as Bunny scowled. Plummergen has experienced more invasions (from Fleet Street) in the seven years since Miss Seeton first came to live there than during the entire period of the Viking troubles. Amateur snoops as The Nuts are, they heartily resent the professionals: especially since most of these are sympathetic to Miss Seeton's cause, and several are positive allies.

"Been lots of strangers, haven't there, after us coming second in the Competition," pointed out Mrs. Spice as everyone else mentally weighed the merits of more royalty or more reporters and couldn't choose between them. There had been more than one interview given and photos in the papers: on the other hand, blue blood was blue blood . . .

"Oh, these aren't common tourists," Bunny hastened to assure her. "Far from it." A resentful look came into her little black eyes. "Mind you, I have to admit that if they are royalty"—with another scowl in Miss Nuttel's direction—"I really can't see why they were talking just now to Miss Seeton, of all people . . ."

Erica Nuttel tossed her head. "Tried to pretend," she said above the gasps of glee which greeted this revelation, "they hadn't expected to meet. Clumsy, though. Wouldn't fool anyone. Didn't fool us—plain as a pikestaff it had all been arranged earlier. Cover story."

"Cover, for why?" somebody demanded peevishly. "What's her reason for not wanting it known as she's acquainted with royalty?"

This struck a chord with almost everyone in the shop, and The Nuts began to fear they had lost their audience. It was Mrs. Blaine who, after a moment's frantic thought, rushed to the rescue. "Maybe they aren't royalty, after all," she conceded in thrilling tones. "Everyone knows the princess, or whatever she is, at The Meadows isn't very rich—how can she be, when she never gives balls or soirees or, well, entertains, does she?"

A general murmur agreed that she did not. Bunny looked smug. "Perhaps we ought to wonder why such sociable, smart people come to visit her when she so obviously won't want anything to do with them . . ." And she paused to let them all murmur again, and looked smugger than ever.

"They can't be reporters, because nothing's happened. Or," she added hastily as Eric caught her eye, "even if it has, they're much too well dressed for reporters. So it has to be clear," she concluded in triumph, "that they must be *criminals* of some sort—who else has so much money they can afford clothes like that?"

"Might be models, or film stars—on holiday," suggested Miss Nuttel halfheartedly while the rest of the shop began to thrill with speculation. Bunny shook her head.

"Mrs. Spice gave us the answer, Eric. It's obvious! Why did Miss Seeton buy a box of birdseed when she hasn't got a bird? What do *you* do with seeds, Eric?"

"Plant them in my—I mean *our*—garden," came the prompt reply. Bunny nodded vigorously.

"And what's in a packet of birdseed? Millet, and sunflower seeds, and—"

"Nothing much wrong with sunflower seeds. Eat them ourselves. Very healthy."

"—and," continued Mrs. Blaine triumphantly, ignoring Eric's interjection, "hemp—*drugs*—and Miss Seeton, talking to those people not twenty minutes ago . . ."

Chapter 8

"THOSE PEOPLE" WERE staying at the George and Dragon, which, since Plummergen's near-success in the Best Kept Village Competition, had been doing excellent business: so excellent that landlord Charley Mountfitchet was busily having the place redecorated, room by room, in celebration of Plummergen's status as one of the county's acknowledged jewels. As each room fell vacant, it was swathed in dust-sheets for the duration. A whole gang of Charley's relatives and friends would descend upon the unsuspecting chamber in a whirlwind of paint, paper, and carpet: and once the tumult had died, duster, air-freshener, and vacuum cleaner were wielded to superlative effect by the multi-talented Doris, headwaitress, receptionist, and general factotum.

Charley's greatest coup had been the creation, in honour of recent events, of the Blue Riband Suite, which sounded splendid. The "suite" had been formed by the cutting of a door between the bathroom on one floor and its neighbouring bedroom. Access to the bathroom via the corridor was blocked off, and people in the other rooms had to trot up (or, if they preferred, down) a flight of stairs to use the hotel's facilities: but Charley was proud of the Blue Riband Suite and charged twice as much as for other rooms despite the late arrival of the expensive carpet he had ordered.

"Those people" had no hesitation in booking the suite for a week and cheerfully paid the deposit which bitter experience had taught Charley Mountfitchet to ask from any guests he had never seen before. The gentleman in the natty brocade waistcoat which had so disturbed Mrs. Blaine signed the register with a flourish, then could not quite prevent a faint blush from rising in his damask cheek as Doris drew in her breath upon reading what he had written.

Mr. Richard Nash, Miss Juliana Popjoy proclaimed the register in an elegant script. Mr. Nash nodded politely to Doris, collected the key, passed it to Miss Popjoy with a smile, and picked up their suitcases. "No lift, I see," he said cheerfully. "Ah, well, no doubt the exercise will do me good."

Just as the brazen pair (as Doris intended to call them, once they were safely out of earshot) reached the foot of the stairs, the front door of the George burst open, and in flew two small boys, grubby, breathless, and excited. They shouted "Hello!" to Doris as they thundered past her desk and then began a bout of what looked like all-in wrestling for a few moments before the younger, an urchin of around eight years old, cried: "Race you!" His brother stopped trying to wrench off his head and nodded. "Ready, steady, go!"

The pair of them ignored Mr. Nash and his suitcases, and the startled form of the personable Miss Popjoy, to charge together, shrieking, up the stairs. It was hard to believe that there was a new Axminster carpet beneath the clattering shoes; as far as the boys were concerned, it could have been bare wood.

Doris winced. "Little horrors," she muttered, all idea of censuring Mr. Nash and Miss Popjoy forgotten. Plummergen will sometimes sympathise with the morals of consenting adults, so long as whatever they do is done in private and doesn't frighten the horses; but badly behaved children are altogether another matter. Doris glared after the disappearing chaos of the two small boys and decided to favour the stately upward retreat of Mr. Nash and his paramour with an indulgent smile.

She did not reinstate the smile, which had faded as she turned back to her work, when the front door opened again to admit an elderly man, arthritic on sticks, sporting an enormous, drooping, white moustache and escorted by a couple who were clearly the parents of the two small boys. It must be supposed that the door had been opened more quietly than before; it was, however, impossible to tell, above the continuing juvenile racket from upstairs. Doris pitched her voice pointedly low as she passed their keys to the newcomers with a greeting.

"Speak up, my dear," requested the elderly man, putting a blue-veined hand behind his ear. His moustache quivered as he smiled at Doris. "Old age, you know, old age—I'm not the man I was."

"Come on, Grampus, enough of such talk," the younger man scolded him at once. "Annabel, tell your papa not to try enlisting our sympathy for his declining years—he could give each of us a run for our money any day of the week, as he knows perfectly well. He grows younger all the time, doesn't he?"

"Indeed he does," Annabel said, smiling fondly upon her parent, who began to preen himself at the flattery. "And it upsets us to hear you talking that way, Papa, as if you were almost in your grave. I wish you wouldn't."

Grampus winked at Doris. "They don't like to admit I won't see seventy again, and I take that as a great compliment. Dragged me out for a walk along the canal and refused to take no for an answer—"

"And had a real effort to keep up with him," the younger man said with a chuckle. "My father-in-law can certainly set a good pace, arthritis or not, and as for all this talk of a dicky heart . . . He's worn us out, hasn't he, Annabel? He'll outlive the lot of us, I'm sure."

Annabel's father looked pleased and chuckled as his son-in-law clapped him on the shoulder. "Besides," added the younger man, "what would the boys do without their Grampus? Which reminds me"—he turned to Doris again—"have they gone up to their room yet?"

Doris scowled towards the foot of the stairs. "Well, as for going up, yes, they have—as I'd have thought anyone could've known without asking—but as regards *to the room*, I couldn't rightly say, not unless it was already open, on account of me not having given them the key. Which is only part of my job, keys, and if you'll excuse me, I must be getting about my business."

With a toss of her head Doris emerged from behind the reception desk and made for the kitchen without once looking back. Thus she missed the knowing looks of the Standon family, and Annabel's murmurs of boyish high spirits, and her father's of the dear little rascals' excitement at their splendid holiday, and her husband's remark that perhaps they really ought to pop upstairs and see what was happening, not that he thought anything was likely to be wrong, but . . .

In the Blue Riband Suite four desperate ears had been resolutely blocked against the rumpus of schoolboys racing up and down the corridor. Mr. Nash, elegant in his brocade waistcoat, had been ordered to keep out of the way while his lady unpacked the luggage; the order was, perforce, given in stentorian tones, far removed from Miss Popjoy's normally melodious voice. Mr. Nash, having settled himself well out of her way by the window, gritted his teeth and made no complaint, though the din from outside was horrendous. As he watched Miss Popjoy assigning various items of clothing to drawers and wardrobes, he wondered (but not aloud) if Plummergen had really been the right choice for a holiday; yet he knew better than to say anything to that effect until his lady showed signs of similar weakness. It had been her idea in the first place, after all.

Juliana closed the last drawer and felt her duty done. She was now willing to permit a slight showing of weakness. "Dickie," she said thoughtfully, "shouldn't we go and see if they're slaughtering each other? Such a noise . . ."

Dickie, with the true-born Englishman's dislike of making a scene, shook his head. "With a bit of luck they are. Slaughtering each other, I mean. But if by any sad chance they aren't, their parents are unlikely to thank us for putting a stop to the little darlings' fun. They surely can't carry on like that for much longer—the manager or somebody's bound to put a stop to it."

"Oh, Dickie." Juliana, despite her irritation, had to laugh. "Why not own up and admit that you just don't want a kick on the shins? From the sound of it those brats are wearing very sturdy boots—hobnailed, probably."

"I'd take a bet on it—I mean, I wouldn't," Dickie said hastily as the laugh in Juliana's eyes changed at once to a frown both worried and warning. "Sorry. What I meant to say was, they're more than likely hobnailed—that is"—and in his turn he frowned—"if anyone wears hobnails nowadays?" Warily he looked at Juliana. He brightened. "Perhaps the boots are football boots, and the noise comes from the studs—although the thought of football in July does rather disturb one's finer feelings, don't you think?"

His nonsense made her laugh again, and then they smiled together in sympathy as the commotion in the corridor came suddenly to a blessed end. Dickie held his breath while Juliana began to count aloud. At sixty they both relaxed.

"After all that I need a drink," Dickie said. "Suppose there's room service in this place?"

"Dickie Nash! When we've barely arrived! Besides," she reminded him, "we're going to need all our wits about us for finding the way—you certainly are, because you're driving. Your bump of location is much more efficient than mine."

Dickie blinked at her. "Good gracious, why should bumps of location come into it? You must know where we're going, surely. He's your friend, after all."

Juliana looked uneasy. She opened her handbag and drew out an envelope: an envelope of a curious purple shade, with the address printed in emerald-green ink. The letter she took from the envelope was written by a flamboyant hand in purple ink, on emerald-green paper. She held the letter out to Dickie, who pulled a face. Juliana laughed. "Oh, yes, I know, but at least he's printed his address so we know what it is. It's just a pity he didn't explain *where* it is, if you understand me—not that I suppose he thought he needed to. This letter's a year old if it's a day. There was no suggestion then that I might want to visit him."

"And no telephone number, I suppose. That would be too much to hope for, after what you've told me about him."

"No telephone number," agreed Juliana. "The postman's probably the only person in the county who knows exactly where we're supposed to be going—and didn't we pass a sub-post office as we drove in? We could go and ask there or try to find somewhere that would sell us a large-scale map. I meant to do it before we left, so it's my fault . . ."

"I'll forgive you, if you'll only let me have a little spot of something before we head off into the wide blue yonder in search of the elusive Mentley Collier." Dickie sighed. "Juliana, my love, it's delightful to be impetuous occasionally, but my instincts tell me that on this particular occasion it might have been as well to be a little less impetuous. I still say you ought to have dropped Collier a line or two—even a post-card would have done—to warn him we were on the way."

"Warn him? Goodness, you make it sound as if I'm one of his creditors. He always used to have dozens, poor Mentley, in the old days. That's why he got into the habit of being, well, inaccessible. I'm flattered he trusted me enough to give me his address, although after all these years he ought to know I'm not likely to sneak on him to the Inland Revenue—though of course," she reflected, "they might have caught up with him after all, and he'll have done another bunk."

Dickie merely looked at her for a moment before saying: "A drink. A stiff one, Juliana Popjoy—and you're paying."

"On condition that we go out and hunt for a map first, I suppose I'll have to agree. I shouldn't have been so quick to come here without checking first, I do admit—but, well, he's not the only reason for our trip, is he? What could be nicer than holidaying in the Garden of England? Especially when it gets us away from the builders and decorators."

Dickie gave her a gentle hug. "It'll be worth it in the long run, you know it will. After all, we'd talked for ages about having the shop refurbished to increase business, and, well, I know it was my fault we never could afford a proper job. I still can't tell you how sorry I am about everything—and it isn't as if I'd exactly expected my uncle to leave me a legacy, was it? So it was almost like the final win to end all wins— and I felt it was the least I could do, to compensate you for all the worries about money you've had on my account over the years. But I really have made an effort to give up gambling now, haven't I?"

"You have, and I'm proud of you, Dickie." Juliana gave him a fond peck on the cheek. "And it was one of the nicest compliments anyone's ever paid me, trusting me with all your inheritance and not keeping anything for yourself. So—so unselfish." There was a quaver in her voice and a hint of tears in her lovely eyes. Dickie, an Englishman to the depths of his innermost soul, hastily thwarted any display of emotion.

"Unselfish? Not a bit, as I keep telling you. I'm just taking a leaf out of Uncle Brummel's book and consolidating my investments—with every expectation of goodness-knows-how-much per cent return on the expenditure. After all, an antique shop in Bath is a nice little gold mine—I'd never have gone into partnership with you in the first place if I didn't expect to make pots of lovely lolly to support me in my decrepit old age. But now"—and Dickie struck a dashing pose—"I'll be able to look forward to a delightfully decadent old age, instead."

"Which is many years away," Juliana reminded him firmly, "and the shop has to make the money first. So stop dreaming about gorgeous young girls, or an unlimited supply of gin, or whatever form your decadence plans to take, and let's go and explore Plummergen—I wish I could remember why that name sounds familiar—to find a decent map."

And it was at the start of this excursion, just outside the George and Dragon, that Juliana Popjoy and Dickie Nash, closely observed by The Nuts, bumped into Miss Emily Dorothea Seeton.

Chapter 9

IT HAD BEEN Dickie who spotted her first, hurrying down The Street with her bundle of purchases held in one hand and her umbrella hooked over the other arm. She blinked vaguely in the direction of the George, sighting strangers on the steps—but, since the Competition, strangers were not so uncommon in Plummergen, and Miss Seeton was never one to snoop. She half registered the pleasant thought that Mr. Mountfitchet, landlord of the George and Dragon, must be delighted with so many new customers, or did one call them clients? Whatever their correct name might be, she was sure he must be glad of them . . . and she would have trotted on to cross The Street in the direction of her own dear cottage, when, to her great surprise, one of the strangers uttered her name.

"Juliana, look—surely that's Miss Seeton! Recognise the umbrella? Miss Seeton—Miss Seeton, hello there!" And Dickie took his lady by the arm, leading her the few steps across the car park in front of the George to stand face to face with someone they had never thought to meet again.

Miss Seeton blinked once more, smiled in response to Dickie's smile, and before he could say anything else said:

"Mr. Nash, what a lovely surprise! And Miss Popjoy, too, of course. How could I forget?" The artist's trained eye is a boon to anyone, such as Miss Seeton, with a large number of acquaintances. "Such an enjoyable time . . ."

But then Miss Seeton, an utterly truthful person, found herself unable to complete the sentence she had so thoughtlessly begun. There was no doubt that she had enjoyed the first part of the cruise she had taken last year around the Greek islands on the liner *Eurydice*; several of her friends had travelled on the same ship, and congenial company had only added to her delight in the Aegean and its glories of nature, architecture, and history. She had made new friends, Dickie and Juliana among them; but, before long, one of the party had been murdered, another found hanging in his cabin, and a third arrested. Those stalwarts who had remained on board the *Eurydice* until the final resolution of the case had completed their holiday on dry land.

Uncomfortable memories drifted into Miss Seeton's mind, and her smile was slightly uneven as she quickly continued: "Are you staying here at the George and Dragon? Such an attractive building, I always feel—so symmetrical, and the creeper gives a charming effect, don't you think?"

"The whole village is charming, from what we've seen of it so far," Juliana said after everyone had finished shaking hands and trying to pass no more than casual remarks concerning that unfortunate cruise. "We were just going out for an exploratory walk, to search the shops for a large-scale map of the area. I forgot to buy one before we came—we left in rather a rush, you see, and Dickie's too much of a gentleman to say it's all my fault we're not sure where we're going."

"Where *are* you going?" enquired Miss Seeton. "That is, if it is not an impertinence on my part to ask. But, as a resident of this area for some seven years now, perhaps I could be of assistance. My cottage is just over there," and she turned, blushing with pride, to indicate nearby Sweetbriars. "You might care, perhaps, to join me for a cup of coffee—or tea, if you would prefer. I have just bought a fresh packet of Earl Grey," and she brandished her brown-paper parcel under their noses.

Dickie raised a questioning eyebrow to Juliana, who said at once: "That would be lovely, thank you, Miss Seeton. And if, over the teacups, you could tell us anything about some little place called Murreystone, which I gather isn't too far from here . . ."

Miss Seeton said faintly, "Good gracious!" and Juliana regarded her with curiosity but was too polite to press for an explanation. She looked at Dickie, who at once offered to carry Miss Seeton's parcel for her, offering his escort instead when she reminded him that Sweetbriars was only a matter of thirty yards away, at most.

Fifteen minutes later the three of them were in the sitting room of the cottage Miss Seeton had inherited from her godmother and cousin, Mrs. Bannet. As they enjoyed Earl Grey tea and slices of Madeira cake, Miss Seeton talked of the Best Kept Village Competition and displayed the scrapbook of newspaper cuttings Martha Bloomer had compiled.

"I had no idea village life was so exciting," Juliana said as the full tale of Murreystone's duplicity came to its breathless end. "I'd always thought of the antiques world as being a fairly cutthroat business, but compared to what you've been telling us, it's positively dull—and as for Dickie in his Cambridge cloisters, he doesn't realise he's born, does he?"

"Oh, I wouldn't say that, exactly," protested Dickie, a Fellow of King's College. "If you read C. P. Snow . . ."

"Don't be silly, Dickie." Juliana shook her head at him as he railed off into silence and, to cover his confusion, helped himself to a further slice of Madeira cake. Intellectual honesty would not let him argue, even in fun, with what was clearly the truth. "*The Masters* is fiction—this is fact, isn't is, Miss Seeton?" Juliana tapped the cover of the now closed scrapbook, smiling at her hostess. "I'm not surprised that *you* were surprised when I asked you all about Murreystone—and isn't it lucky we met you? I might have gone blundering into the post office here and asked exactly the same question—and never have emerged alive!"

"Oh, come now, Juliana," began Dickie, then spotted the appreciative twinkle in Miss Seeton's eye and subsided into a mouthful of Madeira as she said:

"One must allow for a certain amount of what I gather is called journalistic licence, Miss Popjoy, yet it cannot be denied that the . . . what one must call, I suppose, the rival village, did carry matters to somewhat extreme lengths on this particular occasion. It may seem strange to outsiders such as yourselves, and indeed, when I first came to live here, I thought exactly the same as you, but most of the time, from my observation, everybody concerned appears to enjoy themselves a great deal. Not unlike houses," said Miss Seeton, still twinkling, as she poured more tea; thus failing to observe the way her guests exchanged puzzled looks.

"Different colours," Miss Seeton continued to reminisce happily while Dickie blinked and Juliana frowned. "So very childish, sometimes, and no amount of order marks would keep them quiet if they were in high spirits—the girls, I mean. Flour bombs, and throwing rolls of lavatory paper, and once, as I recall, someone hid all the right hockey boots—right-footed boots, that is to say—just before the

House Final, which Miss Edmunds found extremely vexatious. She was the Games Mistress," she explained as Dickie, understanding her at last, sighed with quiet relief, and Juliana hid a smile. "So you see, after a life spent teaching, I am not unaccustomed to these little rivalries. And is not a healthy spirit of competition thought to be good for the development of one's character?"

"The happiest days of your life," murmured Dickie and pulled a face. Juliana chuckled.

"I'm not going to voice an opinion on that, but I still think it was just as well for me I didn't start asking too many questions about Murreystone in Plummergen's post office—and I'm very pleased we met you in time, Miss Seeton, with your being an expert on these parts. I'm sure you can tell us what we need to know, especially as Mentley Collier—the friend we're looking for—is an artist, and so are you. Do you know him, by any chance? It's the sort of happy coincidence that would be useful right now."

Miss Seeton looked slightly overcome by Juliana's statement of confidence. A faint blush rose in her cheeks as she said, "I would hardly call myself an artist in the sense in which I understand you to use the term, Miss Popjoy. I was a mere teacher of the subject—and there is the old saying, is there not? That those who can, do," said Miss Seeton earnestly. "While those who cannot, teach. And in my own view there is more than an element of truth in the theory. And, as for being an expert on this part of Kent . . ."

"You're bound to be more expert than either of us," said Juliana. "Though perhaps it was a bit unreasonable of me to have expected you to know anything of Mentley. He's rather a recluse, so I suppose it's not surprising."

"Recluse?" snorted Dickie. "According to Juliana, Miss Seeton, this leftover beatnik has the Inland Revenue permanently on his heels and spends all his time rushing from one address to another so they won't catch him. The letter she has is a year out of date—the chap could be on the other side of the country by now. But if you did happen to have heard of a place called . . . called what, Juliana?"

"Filkins—it's an old farmhouse, or rather one of the barns. The farm itself was burned down when the previous owner committed suicide, according to Mentley." Miss Seeton shook her head and made regretful noises. "Mentley says," continued Juliana, "that this farmer had delusions of being a bit of an artist himself and much preferred painting to raising sheep. He converted the barn Mentley's living in and turned it into a studio—there are some of his canvases left, huge Turneresque daubs, Mentley says—not that Turner daubed, but you know what I mean, I'm sure—anyway, they're good-size canvases, and Mentley's been painting over them. He says they really aren't much use for anything else, and the poor farmer had no chance at all. Apparently, it was when the Royal Academy refused his thirteenth picture on the trot that he decided enough was enough, and . . ." She made a little gesture of finality.

"How very sad," murmured Miss Seeton. "Not to know the limitations of one's own talent and to react to disappointment in so—so dramatic a fashion . . ."

"Dramatic it certainly is," said Dickie. "I've told you before, Juliana, I think your old boyfriend is pulling your leg. Or he's had his leg pulled by the locals. It's just the sort of joke a gaggle of mischievous rustics would love to play on a gullible newcomer."

Juliana chuckled briefly, then sighed. "I must admit he never was one of the quickest-witted people around—except when it came to keeping a step or two ahead of the tax man—but you're right, he'd fall for anything plausible, and it's such a splendid story it simply cries out to be believed. Don't you agree, Miss Seeton?"

"I think it would depend," Miss Seeton said after hesitating briefly, "on whether he had any particular reason to suppose the story to be true, or otherwise. These canvases, for instance. No doubt there could be some other perfectly good explanation for their presence in such quantities, and in such a very convenient location—but then again, one cannot exclude a considerable amount of dramatic licence, if that is the phrase I want, in the explaining. And if your friend, being artistic by nature, has sympathy with the more dramatic aspects of art, and, by association, with a similar style in, well, in narrative art . . ."

"He'd fall for anything plausible," Juliana said again with a laugh as Miss Seeton fluttered to a halt. "Poor old Mentley. Yes, he was forever getting himself embroiled in all sorts of bother other people had started in the first place—he's a confidence man's dream. He'd be first in the queue to buy shares in the only diamond mine in England, if it looked like an even remotely good thing, so he'd lap up a suicidal farmer and an unlimited supply of canvas that gave him somewhere to paint in peace, because that's really all he's ever wanted to do."

"Which makes him," Dickie said, "the ideal copyist, as you've said before that he is without ever quite explaining why. But now I think I understand. If the chap's already more than halfway to believing any old tale that turns up, he'll believe that what he's doing is the real thing, or near enough. And sincerity in art—as I think Miss Seeton will agree—isn't going to result in rubbish. No wonder he can turn out what you say are near-masterpieces."

"They always were before, so unless he's changed a great deal, I imagine they still are," Juliana said. "Which is why we want to see him, isn't it?" She turned to Miss Seeton and smiled apologetically as she began to explain.

"It was all my idea, Miss Seeton, although Dickie tries to pretend he thought of it now that he's realised how much it will improve our business." She made a face at Dickie's little cry of outrage and winked at Miss Seeton, who smiled benevolently upon them both. "Anyway," Juliana went on, "it all goes back to Dickie's Uncle Brummel, who died recently and left him some money—a real windfall, although it isn't a fortune, by any means."

"Quite unexpected," Dickie chipped in, nodding. "Hadn't shown any more interest in me when he was alive than I'd shown in him." He chuckled. "Which is the reason he gave in his will for leaving me the lot—said I was the only one of his relatives with sense enough not to go badgering him for a share of the loot, and because I'd pleased him in the way I'd behaved, he felt he should return the compliment."

"Absolutely batty," Juliana said while Miss Seeton permitted herself a quiet smile humouring Uncle Brummel's idea of suitable testamentary disposition. "But of course Dickie didn't say no—money's always useful. Especially . . . well, you know a little about that, don't you?" For on the cruise where they had all met, Miss Seeton had played an indirect part in persuading Dickie Nash to give up gambling. "And he said, Miss Seeton, that—"

She broke off at an explosion of coughing from Mr. Nash, who clearly feared himself about to be embarrassed by an emotional expression of Juliana's gratitude. She stuttered, collected herself, smiled at poor Dickie, and merely said:

"Anyway, we decided to blow the lot on a complete overhaul of the shop in Bath. Business seems to be improving, and if we can only bring in more customers, I'm sure it will go on getting better. We're knocking through a wall and building on the back, and the entire stock's been put into store while the decorators are in—the most gorgeous wallpaper, Miss Seeton, and we're even having new lights . . ."

Juliana broke off and laughed at her own enthusiasm. "Well, you get the picture, I'm sure. *Picture* now being the operative word, because I thought we might get a marvellous effect if there were lots of old masters on the walls—the paper will set them off beautifully—but of course the cost would be astronomical. *If* they were genuine, that is."

"Hence," Dickie summed up as Juliana drew breath, "this hunt for Mentley Collier, crackpot but gifted copyist who's always short of money, and—according to reliable information from the lady on my left—daft enough for his old girlfriend to be able to sweet-talk him into doing her a favour without charging the earth."

"Dickie, you make it sound like exploitation, which is hardly fair. You know very well I checked with several galleries and dealers before we came away—I know what the going rate for good copies is likely to be, and I've no intention of doing Mentley down. Neither is it fair of you to talk as if he's crazy. He's just a little . . . eccentric, I suppose, and simply hasn't grown up yet. And, as I have told you repeatedly, he is nothing but a very old *friend*," laying particular emphasis on the final word.

"I'm not jealous," said Dickie cheerfully. "I just hope you aren't going to be disappointed when you catch up with him after all this time. If," he added, "you ever do," and he turned to his hostess. "Any idea of where the beatniks hang out in these parts, Miss Seeton? Or, if you haven't, can you think of anyone who might know? The future of the antique shop," he informed her in thrilling tones, "hangs upon your reply . . ."

Chapter 10

Miss Seeton glanced up at the clock. "What a pity that Bert—such a helpful young man, and not the least hint of a bad temper—in fact, he is one of the jolliest persons I know, and such a great friend of my dear Martha, who is also a cockney, although of course she does not have red hair—but he has finished for today. His round, I mean. Because, you see, he has a van, not a bicycle. So good for fresh air and exercise—a bicycle, that is—besides saving on petrol, as I have found myself—not that I drive, of course, but then, one cannot carry parcels in safety on one's handlebars, so a van is far more practical. In bad weather, especially, as well as being faster, so that one may cover more ground in the same time. And I understand that he delivers the post to Murreystone as well as Plummergen."

Miss Seeton's incoherent thoughts had finally careered to what, Juliana thankfully realised, was a comprehensible conclusion. At least, she hoped she'd comprehended it. She took a deep breath. "You mean that Bert, who is the village postman, could have told us where Filkins is, if only he'd still been at work? And as he doesn't come from Plummergen, he wouldn't have minded too much if we'd asked him about Murreystone?" She gave Dickie a quick look which hinted that he'd better leave all further interpretation to her: he looked as if *floundering* would be a generous description of his mental state.

Miss Seeton smiled at her and nodded. "Oh, yes, but it is still morning, even if a little late, which means that we may be fairly confident of finding dear Mr. Treeves at home—not that he will necessarily be indoors, you understand, as he is a very keen gardener, and most knowledgeable. He" —and from Miss Seeton's lips a faint sigh drifted— "has no need of Greenfinger to point his way—but then, I am so fortunate in having dear Stan to tend the garden for me. And as it is in the afternoons that he mostly goes about his pastoral duties," she concluded, looking pleased, "I could telephone him now."

Juliana missed half a beat before saying quickly: "Don't let us interfere with your plans for the day, Miss Seeton, please. If you want to ring this Mr. Greenfinger, or any of your friends, we'll be on our way—won't we, Dickie?"

But before Mr. Nash had time to agree, Miss Seeton said quickly: "Oh, I don't believe it can be his real name, Miss Popjoy—-so unlikely, don't you think, and I had always been of the opinion that it must be a pseudonym, for professional purposes, and not in the least like, ahem, James Bond." And a delicate blush rose in Miss Seeton's cheeks. "One could not help, you see, noticing the posters—for the cinema—and then there were reviews, and people speaking about the films on the wireless—yet I hardly think that anyone who was fond of gardening would care to paint a young woman in such a—an unusual fashion, do you?"

Juliana hesitated, and this time it was Dickie who came to the rescue. "*Goldfinger*," he said, nodding. "Rather a good yarn, I thought, although not much like the book. But then

I gather that's often the case—sometimes they alter things so much the plot hardly makes sense any more."

Miss Seeton smiled. "Books can be such a blessing, can they not? Although, as Mr. Nash says, not always entirely clear. When I first knew I was coming to live in my little cottage in the country, I went straight round to the local shop and asked the owner for his advice, and Stan has told me more than once that he agrees I could hardly have done better. Greenfinger," she said happily, "has pointed the way for me most knowledgeably ever since my first days here, although I confess that sometimes I find what he says a trifle confusing, but then, I have dear Stan to consult, and when he is at work there is always Mr. Treeves, when he is at home. Would you like me," she enquired, half-rising from her seat, "to telephone the dear vicar now?"

Dickie looked at Juliana. Juliana looked at Dickie. In a quick pantomime of bewilderment, they indicated to each other that they hadn't a clue what their hostess was talking about. They found it hard to credit that a sudden attack of moral fervour had made her realise some desperate need for clerical guidance: Miss Seeton, after all, was hardly the interfering type. She'd accepted their unorthodox relationship without a murmur during that cruise on the *Eurydice*—and afterwards, as well. Or did she feel that shipboard romances were one thing and dry land quite another? Would they next be asked if they wanted the banns called?

"Er," said Dickie at last, words tangled in his throat. He went red and stared at his lady. "What do you think?" he weakly enquired, while Miss Seeton murmured of being sure she knew the number, but she'd better look it up, to be on the safe side. "Although," she added as Juliana wondered what on earth to say, "it must perhaps seem slightly extravagant, as he lives just across the road. One could almost call the request to him over the garden wall—but then, he might not be in the garden, and there is always the chance," she added honestly, "one might not completely understand the reply. One hesitates to criticise the cloth," she concluded, "but it has to be admitted that there are times when the dear vicar is, well, a little muddled about things . . ."

Not for worlds could Juliana and Dickie have met each other's eyes as Miss Seeton said this. "Oh, really?" was all that Juliana could manage, while Dickie cleared his throat with some force and gazed at his shoes. But Miss Seeton noticed nothing strange in their manner as she left her chair and made for the door.

"I will repeat the instructions he gives me, clearly," she told her still-baffled guests, "but perhaps it would be a good idea for Miss Popjoy to write down what I say, so that there will be no confusion. And if it should happen to be *Miss* Treeves who answers, instead of her brother, then so much the better. She is almost as deeply involved in parish affairs as the dear vicar, and her knowledge of Murreystone is sure to be reliable, although I believe she does not attend services there. The problems of the rural clergy," lamented Miss Seeton as she vanished through the half-open door into the hall, shaking her head. "Overwork and scattered parishes— so very vexing to a conscientious parson, which Mr. Treeves undoubtedly is."

Her final words were accompanied by the flutter of pages as she leafed through the telephone directory and by sighs of thankful comprehension from Dickie and Juliana. It had taken a long time, and covered several topics connected only in Miss Seeton's mind, but they'd sorted it out at last. Having lost the chance to pick the brains of Bert, the redheaded cockney postman shared by Plummergen and Murreystone, Miss Seeton had wisely decided that the next best authority to consult must be the clergyman, who also counted both villages among his responsibilities. Just where James Bond and Stan the gardener came into it all, let alone the mysterious Greenfinger of whose views Miss Seeton seemed to think so highly, they thought it better not to ask. Suffice it to say that they looked like finding out, after all, the whereabouts of Filkins, farmhouse studio home to the artist Mentley Collier; and Juliana, pulling a face at Dickie, took the purple envelope out of her handbag and prepared to write down on the back whatever instructions Miss Seeton, from the telephone in the hall, passed on to her.

The instructions were clear and surprisingly concise: Juliana's elegant script had not completely covered the envelope by the time Miss Seeton, with repeated thanks, hung up. It had been Molly, not the Reverend Arthur, Treeves who had answered her call, which was (Miss Seeton had to admit) most fortunate for everyone concerned.

"And we're really grateful to you for going to all this trouble for us, Miss Seeton," Juliana told her hostess with a smile as, having studied it carefully, she put the envelope away in her bag again. "Aren't we, Dickie?"

"Indeed we are," responded Mr. Nash. "I tell you what, Miss Seeton. How about taking a spot of lunch with us, by way of a thank-you for your noble efforts on our behalf, and then running out to this Filkins place with us in the afternoon? Collier's an artist, remember, so you'll have quite a bit in common. I'm sure you'd be interested to meet each other."

Juliana nodded. "He'd love it, Miss Seeton. Do say you can spare the time—you're not too busy today, are you?"

"How very kind of you both," began Miss Seeton but went no further. She suddenly remembered, and frowned, and shook her head sadly. "Birdseed," she murmured. "I bought it specially—though Stan did say . . . but no doubt it would not be too urgent if I left it . . ." As so often seemed to happen, she was torn between the Scylla of duty and the Charybdis of pleasure. An excursion to a real artist's studio would be such a treat, and yet . . . "I'm sure it will be safe enough in the box," Miss Seeton said with a hopeful nod. "Stan said so, and he is nearly always right about such matters . . ."

Juliana caught her eye, eloquent with an unspoken plea for reassurance. "From what you've told us about Stan, I'd agree with you," she said firmly. "If he says everything's going to be all right if you, er, leave it in the box, then I'm sure everything *will* be all right." Dickie mouthed a silent *what?* at her, but she scowled quickly at him and went on: "So that's settled, is it? You're coming to lunch with us over at the hotel, and then we'll head off on our excursion to wildest Murreystone, and Filkins Farm. Only, in the interests of village harmony, we'll be very careful not to let a soul know that's where we're going," she said, smiling to encourage Miss Seeton to smile. Which, after a few more moments of conscience-stricken thought, Miss Seeton duly managed to do.

And then she decided she was looking forward to her lunch. While *cuisine* at the George and Dragon was not particularly *haute*, it was certainly more than just good plain fare; and, when served by Doris in her cheerful headwaitress persona, made for an enjoyable meal, especially when the company was as pleasant as Miss Seeton recalled that Dickie and Juliana could be. After she had collected her umbrella from its clip beside the hall table—on this occasion, she decided, nothing but her best gold-handled brolly would do—Miss Seeton hummed a gay little tune to herself and patted her hair straight in the looking glass with a smile as she adjusted her hat.

Once across the road, however, smiles soon turned to frowns, and for anyone to be able to hear it a little tune would have needed to be bellowed, rather than hummed. The party from Sweetbriars were just studying their menus and discussing whether to share a bottle of wine or to buy by the glass so that everyone wouldn't be forced to eat the same colour meat, when the Standon family made its presence most disturbingly apparent.

It was the clatter of the boys' boots down the stairs which first alerted Juliana and Dickie to the notion that their choice of eating place might not have been a happy one. They gazed at each other in horror when the first shrieks sounded in the reception area, and Dickie groaned aloud as the boys, with their father not too far behind, came rushing into the dining room with a clamour of which table would be best for Grampus to look out of the window, and bags them sit either side of him so's they could try the froth on his beer, because he'd promised.

"You should wait for Grampus to decide where he wants to sit," their father reminded them. "He might prefer not to have you two rascals fidgeting next to him," and he looked round at the other diners with a rueful smile. Doris, who was waiting to show the party to the table she had selected, almost audibly ground her teeth.

"He promised," said the younger boy.

"He won't mind," said the older. "Not if we leave him a seat—he'll know it's for him, and you can order the beer for him before he comes, can't you, Dad?"

"And we can taste it for him," said the younger boy in a loud voice. "In case it's poisoned or anything."

"For heaven's sake, Gary!" His father gave him a brisk clip round the ear, and Gary let out a yell. His brother grinned and pulled his hair. Gary stopped yelling to kick him on the shins. His brother yelled in his turn, then pulled Gary's hair again, whereupon a scuffle ensued with the pair swaying dangerously near the table where Dickie Nash sat wincing and Juliana Popjoy struggled to maintain her poise instead of delivering the forceful speech on Consideration For Others which was boiling up inside her.

Dickie closed his eyes rather than meet Juliana's accusing stare: he hardly felt it was up to him to attempt to control these unruly youngsters when the presence of their own father didn't, even if the code of a gentleman should be to protect the ladies. Juliana could be trusted not to make too much of a scene, he knew, but he felt it was rotten, all the same—and just as rotten for poor Miss Seeton, who was his guest . . .

Then he heard the scuffle die away, without another word being uttered. Had Grampus brought the authority of his enormous white moustache to bear on his grand-brats, limping into the dining room escorted by the daughter who was trying so hard to remain in his good books? Warily Dickie opened one eye and looked for the source of the miracle of silence which had so suddenly been wrought.

Miss Seeton, sitting quietly at the table, had turned on her chair to face the Standon family and fix the rampaging boys with a stare that penetrated even their self-absorbed squabble: a stare perfected through many years of teaching at a girls' school—a stare no child bent on mischief could long resist. Gary and his brother, a look of unease appearing gradually on their faces, acknowledged by their silence the will of another more determined than themselves and stopped the fight without another word. With no prompting from anyone, they fell to rearranging their garments and tidying their hair; whereupon, with bemused and admiring glances in Miss Seeton's direction, Annabel and her husband hustled their children before them towards the table indicated to the party by a highly thankful Doris.

Chapter 11

BETWEEN PLUMMERGEN AND Murreystone there is no single direct route, although the distance between them as the crow flies is only five miles. Dickie Nash, a careful driver, followed every twist and turning described by Miss Molly Treeves and counted nearly eight miles on the clock before arriving, with a sigh of relief, at Filkins Farm.

"I was beginning to think we'd never get here," he told Juliana apologetically. She had been dictating to him from the back of the purple envelope, and he had annoyed her by saying, every now and then, that it certainly was a long way from anywhere, wasn't it; or that he hoped they'd reach the place before winter set in, because he didn't feel confident that even the most skilful St. Bernard dog would find them until it was far too late.

Juliana put the envelope back in her handbag. "Well, we did get here, despite all your moans," she said, wrinkling her elegant nose as she viewed the rustic scene before them. The gate to the farm had originally boasted the traditional five bars, anyone could tell; but rusted hinges had made it sag and buckle, so that the topmost bar, from which depended by one nail a wooden nameplate announcing the entrance to

Filkins Farm, itself depended crookedly by one end, and the middle bar had utterly vanished. Nobody, it seemed, could have moved the gate in years without having the entire structure collapse at his or her feet.

Miss Seeton was gazing about her with bright-eyed interest. "Such a lonely place," she remarked, "but a setting conducive to art, I would suppose, in that Mr. Collier must encounter very few distractions here, and the ability to concentrate is so important, don't you agree?"

Dickie shuddered. "Looks a proper hole, in my opinion, and that's with the sun shining. It'll be a hundred times worse in winter, I bet—that is," he amended, "any hope of concentration must fly straight out of the window, I should think. But I have to hand it to your boyfriend, Juliana. The Inland Revenue would need to be pretty desperate for the fourpenceha'penny he owed them to come all the way out here to collect it."

Juliana ignored the more contentious of these remarks but was forced to admit that, though she bowed to Miss Seeton's superior understanding of the artistic temperament—Miss Seeton uttered sounds of self-depreciation to which Juliana paid no heed—she had to agree that Filkins Farm was not what she called inspirational, and how poor Mentley could expect to produce decent work living here she really couldn't imagine.

"If," pointed out Dickie, "he's still here. I can't see any signs of life at all, apart from the odd bird flapping about over behind those trees—no doubt they're vultures, picking over Collier's bones. Which wouldn't surprise me at all. The atmosphere around this place is enough to make anyone feel like bumping themselves off."

Miss Seeton was shocked. "Hardly vultures, Mr. Nash, if you will excuse me." She coughed delicately. "The vulture, although indeed a bird of prey, is confined to the southern regions, unlike other feeders on carrion such as members of the family *Corvidae*, to which the birds you see there doubtless belong. Crows," she translated, "or rooks—it is not always easy to be sure. One hears it said that if you see a lot of crows together, they are rooks, whereas one rook by itself is probably a crow. *Corvus frugilegus* or *Corvus corone*, anyway, I think we may be fairly certain."

"Oh," said Mr. Nash and cleared his throat.

"Well," said Juliana with only the slightest tremor in her voice, "I refuse to believe they're the only signs of life around the place. Dickie—the gate, what there is of it, is open. If you're prepared to risk your precious suspension on the potholes we can see in the drive, then let's carry on—to whatever fate may have in store for us."

"*Excelsior*," muttered Mr. Nash, who had been prepared to grumble about his car's suspension until his lady mentioned it, and now felt morally obliged not to. Juliana, reflected Dickie, understood him extremely well. He shrugged, sighed, and pressed his foot upon the accelerator. "As you wish, we're on our way," he said. "I only hope it's worth it."

The rutted drive curved gently away from the gate in the direction of a group of buildings, glimpsed through overhanging trees and not properly visible until the car was past the trees and out in the open. Stones spattered up against the shining paintwork of Dickie's car, and he tried not to wince when, avoiding a pothole with his front wheels, he thudded into it with those at the back. Juliana and Miss Seeton bounced on their seats as he dropped the engine into the lowest gear, and the car crawled uncomfortably along.

"Now, isn't this exciting, Dickie? Every bit as much fun as the dodgems," Juliana said very brightly, "and it's not costing us a penny."

Dickie muttered something which Juliana, with consummate tact, did not ask him to repeat. Miss Seeton said:

"I was right—they *are* crows. Or possibly rooks. With all due respect to Mr. Nash, I hardly felt that vultures . . . but of course, your special subject is Byzantine Art, is it not, Mr. Nash?"

"And rally-driving," chipped in Juliana as Dickie gave Miss Seeton the courtesy of a brief acknowledgement, then returned his attention to the potholes. "Poor Dickie! Will it really do the car any lasting damage?"

"Let's hope not, but it's too late to bother about that now. We're past the point of no return, and I shall need a rest before tackling those potholes again. If Collier's not at home after the effort we've made . . ."

The car, with a final judder, came to rest near a large building of weather-darkened oak, into which windows had been cut with a not-too-expert hand. The other three buildings, now that they could be clearly seen, were as dark as the first—but their darkness came rather from stains of smoke, and ash, and all the other scars of combustion.

"Looks as if the chap might not have been making it *all* up," acknowledged Dickie. "Those blackened rafters look perfectly horrible, and there's no proper roof . . ."

"Mentley said the locals don't want to live here because of, well, ghosts," Juliana said, trying not to sound uneasy. The sun was shining, the (admittedly few) birds were flying: yet it was harder than it had been back in Bath to laugh at what she had, with Dickie, dismissed as the exaggerated stories of someone with a suggestible temperament.

"I hardly think," volunteered Miss Seeton as Dickie and Juliana regarded each other warily, "that the gentleman over by that wall can be a ghost." Her audience exclaimed and began to look about them. The man ducked down behind the wall, and they caught a glimpse of purple shagginess as he vanished. "One could not," continued Miss Seeton as Miss Popjoy uttered a little cry of amazement, "describe him as in the least transparent—such a very vivid colour—and a certain degree of transparency, as I understand it, has always been a requirement of supernatural manifestations. Moreover"—as Juliana fumbled with the catch on her seat belt—"he appears to be attempting to conceal himself, which one would not suppose that a ghost needed to do, being by nature in the habit of inspiring fear in the hearts of others rather than in its own—if indeed a ghost could be regarded as possessing one. A heart, I mean."

Juliana lost the remainder of Miss Seeton's reflections on the properties of psychic phenomena as she opened the car door and stepped gracefully out into the yard of Filkins Farm. The purple figure cowered lower behind the wall, a wall so dilapidated that it offered little concealment. As Juliana began to pick her way towards it, the purple figure seemed to recognise this fact, and a pair of suspicious eyes peered through a suitable hole. Juliana waved.

"Mentley, is that you? Remember me? Juliana Popjoy—and I've brought a couple of friends with me. How are you?"

He raised his head slowly, stared, and as she drew close, stood up. Juliana stifled a gasp as she observed his shaggy shoulder-length hair and Rasputin beard, his purple caftan and sandalled feet. "Popjoy?" said the hirsute one at last, doubtfully. "Juliana Popjoy? Why, I know you, man—of course I do. At least . . ." He edged a little nearer, then stiffened. "But who're those cats in the car behind you?"

"Relax, Mentley, it isn't the tax man. It's two friends of mine, Dickie Nash from Cambridge, and Miss Emily Seeton, who's a neighbour of yours, from Plummergen. Oh!" Juliana laughed and gestured pleadingly. "Don't tell anyone about her, will you? I should hate the heavy mob to do either of you a mischief!"

Mentley Collier took two steps back and goggled. "What do you mean with this heavy mob? Why should anyone want to do me a mischief? Like, I mind my own business, I do my own thing, I don't want no hassle any more than I give hassle to anyone else, man. Dig?"

Juliana blinked at the vehemence of his reply, as well as the remarkable mode of speech. Dickie had been right, she reflected: poor Mentley had passed from beatnik to hippie with no indication that he'd even thought about growing up. He really was a bit crazy—decidedly jumpy, too. "A joke, Mentley, that's all it was, an ordinary joke. You're obviously so cut off here you haven't heard about the deadly village feud between Murreystone and Plummergen."

"No. No, I haven't. What do I care about deadly feuds, man? I'm an artist—I don't scramble my brains with this village junk." All the time he was speaking, he edged cautiously nearer. "So, introduce me to your friends," he said at last.

Juliana motioned to Dickie, who climbed out of the car and held open the rear door for Miss Seeton. In silence Mentley Collier watched them pick their way over the rubble and litter of the disused farmyard to stand at Juliana's side. Introductions were made. Mentley stared a little longer, then said:

"Better come into the pad," and turned away from his unexpected visitors without another word. Juliana, silently indicating surprise and apology to her companions, led them towards the windowed building made of dark oak, in which it appeared Mentley Collier had made his home.

Inside the old barn it was as untidy as anyone might have expected from the state of the outside yard. Mentley Collier's talents, whatever they might be, clearly lay in other directions than those of domesticity. There were no internal walls: different areas were indicated by mounds of belongings, set as their owner pleased, spilling carelessly from one "room" to another. The sink was full of unwashed dishes, and the pipes underneath were clearly visible; the tap seemed to be fastened to the wall with string. In what might have been the dining room, tea chests served as table and chairs. Canvases were stacked against the walls, tubes of paint were scattered on the floor, brushes stood in jars of turpentine; the air smelled oily, despite the enormous north-facing window in the studio section, which was wide open. Across the sill were draped a selection of loose garments, possibly bedclothes (if bedclothes came in rainbow colours), damp but drying in the summer sun.

"Mentley, I'm so sorry—we do seem to have come at an awkward time," said Juliana. "But isn't it a little late in the year for spring cleaning?"

He shrugged and pushed his hands into the folds of his caftan. "Spring, summer, what's to worry? The weather's better now, for one thing. Come to help, have you?" The glare he directed towards Miss Seeton, who was studying his studio with an appreciative eye, suggested that he didn't believe the help offered by this little old lady would be anything more than a nuisance.

"Only in a manner of speaking." Juliana smiled at their host. "Rather, we were hoping you could help us—a mutual arrangement, in fact. Might we sit down? This could take a little time to explain."

Mentley Collier, his sandalled feet shuffling, threw a mocking glance in the direction of the tea chests. "Not what you comfort-loving cats are used to, is it? Like, I don't reckon on too many visitors, man—I've no time to sit around talking. But at least you aren't . . . well, who I thought you were when you arrived—and I guess I'm not too busy right now . . . You sit down, if you like, and tell me about this . . . this arrangement of yours. Oh"—as Juliana, leading the way, hesitated by the first of the overloaded tea chests—"chuck it all on the floor. You won't hurt anything, man." He laughed. "You couldn't. I don't dig the valuables scene. Possessions tie you down, right?"

A frown creased the elegant brows of the still-hesitant Miss Popjoy, but Miss Seeton, who had followed close upon Juliana's heels as Dickie ushered them politely before him, was untroubled by this manifestation of the artistic temperament. Mentley Collier had rekindled memories she thought she'd long forgotten: dusty, ill-furnished attics with roofs that leaked and rats in the rafters and the only redeeming feature their strong, northern light; midnight meals cooked on gas-rings and eked out among too many other hopefuls; people painting, drawing, working from sunrise to sunset without a pause, then tumbling fully clothed into bed after swallowing a mouthful of bread and a mug of watery cocoa . . .

Scarcely realising what she did, Miss Seeton moved to one of the few uncluttered areas on the carpetless floor, neatly crossed her feet at the ankles, and subsided, effortlessly and with some grace, into one of her favourite yoga postures, the lotus. And, as she did so, she smiled.

Chapter 12

FOR THE FIRST time Mentley Collier paid Miss Seeton proper attention. He stared at her as she composed herself upon the floor, her umbrella laid carefully across her lap, her handbag beside her on the ground, her eyes bright. "Hey, are you ever an adept, man," he breathed with sudden admiration. "That is about the most impressive . . . Miss Seeton, I've just got to ask how far you've progressed. Man, you must be so far on your way to enlightenment . . ."

Juliana and Dickie did not regard Miss Seeton's smile of happy reminiscence in the same way that the awestruck artist seemed to do. They remembered the *Eurydice*, and the little band of yoga enthusiasts their friend had assembled about her during the early days of that momentous cruise; they did not believe, as Mentley obviously did, that Miss Seeton had some deep psychological insight into the problems of life that had somehow escaped his own studies, whatever they might be. She had made it very plain, on the cruise, that there had been only one good reason for her having begun the practice of yoga . . .

"Oh, my knees, of course," came Miss Seeton's prompt and prosaic reply to Mentley's question. "They have made *remarkable* progress over the years—indeed, I cannot praise the book too highly, and one can feel confident, I think, that the improvement will be long-lasting—but I would hardly consider myself to have taken more than the very shortest of steps along any *spiritual* path. My understanding has always been that it is necessary to be most disciplined from a very early age, and without a skilled teacher . . . one has to be so careful, you see, not to grow *cranky* or *unbalanced* as the book warns may happen without wise guidance, and this point is stressed most carefully. I have always taken note of the warnings—although I did once venture to try . . . but without success, I fear. And it was only the merest attempt at *trataka*, nothing too demanding, I assure you."

She was still sitting on the floor, still smiling as she spoke, looking up at her three companions without any sense of incongruity. She was in an artist's studio; she had been a student of art herself, in those far-off casual days when, should there have been insufficient chairs to go round, some of the party would happily do without them. What could now be more logical, in the absence of adequate seating—poor Miss Popjoy had looked so startled at being asked to throw Mr. Collier's belongings on the floor—than to dispose oneself in a manner to which one had long ago—so very long ago—become accustomed?

As Miss Seeton nodded and smiled, the others came to their senses and began to make room for themselves on the tea chest chairs. At least, Dickie and Juliana did; Mentley Collier had drifted first near to, then away from, that part of the floor on which Miss Seeton sat in her lotus posture. Something about her seemed to unnerve him: he could hardly take his eyes off her.

"Mentley," said Juliana, having briskly dumped a heap of miscellaneous articles in what passed for a corner of the imaginary room, "do stop hovering. We shall start to feel unwelcome." She examined the edge of the tea chest for protruding nails or rough edges, then warily sat down. "Dickie—never mind your trousers, there's a dear. We have business to discuss, remember?"

"Business? With me?" Mentley Collier looked decidedly startled. "Like, what sort of business?"

"If you will excuse me," murmured Miss Seeton, beginning to unfold herself from her lotus pose. A lady should never intrude, however unwittingly, into the affairs of others, and particularly when these affairs wear a financial aspect.

"Oh, no, Miss Seeton, we didn't mean you to go." Juliana looked mildly distressed. "How ungrateful and rude it would be of us to chase you away, when if it hadn't been for you, we might still be wandering around Kent looking for this place—Mentley, you certainly do pick out-of-the-way spots to live in, don't you?"

"Privacy, man," he said, his tone flat, his eyes never leaving Miss Seeton as, with a polite murmur, she subsided again. "And it's peaceful here—plenty of personal space, that's what I need. Cool. Like, no interruptions."

Juliana wasn't sure whether he was trying to be rude or not: it had been a long time since she'd known him at all well, and even in the young days he'd had the reputation for being moody. The artistic temperament, no doubt. "Just the place for an artist," she said with a cheerful nod. "Which is what Miss Seeton thinks, too—she understands your problems every bit as well as you yourself."

"Does she?" Mentley favoured Miss Seeton with a look of nervous respect while she sat smiling upon him in friendly fashion. He blinked. "Like, what problem in particular did you have it in mind to help me with, Juliana?" He managed to drag his eyes from Miss Seeton, and with one expansive gesture indicated the whole of the huge barn-studio. "Man, what more could anyone need than this? Room to breathe, to grow, to develop—to find yourself both as an artist and as a spirit—space and privacy simply to *be*, man . . ." And he shut his eyes, took a deep breath, hitched up his caftan, and folded himself, with a tremendous clicking of his joints, into a poor imitation of the lotus posture adopted with far greater ease by Miss Seeton. "Far out!" he exclaimed, sighing. "Out of sight, man, just utterly out of sight . . ."

Juliana frowned. "Mentley, please don't start drifting away into your own little world like that—I told you, this isn't just a social call. I—we—came to talk business with you, and you aren't making it especially easy."

Slowly the artist on the floor uncircled his fingers, exhaled, and opened his eyes to direct them, with obvious reluctance, towards the statuesque Miss Popjoy. "Juliana, you're trying to hassle me, man, and that's not right, when all I want is the peace and quiet to do my own thing—you ask Miss Seeton if that isn't what an artist needs more than anything else in the world." And, closing his eyes, he took a defiant breath and began to drift away again.

Miss Seeton, startled at having been cited as an authority, had no time to reply before Juliana retorted: "I fail to see how you can make a living from what you call peace and quiet and doing your own thing, Mentley. Even out here in the wilds of the country, you need more than that—you need money. Which I was hoping to be able to put your way, if we came to a suitable arrangement—not vast amounts"— as he opened his eyes again and regarded her with some surprise—"but enough to help pay the odd bill, every time you deliver—assuming that you do deliver, of course."

"Deliver?" Mentley's eyes narrowed. He stared, first at Juliana and then, more warily, at Miss Seeton. "Like, what do you mean, man? Why did you really come here?"

"To ask you if you'd consider putting your best efforts into painting me some of your Old Master copies, for display in the antique shop I own with Dickie down in Bath—and not necessarily just for display, if you could promise to keep producing them when I sold one to a customer." Mentley sat up with a jerk. His mouth dropped open. Juliana flushed and uttered a little laugh.

"Don't be silly, Mentley, of course I'm not asking you to paint *fakes*! I'd want copies—really good copies—which I know perfectly well you can do. Or at least, you used to be able to, when we first knew each other, and I don't see any reason why you should have lost the knack. Copying, surely, can't be anywhere near as demanding as pure creative art," at which Miss Seeton nodded sagely, sighing. Mentley looked from Juliana to Miss Seeton and back again.

Juliana said, "There'd be no need to worry about a thing— I'd choose the paintings and provide you with really good reproductions to work from. All you'd have to do would be to make sure you signed them *After Constable*, or whatever would be legally, well, safe—I wouldn't want either of us to be run in for forgery and fraud!" She smiled, but Mentley did not chuckle. She went on, "You might do rather well out of the scheme, you know. The shop has a nice little turnover, lots of visitors—Bath's a regular tourist centre, and our location could hardly be better. And people who bought one of your copies might start to commission other work from you—original paintings, I hope. You could make your name, at the same time as helping me, of course. And I'd be helping you, too, because naturally I'd expect to pay you a fair price for your work. I'm not asking you for any favours for old times' sake: this is strictly business."

She paused expectantly, but he said nothing, and she was conscious of feeling a little annoyed. Somehow, she'd been expecting a different reaction from this long, uneasy silence. Almost as if he was weighing up every aspect of her proposal, looking for a catch.

"Well, Mentley? What do you say?"

Juliana fixed him with a stern and irritated gaze, and Mentley began to fidget. Evidently the floor was growing too hard for him: or was it that the lotus posture bothered him more than it bothered Miss Seeton? She was sitting as comfortably as ever, cross-legged and calm; but Mentley Collier, his own legs tying and untying themselves in nervous knots, was unable to meet Juliana's eyes. He cleared his throat twice, then coughed and creaked himself upright.

"I'll have to think about it," he said at last.

"He *is* a rum sort of chap," remarked Dickie as the car bounced its way back down the potholes of the drive from Filkins Farm. "Looked to me as if he was more or less on the breadline—I suppose that's why he didn't care to offer us a cup of coffee. But I'd have expected him to jump at the chance of making some money."

"So would I, from what I remember of him." Juliana gave an exasperated snort. "Goodness knows what crazy reason he has for playing hard-to-get. I refuse to believe that he's developed any business sense since I first knew him—mind you, his sense of humour was pretty well developed, even if slightly on the warped side. No doubt he thinks it's funny to keep me—I mean us—on the hop for a while, knowing that it's a seller's market and he's the one who'll be doing the selling—if he does, that is. Yet somehow I'd never really thought of him as being mercenary . . ."

"People change," Dickie said. "For one thing, they grow up, in due course—most people, that is 'Far out, man,' " he quoted in a disgusted tone. " 'Personal space' indeed. Utter tosh and twaddle, if you'll excuse my speaking in this way about your old flame, Juliana. Twitching and writhing all over the floor—oh, I beg your pardon, Miss Seeton." His passenger in the backseat came suddenly to mind, and he turned red. "I wasn't referring to you—very, ah, graceful, you might say. But the chap couldn't even sit still, could he? I'm surprised he even bothered trying to compete with an expert like you."

"Oh, hardly an expert, Mr. Nash," she demurred. "And one would not care to think that a genuine enthusiast such as Mr. Collier, especially as he is a friend of dear Miss Popjoy's, would so far forget the principles of yoga as to practise it—if one could call sitting upon the floor in the company of one's friends *practising*, for the book is most emphatic upon the need to be utterly alone for the greatest benefit to be obtained—but to practise in a spirit of competition, you see, would, from what I have read, be utterly alien to the entire principle of yoga, where one is not even supposed to compete with oneself, although of course the temptation is always there to do just a little more every day—and then, perhaps Mr. Collier is sensitive to changes in the weather. One's knees, you understand. Although, of course, in his case, he is rather young . . . but many people are conscious of climatic variations before they become generally apparent. My own dear Martha, who helps me so much around the house, often finds herself with a headache before a storm—and the birds, as you yourself observed, were wheeling in an agitated manner, which I understand can mean bad weather. Indeed," concluded Miss Seeton, "there are clouds building up—such a dramatic horizon, I always feel. Romney Marsh is so wide and windswept . . ."

"It certainly looks rather dark over to the west, but I'd be prepared to bet on getting you safely home before it breaks," Dickie assured her, then cleared his throat as he realised what he'd said. "I mean, it's not far, is it, so you'll be back indoors in no time. Mind you," thinking it advisable to change tack, "I doubt if it was just the storm that was upsetting the Collier chap, you know. The way he was almost hiding from us when we first arrived, and didn't come out till he saw who we were, I'd have said he was more scared than sensitive to the barometer. He was positively relieved when he recognised Juliana, and most men would run a mile if any of their old girlfriends turned up out of the blue like that."

"Dickie, I keep telling you—"

"Protesting too much, old girl," Mr. Nash informed his lady with a chuckle. "But I can only say how much I think your taste has improved—preferring me to him, I mean. Not a very prepossessing type, to my mind, either physically or—well, perhaps I shouldn't judge his mental state on such a short acquaintance. But the chap seemed to be a bundle of nerves as well as steeped in a load of"—he glanced sideways at Juliana, then amended what he'd been about to say—"hippie claptrap," said Dickie, sounding scornful. "I see plenty of that with the students, but I'd have thought a man Collier's age would be old enough to know better."

Juliana, who was a near-contemporary of the maligned Mentley Collier, wasn't sure how to take this remark and maintained a wary silence while she made up her mind. Miss Seeton, her eye on the approaching clouds, nodded to herself and commented from the backseat:

"No doubt it was indeed the impending storm which made poor Mr. Collier so uneasy—and, of course, the presence of a stranger such as myself . . ." She recalled that Mentley, though an old friend of Juliana, had never met Dickie Nash, either. "You told him you would return for his answer in a few days' time," she reminded them brightly. "I'm sure you will find him in a far more cheerful mood. Provided," she added as the distant sky was lit by a flickering streak of vivid light, "that you take care to visit him on a day when there is no thunder in the air . . ."

Chapter 13

THE THUNDER HAD come, rumbling its way across Kent, with the spears of rain and daggers of lightning and darkening skies of a really spectacular storm. But, though it had been severe, it had not lasted long, moving eastwards to the sea, leaving everywhere in its wake washed and shining in the lazy summer twilight.

Mindful of the recent power cut she had sustained when a thunderbolt struck her cottage just as she was switching on the electric kettle, Miss Seeton invited Dickie and Juliana into Sweetbriars for a glass of sherry, rather than the cup of tea or coffee which Mr. Nash was still lamenting as they left Mentley Collier and Filkins Farm behind them. Juliana, however, refused the invitation, with regret but firmly: she thought poor Dickie had suffered enough that afternoon and needed something far stronger than sherry to sustain him.

After they had left her and returned to the George and Dragon for spirituous refreshment, Miss Seeton pottered from room to room and stared out of the windows at the different views of the storm until it had safely departed. She then sighed, trotted to the kitchen, and made herself a cup of tea, which she carried into the sitting room and was about to enjoy with some of her favourite chocolate biscuits when a sudden thought came to her. She jumped up from her chair with a little cry.

"Oh, dear! Oh, dear, how could I have been so forgetful? That poor creature—all this time—and I promised Stan I would telephone, too . . ."

She hurried to check on the contents of a packing case which stood in the back garden, sheltered by the high brick wall that faced westward and was, despite the recent rain, still warm with the day's soaked-up sun. Having reassured herself, she went back to the cottage into the hall, where, racked by guilt, she began to leaf with anxious fingers through the pages of the classified telephone directory. " 'Biologists,' " she read as she came to the right place. " 'Bird breeders and dealers, Bird cages (see Pet Shops), Birth Control'—oh—oh, dear." And Miss Seeton blushed. "No, I don't think . . ."

She stood frowning for a while, then turned to letter *A* and began to hunt again. " 'Animal feedstuff and concentrates, Animal sundry manufacturers and suppliers—ah! Animal welfare societies—but now, which one should I choose?"

She cast her eye down the column showing the number and exchange and was delighted to find a Rye entry which looked as if it would suit. She checked her watch, crossed mental fingers, and dialled.

"Wounded Wings Bird Sanctuary," came the prompt reply at the other end of the line. Miss Seeton sighed with relief.

"Good evening," she replied thankfully. "I am so sorry to trouble you after working hours, but—"

"We don't have working hours here," said the woman from Wounded Wings. "Birds get sick at any time of the day—or night—so you needn't apologise. I'm Babs Ongar, by the way. Barbara. How can I help you?"

"How do you do, Miss Ongar. That is—er, Mrs. Ongar?" It made it so much more complicated when one could not take a quick look at the speaker's left hand.

"Mrs., for my sins," Barbara informed her brightly, "but my other half is in the Merchant Navy, so it might just as well be Miss. Not that it matters either way, so far as the birds are concerned."

"No, indeed, of course not. You are very sensible, Mrs. Ongar." Miss Seeton cleared her throat before pressing on with the courtesies. "My name is Seeton, Miss Emily Seeton, and I live in Plummergen. Perhaps you know it? Such a dear place, with all the benefits of village life as well as the convenience of being not too far from Town—which is why I am telephoning you now, you see."

Babs didn't see at all. Was this Miss Emily Seeton from Plummergen hoping to sell her a railway season ticket or a new house or something? Before she had time to venture a wary question, Miss Seeton had drawn breath and hurried into the next part of her tale.

"Yesterday, you see, I took a little trip to London and was caught in that dreadful storm—so easy, with a cheap day return ticket, which dear Martha always insists that I should buy—and I would say that it was much worse than today's, though of course, in London one is never too far from shelter of one sort or another, so it is difficult to judge—but today's was almost as violent, though it did not last so long—and now you are the closest person I could find. In the telephone directory, that is. Although," said Miss Seeton, puzzled, "you are not under *B* for birds, which is naturally where I looked first—because when I came home, I discovered a pigeon in my back garden, utterly exhausted, poor thing. The storm, no doubt."

Barbara let out a deep sigh. At last she'd made sense of what Miss Seeton was trying to say. "Oh, yes, we've had several casualties brought in today. They get battered by the rain, when it's heavy, and blown into things as well, by a strong wind—and if yours is a homing pigeon, the electrical disturbance of the storm upsets their ability to find their way back—magnetic fields and so on." She hoped she wouldn't be pushing her luck too far by putting the straight question that had to be asked. "Is this pigeon injured at all or simply worn out?"

"Stan says—he came over at once, so helpful and kind, and with a tea chest which he turned most cleverly into a cage—not that I believe them to be cage-birds, of course, but in the short term it seemed the best thing to do—and the seed which I bought from the shop said that it was generally suitable for birds, not like Quill, which I gather is for parrots. And those, of course, are tropical, although they might be considered cage-birds, too, I suppose, which must mean that Chirrup would do for them as well as for the pigeon. Which has water, too, in its cage—and straw," she added, "for the poor thing to rest on, which Stan says seems to be all that is required. There are no bones broken, he thinks, though he considers himself no expert—which is unduly modest of him, you know, because he looks after my chickens for me, as well as working on one of the local farms. But he tells me he feels he cannot offer much more advice on what to do beyond the provision of food and shelter, so . . ."

"So you rang someone who can," concluded Babs, "which is my job, after all." And she proceeded to demonstrate her efficiency by asking a series of pertinent questions, including whether or not Miss Seeton had happened to notice if there was a ring on the pigeon's leg; did it have a serial number stamped inside its wing; and would Miss Seeton like her to come across to Plummergen to collect her unexpected lodger and deal with it as seemed best.

All of these questions Miss Seeton answered to the best of her ability, and Mrs. Ongar rang off with promises to drop over within the hour, all being well. Miss Seeton went back to her long-neglected cup of tea, reproaching herself for the waste as she poured it away and made another pot.

Though Miss Seeton offered both, Barbara Ongar would not stay for tea, or for coffee. She asked for her congratulations to be passed on to Stan, for his careful carpentry and his sound advice; she explained to Miss Seeton how the plastic ring about the leg of the pigeon was marked with an individual reference number, by means of which the bird's owner could be traced.

"Every owner of racing pigeons has them ringed this way—even the Queen," she told an enthralled Miss Seeton. "You can tell from the letters which of the pigeon unions registered the bird—this one's on the files of the Royal Pigeon Racing Association, I can tell just by looking. I'll phone them first thing tomorrow, and they'll give me the name and address of the owner. He'll be glad to have this chap safe home again, I'm sure—they can be pretty valuable birds, if they're good winners. Do you mind if I mention you? He'll want to write and thank you, I expect."

She added a few snippets of information about microfilm and similar uses for carrier pigeons; touched briefly on the differences between sprinters, middle-distance, and marathon birds; discoursed on the dangers from hawks and other avian raptors; admired the chickens in their henhouse, repeating her praise for Stan's skill; and took her leave, with the pigeon, cooing and fluttering, in the box she had provided for the purpose. Miss Seeton watched her drive off into the near-dark of the summer night, then returned to the kitchen to prepare the evening's third cup of tea.

Somehow, she had lost her fancy for chocolate biscuits and wondered if by any happy chance Martha had made one of her renowned fruitcakes. What she found, as she explored the tins, was a well-sealed, half-eaten slab of gingerbread which she recalled having bought for dear Bob Ranger's last visit. She smiled as she remembered how Anne, her nursing knowledge well to the fore, had scolded her spouse about his incipient tummy and had forbidden him to eat more than four slices, though gingerbread was his favourite.

"Which means," reflected Miss Seeton happily, "that now there is enough left for me," and she trimmed off the dry end, tossing the crumbs out on the flagstone patio for the benefit of tomorrow morning's sparrows. She cut herself a generous slice and repaired yet again to the sitting room.

Where she sat, with only a standard lamp to light her thoughts, drinking tea and musing on Bob Ranger, and dear Anne, and Mr. Delphick, and recent events. For the first time she was beginning to feel that she could think about what had happened yesterday in London without shuddering. "Not blood," Miss Seeton said firmly. "Nothing more than tomato ketchup, as everyone said—although that first man did seem so plausible . . ."

She sat in the lamplight, trying to remember what she could of the plausible man's face and feeling guilty that she, praised—and paid—by the police for her IdentiKit drawing skills, had been unable to produce a likeness of one who, it seemed, was robbing people of their wallets by the meanest of tricks. Pretending to be so helpful—scaring them into believing they had been hurt—taking advantage of their, natural enough, momentary weakness.

"Which is thoroughly immoral," concluded Miss Seeton, rising to go in search of her sketch pad and pencils. She did not switch on the main light—the muted gleam of the standard lamp seemed to have relaxed her; she hoped that now her customary skills might return. She came back to her chair, sat down, and, concentrating, tried to conjure up the face of the man who had stolen the wallet of Arthur Havelock Thundridge.

Her hand hovered over the paper—her pencil made a few uncertain darts at the white blankness before her brooding eyes. Miss Seeton sighed, and blinked, and shook her head. Obviously she was still too bothered, in her subconscious, by the shock she had sustained . . .

She stared at the paper and blinked again. "Gracious," she murmured to herself. "Good gracious me." Somehow, in a moment's abstraction, it seemed that she had managed to draw the required picture, after all.

Or—had she? True enough, there was a face in front of her on the paper, and it was the face of a man: but though she realised almost at once that she was looking at someone she knew, she wasn't altogether sure that what she had drawn much resembled the man who had played the tomato ketchup trick. She had used swift, vivid strokes, giving the clear appearance of a face; yet it was a face surrounded by swirling images and by strange shapes, fantastic in form: animals and birds, rare and gigantic flowers, trees which loomed out of the page and overshadowed the features of . . . Miss Seeton frowned with the effort of recollection . . . of . . .

"Miss Popjoy's friend Mr. Collier," Miss Seeton said to herself, remembering. "Of course! At least—yes, it could really be nobody else, I suppose—the hair—although . . ."

She shook her head again, sighing, as she studied what she had drawn without knowing exactly what she did. Mentley Collier (yes, she was in no doubt now) looked back at her from her sketching pad with vague and troubled eyes, not so much out of focus as out of reach. "Not looking *at* me," she murmured, "so much as *through* me, it seems . . ."

His pupils were dark and wide, penetrating yet somehow blank. There was no life, no interest in them: which seemed strange, for an artist. "Unless he is looking through right to the heart of the matter," mused Miss Seeton. "Seeing the true nature of what he is trying to portray, no doubt—and yet . . . if what he sees is as, well, as *peculiar* and so very uncomfortable as these strange plants and creatures . . ."

Mentley Collier appeared to be looking upon life with a jaded and distorting eye, seeing nothing in the way more, well, more *normal* people might be expected to do. "Which is no doubt the artistic view of life," Miss Seeton tried to reassure herself. "Modern art, perhaps—although, from what Miss Popjoy said of his copying skills, one would have supposed him to prefer . . . and yet, one had no real chance to study his work. Perhaps he has so altered his style from the time when Miss Popjoy and he were friends that now he cannot . . . which would explain why he did not feel able to accept her commission at once. So very disconcerting, however, the anger and, well, fear—there is almost a hurricane blowing in the branches of the trees—those flowers might be huge mouths, ready to devour the poor man whole—and the claws and beaks of those birds . . ."

She had taken the swooping avian forms at first for the rooks (or crows) which had fluttered around Mentley's studio farmhouse, but closer inspection showed them to be even more raptorian in form. "Like the vultures about which Mr. Nash made his little joke," she comforted herself firmly. "I am simply muddling our conversation today with, well, with other things—which is hardly surprising, in view of the spectacular storm—and of course," she reminded herself with a smile, "Mr. Collier's sensitivity to the weather will have made him feel so very uncomfortable—just like my picture." She gazed again at the distorted images and the face of the fearful man. "Exactly like dear Martha," said Miss Seeton. "Thunder upsets her, too—oh, dear." She cocked her head to one side, listening. "Oh, dear . . ."

In the warm distance of the summer evening, another roll of thunder sounded low.

Chapter 14

AFTER THEIR FIRST surprise and pleasure at renewing the acquaintance with Miss Seeton, Dickie and Juliana had fallen to discussing some of the other friends they had made during that momentous Aegean cruise on the *Eurydice*: foremost among these, in the memory of Mr. Nash, being Sir George Colveden, KCB, DSO, JP. Sir George it was who had helped Dickie to stop gambling: he had offered odds of a hundred to one that a Scotland Yard detective would be sent out to the ship and would solve the murder. Out of all the company it had been Dickie who stepped in and cheerfully wagered a tenner.

The sight of the baronet, chequebook in hand, just as cheerfully prepared to pay out the thousand pounds he owed (since it had been not Scotland Yard but Miss Seeton who eventually solved the mystery), startled Mr. Nash into a flutter of protestation from which he was rescued by the good offices of Mel Forby, the *Daily Negative's* demon reporter. Mel was as shrewd as she was pretty and knew of his little weakness. She therefore proposed that Dickie should only accept Sir George's cheque on condition that it was the last money bet he would ever make. Mr. Nash agreed; and had kept nobly to his promise ever since.

Dickie and Juliana had learned from Miss Seeton that the Colvedens lived not half a mile from their hotel, and resolved to telephone Rytham Hall with an invitation to dine at the George and Dragon one evening soon. By some hospitable sleight of hand which, afterwards, Juliana could never quite work out, this invitation had been changed by Lady Colveden into a proposal to eat *en famille* at the Hall the next day; a proposal which had been gratefully accepted.

"And really," said Juliana as Dickie zipped her into a delightful little black dress, "it's just as well that we're going there, rather than the Colvedens coming here. I'd be a bit embarrassed for them, having to submit to the assault and battery those ghastly brats will keep committing on everybody's ears." For the Standon boys were running as much riot as on earlier occasions, and this time there was, to the great regret of almost all who had to hear them, no Miss Seeton to quell them with one of her glances.

"I blame the parents," said Dickie, smoothing creases from his lady's sleek satin shoulders. "I can't think how their poor grandfather puts up with that rumpus day in, day out—it's odd, isn't it? He doesn't strike me as in the least bit deaf, which might have excused it."

"He's not deaf, he's doting. He thinks those rackety little monsters are absolutely wonderful, and anything they do is all right by him. So of course his daughter and her husband have to humour them, which is what makes it so awful for the rest of us." Juliana sighed, then brightened.

"Why 'of course'?" enquired Dickie, watching her fondly as she slipped a pearl necklace from its velvet-lined box and held it out to him with a smile, then turned her back on him. "I do like these on you, you know."

"Mm." Juliana was noncommittal: the necklace, which was indeed beautiful, had been paid for by one of Dickie's rare winning streaks. She would far rather he had given her a string of cultured, cheaper pearls, or even some from a Christmas cracker . . . but, she reminded herself, his betting days were over. "Yes," she said, turning to place a loving peck on his cheek. "I think they suit me, Dickie darling—you have excellent taste. Thank you."

"And thank *you*," he returned, "for explaining—explaining why *of course*," he added as she looked at him with a puzzled expression.

"Oh! Oh, yes, of course—well, Dickie, do think about it. Can't you see that it's the old man who has the money, and *he* seems to think the boys can get away with murder, and his family goes along with him so that he won't cut them out of his will? Which is the sort of thing tyrannical old gentlemen are doing all the time."

Dickie rubbed a thoughtful nose and frowned. "I admit I was unusually lucky, with Uncle Brummel. But do you honestly think Standon's daughter and her husband have such a . . . a calculated eye to the main chance? I'd have called them more . . . overindulgent, the mother in particular. After all, nobody puts up with such a commotion unless they, er, like it. They must be able to shut those kids up properly, if they really want to—Miss Seeton just took one good look at them yesterday, and they went quiet, remember."

"A few more clips round the ear at the appropriate time might have stopped them ever reaching the stage when they needed one good look. But now the old man thinks it's just high spirits, and his daughter makes no attempt to shut them up, and her husband never stops them when the old man's around, which is most of the time, unfortunately. You'd think anyone as frail as he's supposed to be would hate all that racket—and the parents," said Juliana darkly, "seem to be actively encouraging the brats. I think it's creepy, the way they hover round him waiting for something to inherit—like vultures, circling over a man in the desert."

"Or," Dickie said with a chuckle, "rooks, perhaps, or do I mean crows?" Which made her laugh as she remembered the previous afternoon's little lecture from Miss Seeton on the habits of birds. "That's better, Juliana. You know I don't like to see you so glum—let's start looking forward to our night on the town, if you can call Plummergen a town, instead of worrying about other people's problems. We've only just over-come our own, after all—we deserve a bit of cheering up."

He slipped her light summer coat around her shoulders, hugged her gently, and ushered her out of the room.

The day of Miss Seeton's adventure in London had herald-ed a band of short yet intense thunderstorms, but this evening the air seemed to be clear as Dickie and Juliana left the hotel and elected to walk the few hundred yards to Rytham Hall. Dickie would have happily driven the distance, but it seemed a shame, they both felt, to miss the chance for a gentle stroll down a country lane, in the deepening summer dusk. Dickie beamed as Juliana took his arm, and thought himself the luckiest man in Kent.

"Sir George will be green with envy when he sees you," he murmured, holding his lady close. "You look utterly gor-geous tonight."

"La, sir, such compliments!" replied Juliana, giggling. Mr. Nash had not been the only one to partake of a little liquid refreshment on their return to the George and Dragon af-ter a day's sight-seeing. "And you look especially handsome tonight, Dickie. Even if Sir George offered to carry me off to Gretna Green, believe me, I would refuse his kind offer," and she gently squeezed his arm.

They walked along in perfect companionship, admiring the view as it faded into the slow darkness of the night, smelling the heavy scents of hedgerow flowers, listening to the songs of drowsy birds as they prepared to roost.

"Miss Seeton would know what they were," Dickie said on hearing an especially musical trill. "Nightingales, maybe?"

"Not vultures, anyhow," said Juliana, and they laughed together as they walked.

A young man appeared out of an imposing gateway which, as it came into view, they had assumed was the entrance to Rytham Hall. "Good evening," said the young man in a welcoming voice. "Miss Popjoy—and Mr. Nash, I presume?" His eyes lingered in admiration upon Juliana's black satin curves, and the creamy whiteness of the pearls against her throat. "I'm Nigel Colveden: my parents asked me to keep a lookout for you, just in case you missed the place. Not that you could, really, with there being nothing else along this road until you hit Stone and Wittersham, but it's such a splendid evening I'm glad of any excuse to be out and about in it." And his eyes settled wistfully upon Juliana again as he sighed a quiet sigh.

By the end of dinner, during which Nigel demonstrated that, as a working farmer, he had certainly not lost his appetite, he had obviously lost his boyish heart to the charms of Miss Popjoy. When the time arrived for coffee to be poured, he came leaping to his feet to carry Juliana's cup all of seven paces round the table, rather than have her make the effort to lean across and receive it from his mother's hand. Lady

Colveden watched in amusement as her son demonstrated his belief that she could not be trusted to arrange the bitter mints in sufficient elegance on their plate, adjusting the little display into a more perfect circle before handing it, with a reverent bow, to Juliana.

"Port, brandy, a cigar?" suggested Sir George, looking on Nigel's gyrations with as kindly an eye as his wife. The boy took after his father in his liking for an attractive woman, no doubt of that: a regular chip off the old block. No need, of course, for Nash to feel annoyed about it, or Miss Popjoy, either—seemed to be flattered by the boy's attentions, the pair of 'em. And who wouldn't be, having a good-looking youngster like Nigel dancing attendance? Miss Popjoy was a regular charmer—Sir George stroked his moustache with a thoughtful finger and smiled—and Nash was a very lucky man.

"I hope," said Lady Colveden, "you aren't proposing to send the pair of us away while you three males fill the room with smoke and tell smutty stories, George. Miss Popjoy and I intend to stay right here and drink port with you—don't we, my dear?"

"Certainly we do," replied Juliana at once with a nod and a friendly smile in Nigel's direction. Dickie, who had enjoyed his meal and the accompanying wines, grinned at his hostess and remarked:

"Better beware of the pewter pots, then, Lady Colveden. But we'll do our best not to embarrass you."

"Dickie," Juliana warned her paramour, "you're starting to talk nonsense—I don't think you ought to have any port or brandy. Which people don't drink out of pewter pots anyway, as far as I know."

Meg Colveden was frowning. "I'm afraid we only have ordinary glasses, Mr. Nash, so—"

"No, no, nothing like that," Dickie interrupted her with a chuckle which made Juliana glance at him sharply. "D'you mean"—he gazed round the table at the four puzzled faces—"you've never heard the real reason why ladies leave the room? It's not simply, um, to allow the gentlemen to enjoy a spot of naughty talk. There's more to it than that."

He paused and helped himself to a mint. Everyone gazed at him as he slowly unwrapped the silver foil, which seemed to be giving him a spot of bother. "Dickie," said Juliana once more, in that admonishing tone. "What on earth are you talking about?"

"Sideboards," replied Dickie, sounding muffled as he put the mint, whole, into his mouth. "Sheraton sideboards, and Chippendale, and that other furniture chap in the eighteenth century . . ." He frowned and clicked his fingers.

"Hepplewhite," supplied Juliana, not sure whether to scold him or to laugh. "Of course, yes, pot cupboards—how silly of me." She glanced at Lady Colveden, who was listening politely. "We've had one or two rather good examples in the shop over the years—mahogany, mostly. And all with a little cupboard door round the back, and"—she giggled, for she, too, had enjoyed her meal—"a little pewter pot inside. For when the men had drunk so much that, well . . ."

"And the ladies left the room," concluded Meg Colveden as Juliana allowed her explanation to fade away, "so the men wouldn't be embarrassed. What a sensible idea."

"A simple matter of cubic capacity," ventured Nigel, his eye on Juliana to see if she would be shocked by his worldly air: which she did not appear to be. "Shall I fetch the drinks over to the table, then?" he asked his father.

Sir George nodded his assent, adding that it was interesting to learn about these old customs, but if anyone asked him you couldn't beat twentieth-century plumbing, because apart from anything else it didn't get woodworm. "Freezes up in winter, though," he had to admit as he opened a box of Havanas and offered it to Dickie.

"My goodness, how it does," agreed Lady Colveden. "Last winter—do you remember, Nigel? Having to climb up into the roof with all those hot-water bottles and towels to thaw out the pipes?"

"And Dad wanting to cut them with a hacksaw and hammer them flat, and you saying over your dead body," Nigel said with a grin. "And the language that plumber from Brettenden used—oh, yes, I remember all right. Still, there's no risk of having the pipes freeze for the next few weeks, is there, with the thermometer in the eighties. I'd say we're in for a regular heat wave—I wouldn't mind betting there'll be some records broken before the summer's out."

Dickie leaned forward, his eyes bright. "How high d'you reckon the mercury's likely to go?" he enquired eagerly.

"Oh," said Nigel, who had merely been hoping to impress Juliana with the weather lore of a working farmer. "Oh, er, well, I'll hazard a guess and say ninety-three before the end of the month—though that could," he added honestly, "just be wishful thinking, I suppose. We need dry weather for the harvest, you see. We can certainly do without any more storms like the one this afternoon."

"But surely, after that little lot," said Dickie, failing to spot the anxious expression in Juliana's eyes as she sat and watched him grow more animated, "there can't be anything left up there? I'll wager you won't see another drop of rain for two weeks, at least. When's your harvest? Ten to one you get it in safely, Nigel."

Nigel, who hadn't expected his casual comments to be taken so seriously, looked surprised. "Good heavens, I'd love to think you were right, but with the English climate as temperamental as it is, I'm not very hopeful. Still, I don't mind risking a fiver on it—with odds like those, if you turn out to be wrong at least the fifty pounds will help to cheer me up while I stand and watch the fields trying to dry out."

"Oh, Dickie," said Juliana in reproachful tones. "Sir George—Lady Colveden—"

Sir George, responding with characteristic gallantry to the unspoken plea of a lady, shook his head warningly at his son. "A joke's a joke, Nigel, but Nash is no farmer, as I'm sure he won't mind my saying. Hardly fair to take advantage of him—specialist knowledge, you might say."

Lady Colveden was nodding agreement with her husband's views, and Nigel, who knew nothing of Dickie's unfortunate habits, was puzzled but perfectly happy as he said:

"Oh, well, it was just a bit of fun, after all. I mean, how annoying for you if I turn out to be right, and it rains on you both on your way home—"

"Then I," Juliana said grimly, "will borrow an umbrella, and Dickie will just have to get wet—because, in any case, he seems convinced it isn't *really* going to rain. Never mind the thunder we've been hearing on and off for the past half-hour."

"Oh, Miss Popjoy," Nigel said at once, "I'd be only too happy to drive you back to the hotel—both of you, that is, if you don't mind the squeeze. It's only a little MG."

Juliana directed the full force of her beautiful smile towards him. "Nigel, you are a perfect sweetie, and thank you in advance for your kind offer—which I, for one, know I'm

130

going to be delighted to accept. Dickie, however"—with a frown—"will be only too happy to walk—because in that way," she said sternly, "he can find out for himself whether his bet was worth making or not."

And, as she finished speaking, in the warm distance of the summer night another roll of thunder sounded low.

Chapter 15

WHEN THE PARTY eventually broke up, it was a rapturous Nigel who opened the passenger door of his sports car for Juliana to take her place. Despite the now steady downpour which had followed inevitably upon the thunder, Dickie, a sheepish expression on his face which only Nigel failed to comprehend, elected to walk the half-mile or so from Rytham Hall to the George and Dragon: insisted on walking, in fact.

"Too much of a squeeze for the three of us in there, old chap," he assured Nigel, who had to agree with him. "Better let the lady ride in style—a spot of rain won't do me any harm, honestly. It's not as if I'm made of marshmallow."

Juliana muttered something which sounded—to the adoring Nigel's bewilderment—like a reference to the consistency of Mr. Nash's brains, but before he had time to ask what she meant, she had smiled graciously upon the young man she now addressed as her knight-errant and said that she felt utter confidence in his ability to take care of her. Nigel, delighted, did not see the guilty flush which stained the already glowing cheeks of Mr. Nash; while his parents, in some discomfort, met Juliana's magnificent eyes with apology in their own.

Since he seemed bent on making amends for his lapse by this martyrdom, Lady Colveden offered Dickie the loan of her torch, which he accepted; less acceptable, however, was Sir George's offer of his golfing umbrella. Maybe Mr. Nash felt that his suffering should not be eased too far—or maybe, in his subconscious, memories of Miss Seeton, and the Greek cruise, lurked to increase his guilt.

Whatever the reason, Dickie plodded resolutely off into the storm as Nigel panted back down the stairs with a large plaid travelling-rug normally used on picnics. "You mustn't catch a chill, Miss Popjoy," he said as he wrapped the rug about her elegant knees. "The old bus doesn't have a very efficient heater, I'm afraid. We'd have to drive a lot farther than the pub for it to start warming up."

Juliana was too flattered by his chivalrous intentions, and too annoyed with Dickie, to remind Nigel that the distance to the George and Dragon was hardly enough for the most sluggish circulation to freeze to a halt: and so young Mr. Colveden was rewarded by a smile of thanks that made him want to snatch up spear and shield and gallop off to glory. The drive along Marsh Road seemed very tame, compared with the Galahad-like visions before his eyes, and all too short.

They passed Dickie quite early on: the beam of his torch seemed very feeble through the driving lashes of rain, but Juliana hardened her heart as she remembered her paramour's broken promise, and urged Nigel to drive on. Which Nigel duly did, though he resolved that, on his way back, he would collect Mr. Nash to spare him the rest of his soaking.

"It's certainly a night for staying indoors," he said as the car, windscreen wipers frantically a-flick, neared the end of Marsh Road. "I see Miss Seeton's gone to bed—can't say I blame her, can you?" This last, as they passed beneath the windows of Sweetbriars. Ahead of them, through the rain, they could just make out the lights of the George and Dragon. "If I drive up to the door," said Nigel, "would you mind making a dash for it? If Miss Seeton hadn't put her light out, I'd pop across and borrow an umbrella, but I could slip my jacket off for you to throw over your head, if it didn't matter too much about your hair—"

"Nigel, dear, don't worry about me. I'll be fine—it's not as if it's all that far. I'll survive."

"You must be sure to change your wet clothes as soon as you get in," insisted Miss Popjoy's knight-errant, thinking that Sir Galahad would rather have slaughtered dragons than hint of damp underwear (in the darkness, Nigel blushed) or waterlogged shoes. Still, people had to adjust themselves to the times they lived in, and it didn't seem that Miss Popjoy had been offended, thank goodness . . .

For, even as Nigel manoeuvred the MG so close to the steps of the George's main door that any closer would have seen him on the mat, Juliana leaned across and pecked him on the cheek, very kindly. "What a nice young man you are, my dear," she said. "Thank you for being so sweet to me— and do thank your mother again, won't you, for such a delightful evening? I enjoyed it so much."

"Oh, gosh," said Nigel, before collecting his wits sufficiently to rush round and open the car door. He had quite forgotten his offer of a sheltering jacket, but as it took only five careful steps before Juliana was standing in the tiny porch of the hotel, it hardly mattered. Nigel pressed the doorbell, greeted Charley Mountfitchet with effusion, and bade Miss Popjoy a devoted good night.

Such was his state of rapture as he drove homewards that the sight of Dickie Nash, still struggling through the storm and wishing his smart shoes were better adapted to country life, failed to remind him of his intention to offer a lift. Nigel drove homewards with an uplifted heart; and Dickie, who was by now beginning to regret his self-imposed penance, trudged onwards without a dry or comfortable square inch to his unhappy self.

Juliana had warned Charley Mountfitchet that his second guest would be arriving before too long, so the landlord of the George and Dragon was ready for the anguished tintinnabulation which heralded poor Dickie's dripping manifestation on the front step. Mr. Nash tried to carry off his squelching and solitary appearance with an air of insouciance, but Charley was not fooled.

"Miss Popjoy got in ten minutes or so ago," he advised the wretched Dickie. "I offered her a hot toddy to keep out the cold, but she said no—said as how you might fancy one, though. Walked down from the Hall, haven't you?" Charley's grin was knowing. "A nasty night for a stroll, some might say, but Miss Popjoy tells me you're . . . fond of fresh air."

Dickie sneezed. As water trickled from his hairline to drench his eyebrows and drip to his cheekbones, he felt more sorry for himself than he had in years. Regret and guilt for the bet he had made with Nigel were overlaid by physical misery—of which, he told himself suddenly, Juliana seemed to be well aware. As long as she was prepared to accept his soaking as reparation for the broken promise . . .

"A stiff whisky, that's what you need, Mr. Nash," Charley told him as Dickie sneezed again. "On the house—come on through, and I'll pour you a double." And Dickie, brightening at the thought that Juliana would forgive him the moment she realised how he had suffered, gladly followed the landlord through into the bar.

It was several double whiskies later that Mr. Nash made his eventual way to bed. He still felt wet, decidedly so, but at least he could accept the fact with equanimity, he told Charley Mountfitchet as the latter followed him up the stairs and made sure he put his key in the correct lock. The landlord bade his guest good night, then hovered in the corridor for a few moments in case Miss Popjoy's greeting of her sozzled, still-soaking paramour would be lively enough to make a good Plummergen story once the participants were well out of the way; and also in case the nearby Standons should wake, disturbed by a tumult which would be, for once, not of their making.

However, nothing but a stony silence resounded through the walls of the Blue Riband Suite—apart from a clatter and a curse, as Mr. Nash tumbled over some piece of furniture—and, keeping his fingers crossed that nothing else would happen, Charley went away.

The piece of furniture over which Dickie had tumbled proved, once he had groped for the light switch and turned it on, to be the comfortable couch which Juliana had pulled across from its place by the window to stand as far from the king-size bed as possible. And on the couch, wrapped in blankets which were pulled pointedly over her head, Juliana lay, very much asleep.

"Sssh," Dickie admonished himself, realising that he was not to be forgiven as easily as he'd hoped. "Mustn't wake her up—things'll look so much better after a good night's sl—sl—ah, ah*choo! Ahchooh!*"

This resonant aural onslaught failed to arouse his lady from her deep slumber, though the blankets twitched slightly and an acute listener might have heard the click of an angry tongue. But Dickie in his present state was far from being an acute listener.

"Hot bath, before I die of pneumonia," he announced, his eye on the blanket-muffled form on the couch, which did not stir. He sniffed loudly, stifled another sneeze, and permitted his teeth to chatter: he was starting to feel very sorry for himself. Yet even this evoked no response.

He found himself swaying where he stood and thought it prudent to adapt the motion into a forward progress. He set one careful foot in front of the other and made his uneven way towards the window. He felt the radiator: it was cold.

He pointed out, in tones that were but slightly slurred, this sorry state of affairs to the adder-eared blanket on the couch, but there still came no hint of sympathy for his plight. He sighed and sneezed once more: which jogged his memory, so that he exclaimed again:

"Hot bath!" And he headed for the bathroom. This was on the far side of the suite, which meant that his back was towards Juliana, and thus he did not observe a baleful eye watching him over the top of a fractionally lowered blanket. He closed the door with something more than a thud, and Juliana held her breath.

And lay, listening and worrying, until his bath was done and he had reappeared without drowning himself in a drunken stupor. So relieved was his lady at seeing him that she allowed herself the luxury of a brief remark.

"Washing away your sins, Dickie dear?" she enquired, but before he could reply had pulled the blankets up over her head again. Mr. Nash, sobered by steam, found himself lost for words, and, with a muttered apology, collapsed into his shamefaced sheets and fell heavily asleep.

After two hours he awoke, shivering. The rain was still falling, and the radiator was still off: it was summer, he reminded himself, albeit an English summer. He felt too tired to take another bath . . .

But, as he mused on the pleasant warmth that had crept into his bones as he bathed, he was struck by a brain wave. He crept from his bed into the bathroom, put the plug into the bath, and turned on the hot tap as far as it would go. When the bath was full, and the steam was swirling mistily all around him, he propped open the door to allow every atom of warm moisture to reach the bedroom, where he had felt so cold. If only Juliana had not taken half the blankets— but she was right, he supposed, to feel a little annoyed with him—a promise was a promise, and he couldn't really blame it on Sir George's fine claret, although young Nigel might have been egging him on a bit—not that they'd been eating eggs, but—but eggs—birds . . . rooks, crows, vultures . . .

Dickie's eyes closed, and he drifted cosily once more into sleep. From which, some time later, he awoke, shivering again. The bathwater was no longer hot; and he, poor Dickie Nash who had been soaked to the skin, was cold.

Twice more during the night he repeated his performance with the hot tap, wondering that Juliana did not wake up at the sound of the gurgles of an emptying bath. But Miss Popjoy was worn out by tiredness and emotion, and slept now in truth as deeply as she had pretended before. As deeply as, eventually, Dickie Nash slept . . .

To be awoken by shrieks and a clatter from the corridor, where the Standon boys were up to their usual tricks. They erupted from their bedroom shouting of bacon, baked beans, and fried bread with an enthusiasm that sent shivers down Dickie's fragile spine into his even-more fragile stomach. They indulged in an all-in wrestling bout which sent various hard and energetic portions of their small selves bouncing off the door of the Blue Riband Suite and were only quelled by a roar from their father that if they didn't get a move on, they'd find all the breakfast gone. With hungry yells they hurtled down the corridor towards the stairs, leaving Mr. Nash feeling worse than he had felt for years.

He had not thought himself able to move before, his eyes still tightly closed against the horrors of the day. With a groan, he now acknowledged the presence inside his head of a small pneumatic drill, wielded by a sadist with hobnailed boots. His eyelids felt like lead. He groaned again. The hobnailed boots did a little dance. He gulped and forced his eyes—behind which the pneumatic drill was working at full throttle—open.

To discover, to his horror, that he had overnight been struck blind.

Chapter 16

DICKIE UTTERED A little cry and promptly closed his eyes again. He squeezed the lids tightly together, setting crimson golf balls bouncing before him; counted in a nervous silence to ten; gritted his teeth; and, slowly, holding his breath, once more opened his eyes.

He was still blind. And—he'd heard those Standon kids say so—it was breakfast time. It ought to have been daylight—the curtains hadn't been anywhere near thick enough to make everywhere so black, everything so heavy . . .

"It's a judgement on me," he gasped, lying trapped and motionless in his bed. "Oh, my God, I'll never make another bet in my life—Juliana, where are you? Juliana!"

There came the rustle of angry skirts, and then her icy voice sounded close by his ear. "Dickie, I wonder if I will ever speak to you again after today. How could you? Apart from breaking your solemn promise not to gamble any more—and in front of the Colvedens, of all people—to do a thing like this . . . Dickie, I—I don't know what to say. And as for knowing what to do about it, well . . ."

"I need a doctor," ventured Dickie at last, when she had blown her nose crossly and stamped—at least, to his stifled senses it sounded as if she had stamped. "Juliana, I don't know what's happened—but I need a doctor!"

"You need black coffee," retorted Juliana promptly, "and you will just have to suffer the way everyone else with a hangover does. I can't see any need for a doctor—"

Her words sounded ominous, and he interrupted her with a desperate shout. "Juliana, I can't see—and I can't move—I've had a stroke, or something! It's awful!"

"It certainly is," she agreed. "The mess you've made of this room—it's not only awful, it's embarrassing. What on earth are we going to say—are *you* going to say, that is—to Mr. Mountfitchet? We'll never be able to come here again, and when everyone hears about it, which they're sure to do, we shall be a laughing-stock."

"Juliana—"

"I can just about excuse your broken promise by saying that the Colvedens' cellar contains a very strong claret, and you might not have noticed it creeping up on you—but the fumes you were breathing all over me last night certainly blended more than claret and the odd glass of port. Whisky, perhaps? Mr. Mountfitchet offered me a hot toddy to keep out the cold, but I had sense enough to refuse it. You, I gather, did not—and this," she concluded bitterly, "is the result!"

"Juliana—I'm ill," he managed to quaver as she paused for further stamping. "I can't see! I can't move! I don't know what's happened to me . . ."

There came a sudden movement above his head, and a damp, furious, ripping sound. "Open your eyes, Dickie Nash," came the stern command. "Stop feeling sorry for yourself, and open your eyes—and just *look* at what you've done!"

Miss Seeton had finished her breakfast long ago and (since it was not one of Martha's days for obliging her) had washed up every dish, plate, and utensil. Her coffee cup, rinsed and dried, sat waiting beside a kettle primed with freshly drawn water, ready for when their owner returned from what she had planned as a little shopping expedition.

"A bus trip to Brettenden," said Miss Seeton to herself, gazing through the window at the cloudless sky and thinking how clean and fresh everything seemed after last night's storm. "The scheduled bus runs today—I can be there and back in only a few hours, instead of having to wait for Jack Crabbe, who is so kind, but with those crossword puzzles he compiles—so very clever—he is quite happy to wait all day for everyone to complete their shopping, and today, I do have rather a lot to do . . ."

For, after further abortive attempts to recall the face of the man who had perpetrated the tomato ketchup crime, Miss Seeton had decided that a change of scene, and the purchase of fresh drawing implements, might serve to shift her artist's block and help her achieve that worthwhile likeness which her colleagues—she blushed guiltily—in the constabulary must surely have expected of her.

She sighed. "The retaining fee—so generous, and in this instance so undeserved—but I must try to do my best, and more than my best, if possible . . ."

She sighed again as she adjusted her cockscomb hat in the hall mirror and picked up her basket from the little table beside the umbrella rack. She selected one of her second-best brollies for the Brettenden excursion and could not help smiling as her eye lighted upon that gold-handled best umbrella given to her so many years ago by her now good friend, Chief Superintendent Delphick. And, greatly cheered by the sight and the memories it evoked, she resolved for dear Mr. Delphick's sake to do her utmost, on her return from Brettenden, to draw the likeness of the tomato ketchup man.

Miss Seeton had allowed herself plenty of time to catch the bus. Having locked the door of her cottage, she closed the garden gate and was starting northwards up The Street, when outside the George and Dragon opposite she was rather surprised to observe the two young Standon boys waiting by what she took to be their parents' car: waiting in perfect peace and quiet, not fidgeting, not fighting—which, to the experienced pedagogic eye of Miss Seeton, suggested only one thing.

"Mischief," murmured Miss Seeton as she hesitated for an instant only, then crossed The Street and headed for the car, as if to greet the youngsters. Who, at her approach, shuffled their feet, dropping their gaze. Mischief, undoubtedly: she recognised the signs only too well; and, in the apparent absence of their parents, she felt it her clear duty to nip any mischief firmly in the bud.

It had taken half an hour or more for Dickie to collect his scattered wits, and for Juliana to chivvy him into shaving, dressing, and going downstairs to face the music. She, he observed glumly, had woken far earlier than he had and was looking her best even before he had stumbled out of bed—which gave her, he thought, an unfair advantage. And now she was insisting that as he had (without meaning to in the least, as he kept trying to tell her) caused all the bother, it was for him to confess his fault to Charley Mountfitchet: which Juliana was prepared to see that he did.

Clutching a still-throbbing head, poor Dickie groped his way to the bedroom door; fumbled with the handle, and half-opened it; saw the startled faces of the adult Standons whisk back into their own room; and shut the door again.

"I feel terrible," he groaned. "And I must *look* pretty terrible, too—scaring people half to death—don't you think it might be better to inflict myself on Mr. Mountfitchet when I'm a bit less—"

"No, Dickie, I don't. It's no use putting it off—this isn't going to disappear all by itself, you know. Hurry up." And Juliana's tone was so grim that, though he still secretly groaned, Dickie once more made his way to the door: and, this time, forced himself through it.

Juliana was right behind him as he tottered down the stairs and reached the comparative safety of the reception hall. Charley Mountfitchet was there, kneeling beside the desk with a watering-can in his hand, tending a rather sad-looking cheeseplant.

"Never be the same again," he muttered, pouring a libation from the can into the cheeseplant's rich compost and with a surprisingly gentle hand stroking the plant's drooping leaves. "Not that I mind a spot of fire-fighting, in a good cause, but . . ." He turned a deep red, which might have been caused by stooping, set down the can, and rose to his feet. "Good morning, Miss Popjoy, Mr. Nash—and how are you both today? A little late for breakfast, but I don't doubt we can persuade Doris to rustle a little bite of something for you."

"Thank you, Mr. Mountfitchet, but before we take you up on your kind offer," replied Juliana, "my friend here has a confession to make. Go on, Dickie." She clicked her tongue as he seemed suddenly dumbstruck. "Dickie, go on!"

"Come now, Mr. Nash," Charley said in his most soothing tones. If he couldn't tell a hangover when he saw one, then thirty years in the licensing trade had taught him nothing at all—but there wasn't no need for Miss Popjoy to nag the poor bloke for having taken one over the eight last night. Anyone could see that Mr. Nash was the old-fashioned sort who knew how to hold his liquor, without causing any trouble . . . "So what seems to be the trouble, Mr. Nash?" enquired Charley kindly, as Dickie could do nothing but gulp and goggle at the landlord and fiddle with the knot of his tie.

Juliana let out an exasperated snort. Her magnificent eyes flashed. "Dickie, honestly—how like you, to leave it all to me—but, so long as Mr. Mountfitchet understands that it was nothing whatsoever to do with me, I suppose I'll have to explain."

"Understood, Miss Popjoy," Charley assured her, starting to wonder if this confession was going to be for something a bit more serious than he'd supposed. He folded his arms and fixed her with an increasingly stern gaze, beneath the reflection of which poor Dickie wilted even more. Charley, however, had eyes for nobody but Juliana as she began:

"Last night, you see, Mr. Mountfitchet, Dickie got rather wet coming home from the Colvedens'—we all tried to stop him, but he insisted on walking," she added meanly, feeling he deserved a little punishment for making her do his dirty work for him. "Anyway"—as an anguished cry of betrayal burst from Mr. Nash—"he got soaked to the skin, and he was absolutely frozen, poor thing"—involuntarily—"so he had a lovely hot bath to warm himself up . . ."

"Very sensible." Charley nodded as Juliana choked and fell silent. "I'm bound to say I thought last night he'd be the better off for a hot tub—reckon I said as much to you, didn't I, Mr. Nash, while you were drinking your toddy?"

Juliana wished that Charley had never thought of making Dickie the offer of whisky, because without it he might not have behaved quite so foolishly—but she could hardly blame the landlord for his generous attempt to prevent the death of one of his guests from double pneumonia.

"I—I believe you did," acknowledged Dickie, in a near-whisper. Juliana prodded a forceful finger into his spine: now that he'd started to talk, he could carry on talking. "So—so, well, I did. Have a hot bath, you see." Juliana prodded him again, as he gulped. He dragged his shoulders back and stood upright, facing the firing squad. "And then I went to bed—and I woke up in the night, and I was still cold—so I ran another hot bath, only I didn't want to get in it, because I was so tired—and I thought, well, I could leave the bathroom door open, and the steam would warm the bedroom—I'm very fond of a Turkish bath," he added, as if this might explain his unusual solution to the problem of a chilly summer's night.

"Look, if you're bothered that you emptied the hot-water tank," Charley said quickly, "there's no call for you to go upsetting yourself, Mr. Nash." If this was the great confession, he could afford to relax and cheer the poor bloke up a bit. Above the increasing roar of a motorbike engine outside, he said proudly: "Got the very latest in gas boilers down in the basement, I have. Hottens any amount of water quick as winking. Just forget about it, and don't you fret—I'll not go putting extra on your bill."

He scowled at the motorbike throb as it seemed to have found a comfortable spot right outside the hotel, then gave Dickie a reassuring smile. Poor Mr. Nash, worriting that way—nice of him to bother, though; there were some who'd never think of letting a bloke know what they'd done, but—but why was he shaking his head, daft beggar, looking like a wet weekend, and Miss Popjoy no more cheerful, neither?

The throb increased to a sudden roar, then began to fade as the motorbike evidently roared off up The Street. Somebody pushed open the front door and slouched into the hotel, nodding casually to the little group. Charley frowned.

"You're late, Maureen," he greeted the young woman who had made this unceremonious arrival, tossing a crash helmet on the reception desk. "And you know I'm not so keen on your Wayne and that daft machine of his, spilling oil on my new tarmac—that car park's not a racing track, my girl, and the pair of you'd do well to remember that. Anyway"—as she opened a heavily lipsticked mouth to protest—"no time for all that now. Get along to the kitchen and check with Doris what needs doing, will you?"

As Maureen flounced away, Charley turned back to Juliana and Dickie, exchanging the frown of irritation for one of polite mine-hostial enquiry. "Was there anything else seems to be the matter, Mr. Nash, Miss Popjoy? Only, I'm a bit on the busy side this morning . . ."

"I'm afraid you're going to be, well, quite a lot busier before the morning's out," Dickie told him as he seemed set on leaving them at last. "You see . . . the bath—the steam—I really am most frightfully sorry, and of course we'll—I mean *I'll*"—as Juliana prodded him more sharply yet—"pay for whatever needs to be done, but . . . but all the wallpaper has soaked itself off the walls, and it's lying in great wet tangles all over the floor, I'm afraid," Dickie said and closed his eyes with the relief of having finally managed to explain. And also so that he would not have to look at Charley Mountfitchet's face.

And there followed a long, pregnant silence.

Chapter 17

THE LANDLORD OF a hotel sees many strange things during his lifetime, and Charley Mountfitchet lived, after all, in Plummergen, where almost anything might happen (and, since Miss Seeton had come to live there, frequently did). Dickie and Juliana were nevertheless surprised at the equanimity with which, after what felt like forever, Charley reacted to the tale of Mr. Nash's slight mishap, and his calmness as he ushered the pair back up the stairs to view the damage. He seemed more disturbed by the dilatory manner in which young Maureen seemed to be setting about her morning's work than by the rampant wallpaper coiled about the room.

"Lucky we'd not got round to replacing the carpet just yet," he said, surveying the wreckage from the threshold. "Now, paste all over my Axminster's something I can't say as I'd care for—but, well, there you are, these things happen—and we're insured, so it could be worse. Won't take no more than a day's work to put this little lot to rights, not if I get hold of my brother-in-law and a couple of his mates—and you two won't mind moving into another room while we get it all fixed, will you? So how's about you popping off for a bite of breakfast—tell Doris I said so—and I'll be getting busy on the telephone?"

It was a shamefaced, though relieved, couple who crept at last into the dining room of the George and Dragon and sat at one of the tables, speaking in hushed voices and glad the worst was over. Doris, who had been laying tables for lunch, agreed to prepare toast and strong coffee and seemed glad not to be asked to cook anything complicated at this late hour or to have to ask Maureen to do so. Doris accepted the order cheerfully and bustled away to fulfill it at once; which enthusiasm for work drove Maureen (who had been at Wayne's birthday party last night and had sapped most of her energies there) out of the kitchen at last and into the reception area.

Here, she hovered with a duster, trying to look as if she had serious intentions about working. She stood by the cheese-plant and flicked its leaves with listless feathers, listening to Charley with her mouth half open.

By the time the landlord had alerted his full decorating team, even Maureen understood what had happened to the Blue Riband Suite. "Coo, Mr. Mountfitchet, how funny," she summed up the entire episode. "What a laugh, innit?"

"Not really, no." Charley eyed her sternly. "To start with, it'll mean extra work for you, my girl, because you'll have to change all the bedrooms round, and Doris hasn't the time to help like she usually does. Though where's best to put them," he added, to himself, "I'm not sure . . ."

Maureen shrugged. "If we got to change the Standons' rooms anyway, I can't see as there's any problem. I mean, I don't want to be swapping sheets backwards and forwards all the time, do I? Not as if I'm on overtime—"

"The Standons?" Charley frowned. "Don't talk so daft, Maureen. The Standons are still using their rooms—booked till the end of the week, they are."

Maureen gaped at him. "Then why was they loading up the car with their suitcases just now? Me and Wayne, we both saw them—they drove away just before—"

"What!" Charley's cry silenced Maureen completely, and she dropped her duster in surprise. He ignored her as he hunted through the pages of the hotel register; checked the receipts on the iron spike; checked them again—and then shouted towards the kitchen for Doris.

The crystals of the hall chandelier were still ringing as the green baize door was pushed open and the headwaitress came hurrying out. "What's wrong, for goodness' sake? I'm right in the middle of making toast—"

"Never mind that now," Charley broke in. "The Standons—Maureen says they've gone. Did they check out with you?"

"No, they didn't. You don't mean . . . No, they wouldn't, surely. The kids may've been little horrors, but the old man was a regular gent—"

"Maureen, are you quite sure?" The anguished landlord fixed the startled slavey with a burning gaze. "Anyone can make an honest mistake, girl—they weren't really driving away with their cases in the car, were they?"

Maureen tossed her head. "Best check in their rooms and see for yourself, Mr. Mountfitchet. I'm not one to imagine things—you go and look, and you'll find I'm right."

Charley thumped his fist on the hotel register with an oath. "Oh, I'll do that, never fear—and before I do, I'm locking the front door! You stay here, Doris, and don't you let that precious pair in the dining room try to sneak out. Maureen, you get along into the kitchen and keep a watch on the back door . . ."

He was halfway up the stairs before he had finished and did not hear Doris countermand his orders with the suggestion that it should be Maureen who stayed in reception while she herself checked on the state of the toast, which she now feared in her haste she might not have switched off properly. Maureen could hardly be trusted to use the toaster in the normal manner, let alone cope with it if it had caught fire: but a locked front door (and Charley had pocketed the key) ought not to tax her intellect too greatly.

Charley came back down the stairs with a grim expression on his normally cordial countenance. "Done a flit," was all he said and headed straight for the telephone. Maureen's presence in lieu of Doris did not seem to worry him as he set his finger in the dial and, without having to look up the number, rang the house of Plummergen's PC Potter.

Juliana and Dickie were on their third cup of coffee, wondering what had happened to their toast but not wishing to make a fuss, when the door of the dining room juddered open and Charley Mountfitchet marched in, flanked by Maureen (still armed with her feather duster) and a uniformed police constable.

Dickie pushed back his chair and leaped to his feet with a cry of alarm. "I say—I mean, I told you we'd be glad to pay for the redecorating—surely we can come to some suitable arrangement! Couldn't we talk it over? Aren't you being a bit, well, hasty?"

"I'd say that depends, Mr. Nash," replied Charley while Maureen brandished her duster and Potter favoured these dubious guests with the official glare he found so useful at chucking-out time. Dickie, aghast, subsided; Juliana, with a surge of desperation, said:

"I know it's absolutely no use our apologising without some more practical expression of—"

"Never mind all that now!" barked Charley. "Just part of the camouflage, isn't it? How often have you played that trick before, Mr. Nash? Got it down to a fine art, you have! Regular little decoys, the pair of you, and me so busy listening to your tale I never spotted your pals sneaking off with their cases—very clever, you must think yourselves! The row those kids were kicking up all the time, when they kept quiet anyone'd be thankful for it and pay no heed—and that's what you all rely on, don't you? Only this time you tangled with Charley Mountfitchet, and he's not one to take such shenanigans lightly—there's a police cell waiting for you two, make no mistake!"

At this ominous point in the proceedings Doris emerged from the kitchen with soot in her hair and a frown on her face. "Just a minute, Mr. Mountfitchet," she said formally above the gasps and horrified exclamations of Juliana and Dickie as PC Potter flexed his muscles and prepared to play his part. "We've had little enough time to think about this—but one thing I've got to say, and that's as how these two had lunch with Miss Seeton yesterday and took her out in the afternoon for a drive, so she must know them and could maybe speak for them, and perhaps it's nothing more than a queer coincidence, what's happened. I thought."

"Oh." Charley looked at Doris with some interest. "Did they? And they dined at the Hall last night, too—but then, Sir George is a magistrate and must know all manner of folk—still, it might just be there's been a bit of hasty speech on my part, and an apology due—yet I don't know," he said slowly as looks of tentative relief began to appear on the faces of Dickie and Juliana. "I don't know . . ."

"So what if they're friends of Miss Seeton's?" demanded Maureen, scowling. "She's one as has any number of queer friends, everybody knows that. The Standons, for one thing—she was only talking to them just before they drove away, wasn't she!"

Sensation. Miss Seeton's general "queerness" had been hotly debated in Plummergen from her earliest time there: a debate which had split the village in two. Some said that at the very least she was a witch; others maintained her to be a perfectly normal gentlewoman to whom adventures merely happened, without her instigation, and that her response to said adventures made her a credit to the place.

Maureen was not of the latter opinion. "Chattering away nineteen to the dozen, so she was, friendly as you please, and if you don't believe me, you can ask my Wayne, because he saw them at it as well."

The frown was creeping back into Charley's eyes, and he turned to PC Potter. "Reckon there's still something here ought to be looked into, I do."

"Well, I don't," Doris informed him roundly. "If Miss Seeton thinks these two're all right, then all right they're sure to be—everybody"—and she glared at Maureen—"knows that. Why, when she was here with them yesterday, she'd got her gold-handled umbrella along of her, and she'd not bring that out for any queer folk, now would she?"

Which successfully quenched Maureen and convinced the rest of the company: even Dickie and Juliana were impressed. PC Potter remarked that it might be worth Mr. Mountfitchet's time—for peace of mind, nothing more—just to step across the road to Sweetbriars and ask Miss Seeton for her views, but for himself he was prepared to accept the evidence of the gold umbrella, and would suggest Mr. Mountfitchet did the same. "Or"—as Charley muttered something—"you could give Sir George a ring, though I don't doubt you'll hear the same from him, a bit on the shorter side, of course"— with a grin—"but to the same effect, you can be sure."

Charley supposed that he could, adding that, taking Miss Seeton's umbrella into account, he reckoned he didn't really see the need to go bothering people, either. He was sorry for any little misunderstanding, but he hoped Miss Popjoy and Mr. Nash would look at it from his point of view . . .

Which, of course, Dickie and Juliana said that they did.

"So now there's only these vanishing guests of yours to be sorted out, Charley," said PC Potter, accepting a cup of coffee and amiably joining the late breakfasters. Maureen, sniffing with disapproval, drifted away on some unspecified errand of her own, leaving Doris to produce vast quantities of hot buttered toast which the landlord intimated that he, too, would share with the suspects of a few moments ago, to show there were no hard feelings.

"Besides," said Potter, spooning marmalade with a lavish hand, "we'll not catch these here Standons—if that's their real name, which I take leave to doubt—without statements from everyone as saw them, so while we're having our bite to eat, you can be thinking what they looked like, ready for me to write it all down. Saves time, you see," said PC Potter, and everyone agreed with him, although Charley secretly had doubts as to whether anything useful could be achieved.

Everyone was getting on extremely well with everyone else, and had even managed to recall a few details about the Standons which Potter thought would be useful, when the door of the dining room was flung open with almost as much force as before. They all stopped eating and turned to stare.

Maureen, her eyes bright, her cheeks almost as red as her lipstick, came rushing in, more excited than either her employer or PC Potter (whose instinctive thought was *drugs*) had ever seen her.

"I told you so," she said breathlessly to Charley Mountfitchet, "only you wouldn't listen—I said as how she was in it with them, and you didn't believe me, did you? Well, you was wrong and I was right!"

"Talk sense, girl. Wrong and right about who? In what with who else? Getting yourself worked up about nothing, that's what you're doing."

"Oh, no, I ain't!" Maureen glanced round the table with triumph in her eyes. "I just done what you should've done, Charley Mountfitchet, but you can't say as nobody warned you—Miss Seeton, that's who I'm talking about!" There was a sudden, intense silence. She smirked. "Went to ask her, didn't I, only across the road, not five minutes away—and was she there?" She did not wait for them to answer. "No, she wasn't—and that's why she was talking to them Standons when Wayne and me saw her. She was getting ready to skip, that's what she was doing!"

Only a brief flicker of doubt crossed Charley's face: he was still prepared to accept the verdict of the gold-handled umbrella, which the whole village knew to be Miss Seeton's pride and joy. But the face of PC Potter wore an anxious aspect. Not that he dreamed for one minute of Miss Seeton's being in league with the defrauding Standons—but if the evidence of Maureen was correct, and the old lady had been in conversation with them just before they absconded . . .

With anyone else it wouldn't have mattered: but Potter knew Miss Seeton of old. The marmalade suddenly tasted very bitter. Things tended to happen to Miss Seeton that would—that could—never happen to anyone else.

He swallowed his mouthful of toast and got hurriedly to his feet. "We'd best be on our way to Ashford," he said, to everyone's surprise. "More sensible to give the statements there, see, about how these Standons looked, and the sort of car they was driving and all. And the sooner we can be on our way, the better."

But he did not add his silent reason for this unexpected change of plan: which was his fear that Miss Seeton had been kidnapped . . .

Chapter 18

AT ASHFORD THE Plummergen party discovered that Superintendent Chris Brinton was out and likely to remain so for an unspecified time. Desk Sergeant Mutford took great pleasure in dwelling upon this inconvenient fact.

"A horrible murder, we've just had reported," he said, gloating. "Chap cut to ribbons, Ruckinge way—couldn't give you the slightest idea when Mr. Brinton'll be back, I'm afraid. Course, there's young Foxon just come in—that is, if you didn't mind the glare . . ."

PC Potter had dealt with Detective Constable Foxon on previous occasions and was untroubled by that young man's idea of "plain" clothes. Foxon it would have to be, since it was not possible to follow standing orders: the lad was, after all, acquainted with Miss Seeton, and one of Brinton's regular team.

The standing orders had been issued by the superintendent some years ago, to the effect that he was to be informed—if necessary by telephone, at home—of any (repeat, any) untoward occurrence either in Plummergen or involving Miss Seeton. (This was in addition to the regular weekly reports which, shortly after Miss Seeton's arrival in the village, he had insisted that Potter should supply.) Brinton had, at the time of issuing the orders, thought it far better to be safe than sorry: but there had been several occasions since then when he had felt ignorance to be decided bliss.

It was not long before Dickie, Juliana, Maureen, and Doris were in various interview rooms, looking at mug shots and giving statements. Potter had agreed Charley could come over later, under his own steam: the landlord was understandably reluctant to leave his hotel unoccupied for any length of time, in view of what had happened: the details of which, gleaned from the others, Potter was now explaining to Foxon, describing the Standons, and their swindle, and the possibility of Miss Seeton's involvement with them.

"And I wouldn't care to say for certain whether or not she's been kidnapped," he concluded, "but I thought as you, or Mr. Brinton rather, should be told about it, her being one of us, as you might say."

Anything less like a regular member of the constabulary, with their truncheons, than Miss Emily Dorothea Seeton, with her umbrella, Foxon could hardly imagine. As he glanced at his watch, he chuckled. "Well, unless they've chased her into Brettenden and nobbled her there, she's perfectly safe, for once. I met her myself, not forty minutes ago. She'd popped in for an hour or two's shopping—"

Potter slapped himself on the forehead. "Market day, of course, and she'll have taken the bus—fool that I am for not thinking of that! Only, with it being Miss Seeton, and knowing what she can be like . . ."

Foxon nodded. He knew, all right: few better. "I'll give your report to Mr. Brinton the minute he comes back, of course—we don't really want to take chances where Miss Seeton's concerned, no matter how indirectly. When you drop the others back to Plummergen, better check she's got safely home again—the bus runs every couple of hours on market day, doesn't it? She told me she didn't plan to stay long—just fancied a change of scene, she said." He did not add that she had been coaxed into using her artistic abilities to help him make his latest choice of plainclothes fashion, steering him away from his favorite pinks and purples towards a more decorous (by his standards) deep orange shirt with green polka dots. "Suppose we leave it that you'll ring in if she's not on the next bus? Otherwise, we'll just concentrate on the swindle and assume that Miss Seeton's chat with the Standons was pure coincidence."

With this suggestion Potter was content: but Superintendent Brinton, when he returned shortly after Potter had gone, was not. He turned a withering glance upon his subordinate, who looked (to Brinton's mind) too cheerful by half.

"Coincidence be damned! As if I didn't have enough on my plate, with this knife murder—and you swanning off to the shops when for once in your life you might have been of some use . . ." He snorted, and scowled. Foxon hid a grin.

"I'm sorry, sir. But if I'm to hang around that new disco without anyone knowing who I am, I need some smarter gear—and they had a sale on—and," he added wickedly, "Miss Seeton helped me choose it, sir. Very good eye for colour she's got, sir—the artist's eye, of course."

Brinton's own eyes were sideways slits. "You're trying to wind me up, Foxon, and you think you've succeeded. Just because Potter's brought us the gypsy's warning that Miss Seeton's about to start up again—and you know there's no such thing as coincidence where she's concerned—"

"Oh, yes, sir, I couldn't agree with you more. But I thought you'd be glad to have your mind taken off everything else, just for a moment or two, sir—along the lines of, er—banging your head against a brick wall, sir."

Brinton groaned and clutched his hair. "Lovely when it stops, laddie? You're mad—stark, staring mad. You know as well as I do there's absolutely nothing that could make me forget for an instant that Miss Seeton's found herself in another case—even if it isn't," he added, frowning, "quite up to her usual standards."

"Yet, sir," supplied Foxon; then, as the superintendent glared at him, "Sorry, sir. Seriously, I know what you mean—swindling hotels just isn't in the same league as some of her other cases—or even this knifing, sir, that you were going to tell me all about." And he sat waiting for Brinton to enlarge on the murder which had spared him the first manifestations of Miss Seeton's latest effort.

"Ugh." Brinton made a face, then shook his head briskly and snatched up the telephone. "Switchboard? Plummergen police house, and make it sharp." He caught Foxon's look of astonishment. "Yes, I know murder's supposed to be priority number one, and normally I'd agree, but not this time. Our corpse is no great loss to the world, believe me, and with Miss Seeton involved in the other, I think— Hello? Is that you, Mrs. Potter? Brinton here. Your husband back, is he? . . . Oh, I see. Well, when he comes in, could you ask him to bring Miss Seeton over to Ashford as soon as possible?. . . No, nothing serious, but if she wouldn't mind . . . Thank you, yes, please pass the message on."

He banged down the receiver, uttered a sigh of relief, and wiped his perspiring forehead with a large white handkerchief. "Well, I've done what I can to defuse her for the time being," he growled. "And until she shows up, there's nothing else to do—so we can turn our full attention, if we must, to the knifing that seems to have taken your fancy. Goodness knows why—I told you, we're well rid of him. You might almost say I'd be glad to shake the hand of the bloke who did away with him—almost," he repeated, with a sigh.

"Why, sir? Who was he?"

"Gerald Sacombe. Yes"—as Foxon exclaimed—"the drug dealer—and, it turns out, a thoroughly horrible piece of work, quite apart from the dealing. Pornographic photos on the side, going by what we found when we searched the place. And from the way he was carved up, it seems that whoever did it really enjoyed their work. He looked just like a piece of raw steak wearing pale pink ribbons."

Foxon made a face. "A crazed junkie, sir?"

"Could be—but, as I said, who really cares? The world is a better place without our Gerald, in my opinion, though if you tell anyone I said so, I'll have you back on the beat right through the summer, when all the tourists ask daft questions and drive the wrong way round the town centre."

Foxon paled. "Your secret's safe with me, sir, and in any case I reckon I'd agree with you about Sacombe. We've been after him for ages, haven't we?"

"And somebody else got to him first." Brinton shrugged. "Pity—I'd dearly have loved to feel his collar, but the blighter was always too clever for us. I'd give a lot to know how he worked his supply route, but I don't suppose we stand much chance of finding out anything now. Which is one of the two reasons I regret his passing, Foxon. The other, before you ask, is that whoever it was really did make quite a revolting mess of him. Even the photographer looked pale, and you know they always make out they've seen it all before—so I can't say I care much for the idea of a weirdo like that running loose around these parts. We could be in for a nasty time of it."

Foxon pulled an expressive face and shuddered. "As you said before, sir, ugh. Let's hope you're wrong . . ."

PC Potter, having delivered his witnesses to the George and Dragon and told Charley to pop along to Ashford when he felt like it, decided that his Panda car could do with a checkup. Which gave him an excellent excuse for loitering on the forecourt of Crabbe's Garage (outside which the bus stop was situated) while Jack Crabbe polished the windscreen, peered under the bonnet, and tested the depth of the tyre treads. Jack, who could take an official hint, was glad to go along with the fantasy that the Kent police took poor care of their patrol vehicles; and enjoyed himself greatly by uttering loud remarks about the appalling state of Potter's big end and similar insults.

The Brettenden bus arrived, decanting a parcel-laden crowd of passengers. Among them was Miss Seeton, with her small wicker shopping basket: not heavy or awkward enough, thought Potter, to need an offer of help. But she was back home in safety, which was the main thing. He thanked Jack for all his hard work, threatened him under his breath with a speeding ticket next time he took the family bus to town, and drove cheerfully away to the police house.

Where his wife greeted him with the message from Superintendent Brinton, instead of the cup of tea he'd been looking forward to. "The sooner the better, he said," she told her husband as he looked disappointed. "You'd best be off to Sweetbriars to fetch her—it might be something really urgent. Suppose they want her at Scotland Yard again?"

"They'd send a car for her, like they've done before."

"Not if it was one of them secret cases she does for 'em sometimes, not wanting anyone to know that's where she's gone. Mr. Brinton sounded a bit, well, distracted—didn't want to go into details over the phone, I reckon." Mabel Potter nodded sagely. "Mark my words, it'll be Scotland Yard for Miss Seeton, and the Battling Brolly in the papers again before much longer, you see if I'm not right . . ."

Which sounded so plausible to her husband that he forgot all about his thirst, and the hot weather, and without even stopping to polish his buttons, jumped straight back into the car and drove down The Street to Miss Seeton's cottage.

Miss Seeton had enjoyed her trip to Brettenden and had bought a fresh set of pencils, varying in hardness, as well as a new sketching block. Now, perhaps, she would be able to draw the face of that man who had startled her with his wicked, bloody (she blushed) trick . . . perhaps she would no longer feel that she had let everyone down by her failure to remember what he looked like. Dear Mr. Delphick had seemed so, well, one could not exactly say *reproachful*, for he was too understanding not to know that there were times when, try as one might, the inspiration simply would not come, but he had every right to expect—

"Oh, dear." Miss Seeton, bustling about her sitting room, had glanced out of the window and seen the Panda car pull up outside. The police! Mr. Delphick was obviously more upset by her failure than she had supposed. PC Potter—her colleague—had been sent to take her to task . . .

Miss Seeton's eyes were anxious as she opened her front door to Potter's cheerful knock. "Oh, dear, Mr. Potter, has Mr. Delphick asked you to call?" she greeted her visitor, sounding as anxious as she looked. "I'm so sorry, but—"

"No, I don't think so," Potter cut in quickly. He knew only too well how her speech could wander if people didn't hurry to divert her. "No," he said more slowly as he recalled what his wife had been hinting at. "No, it was Mr. Brinton said he'd like to see you, if you wouldn't mind, and as soon as possible, please. I'm to take you there by car—had it serviced specially," he added, thinking of Jack Crabbe and his comments about big ends.

Miss Seeton saw his grin and misinterpreted it as a knowing smirk: which reason told her was so unlike dear Mr. Potter, but which guilt insisted she deserved. "Oh, dear, yes, I noticed you at the garage, but I had no idea . . . and yet"—with a sigh—"it is useless to procrastinate. I will put on my hat and collect my umbrella, of course, so that we may be on our way immediately."

And her guilty conscience troubled her so much that she quite forgot to take her sketching gear with her.

Chapter 19

IN FACT, MISS SEETON seemed so glum and thoughtful on the journey that Potter was prompted to tell her one of his more recent, and repeatable, adventures in an attempt to cheer her up. Poor old girl, looked like she'd lost a shilling and found sixpence: but this oughter make her laugh . . .

"It was on the motorway, see, chap driving to Dover with a load of racing pigeons, new stock he was starting to train for some big race or other up in Yorkshire. Well, he breaks down halfway between two emergency phones, and what should happen as he's running on to the hard shoulder with knocking under the bonnet and blue smoke coming out of the back, but a patrol car—couple of my mates—pulling in behind him, and say they'll radio for the RAC or the AA right on the spot, save him having to walk to the telephone."

"How very kind of your colleagues," said Miss Seeton, "although only to be expected, of course."

"Well, that's what anyone'd think, wouldn't they? But this chap, he says thank you for the offer, he's got a better way of calling for help, seeing as it's just that he's been burning oil and a couple of gallons should set him to rights again. He'll fly off the pigeons to his old dad, lives at home and helps to train 'em, you see, and there'll be messages tied to their legs for the old chap to bring a can of oil along, save paying the RAC, because of course they have to charge, call-out fees and everything."

"I suppose they would," Miss Seeton acknowledged, though she really had little idea of what he was talking about.

Potter began to laugh. "They say time's money, don't they? Must've cost this pigeon chap a fortune, I reckon. He told my mates they'd be home in about ten minutes: still learning, they were, so not too far from home. Well! Two hours later he was on the telephone, asking for help, never mind having to pay for it, and not very happy either, thinking his birds'd got lost on the way home, and must be dud stock and no good for racing, when he'd paid upwards of two hundred quid each, if you can believe it."

Miss Seeton could. Since her move from London to the country she had developed her study of birds, and in any case had, at the moment, a particular interest in racing pigeons. "Oh, dear, I do hope he didn't lose them all—and that he didn't, that is to say, that they all survived their ordeal . . ." Visions of pigeon pie, an Elizabethan delicacy, floated horribly in front of her eyes.

Potter chuckled. "Bless your life, they survived—done just what was asked of 'em, they had. Prime stock, he said they were, and I believe it. Started arriving home within ten minutes of letting 'em fly, with their little notes tied to their legs—and did you know, Miss Seeton, a pigeon can carry a fair weight, what with the canister and all, never mind a screwed-up bit of paper fixed with an elastic band, which is what he'd done with the lot of 'em. Only his dad, see, he never thought to look for messages, so the bloke's trouble was wasted. The old man knew his son had gone off on this training flight, so that's what he thought they were all doing when they came back one after the other. And he still"—Potter chuckled—"had to pay the RAC to bring him the oil for the engine, after all that!"

Miss Seeton smiled politely, though she saw nothing very amusing in the poor man's predicament. He must have been so worried, thinking the birds were lost—not that they *were*, as he had found out later, but she knew from what Mrs. Ongar of Wounded Wings had told her that racing pigeons could be very valuable. Carrier pigeons, too—not that it made much difference, if you were stranded on a motorway and running out of oil. Which she imagined must be necessary for a car to run properly, and certainly Mr. Potter thought so—or why else would he have told her this little story?

She supposed it must be her turn to tell him something in exchange, and (thoughts of Wounded Wings still very much in the forefront of her mind) described to PC Potter her discovery and rescue of the stranded, storm-weary carrier pigeon which had been fed on Chirrup and stayed with her overnight, while it regained its strength.

"Just as well it's gone," Potter said. "Tibs is in one of her moods recently, and there's no accounting for what she might do." Tibs was the Potters' cat. The only person in Plummergen who had any control over the creature, a large vindictive feline thought by many villagers to be possessed of evil spirits, was Miss Amelia Potter, age five. There had been occasions when Miss Seeton had worsted the beast, but they were not, on the whole, occasions she was in any hurry to repeat.

"Cats," said Miss Seeton, "have strange moods, indeed. They are mysterious creatures, and unaccountable . . ."

"And so are some people," Potter said. "Why, they were telling me only this morning, Sergeant Mutford it was, some bloke the other day went right off his head, blamed it on the storm—rushed round with a shotgun and peppered one of the neighbour's cats, yelling and screaming at the poor beast, he was."

"Oh, dear," said Miss Seeton faintly. PC Potter felt very cross with himself. Far from cheering her up, poor old lady, he seemed to be making things worse . . .

He was a thankful man when, a few silent minutes later, he delivered his passenger safely to Ashford police station and headed back to Plummergen for a strong cup of tea.

Superintendent Brinton greeted Miss Seeton politely, but absently, for his mind was, despite himself, preoccupied with the late (albeit unlamented) Gerald Sacombe. His face briefly wore a frown as he observed the absence of her sketching gear; then he told himself that of course she'd be able to make do with what they could find for her around the station: the English were very good at making do. He smiled at Miss Seeton in what he supposed was a reassuring manner.

"If you're sure you wouldn't like a cup of tea or anything, I'll just take you along to the interview room and leave you to it, if you don't mind. Rather a nasty case has come up, and it's all hands to the pump, I'm afraid. You'll be all right by yourself for a while, won't you? You see, we need my office to investigate the murder."

"Murder? Oh, no—I mean, surely not." Miss Seeton's hands fiddled with the clasp of her handbag. "I mean, the poor man wasn't *really* stabbed, was he?"

Brinton gazed at her in astonishment. "If he wasn't, then he must've put on razor-blade underwear and rolled down a very steep hill, instead. I've never seen such a sight."

"But—but wasn't it only tomato ketchup? I'm sure poor Mr. Thundridge said—oh." Brinton's astonishment had registered at last. Miss Seeton blushed. "Oh, dear, how foolish I must have sounded. I'm so sorry. You see, I thought you—that is, Mr. Delphick had asked you to ask me—after what happened the other day, you see—when I was arrested . . ." Miss Seeton blushed again.

Brinton's reaction was even more extreme. His jaw fell open and his eyes popped. His voice, when he finally found it, emerged as a faint gasp. "Arrested? Miss Seeton, you surely don't mean . . ." And he stood shaking his head while she blushed even more.

"Oh dear, yes, such a silly mistake—on my part, that is to say, for one must excuse poor Mr. Thundridge. His suit was ruined, but it did look so like blood, and he sounded so very convincing—the man with the tomato ketchup, that is. And poor Mr. Delphick, although of course he is far too kind to say so, was very disappointed at my failure to produce a good likeness—or, indeed, any likeness—of the man, so I naturally thought that when Mr. Potter came to fetch me here, he must have telephoned from Scotland Yard to make me try again—Mr. Delphick, I mean, not Mr. Potter, although he, too, should be considered a colleague, should he not?"

Miss Seeton drew a deep breath, which gave Brinton time to jump in before she could say anything else. He raised an arresting hand and said:

"Please don't trouble to explain further, Miss Seeton—I'd much prefer it if you'd let *me* explain to you." Which he proceeded to do, slowly and carefully, as he escorted her down the corridor to the interview room with the largest window, where he had ordered a comfortable chair to be installed. He sent out for pencils and paper, not daring to ask why, if Miss

Seeton had supposed herself to be required to draw pictures for Scotland Yard, she had omitted to bring her requirements with her: he knew of old how easily she was flustered by the unexpected, and from what he'd understood of her remarks, she'd been more than flustered by the arrival at her cottage of PC Potter in his Panda car.

"So we'd like you to draw these people for us, if you can," he concluded as Miss Seeton listened to him with a slight smile of relief on her face and a faintly shocked look in her eyes. "Do you think you'll be able to do it?"

"Certainly I will try my utmost, Mr. Brinton, in such a . . . a very deceitful matter—one does not like to think that the Standons—and they seemed such a normal happy family—but to cheat Mr. Mountfitchet in such a way . . ." Her eyes were bright, and her cheeks were pink. "It is clearly no more than my duty to do what I can to be of assistance, even if I only saw them on that one occasion—though it was not, of course, in quite as, er, fraught an atmosphere as that of my little . . . misadventure the other day . . ."

So Brinton left her to it, while he hurried back to his office and busied himself with the case of the murdered drug dealer, Gerald Sacombe.

He became so deeply involved that he lost all track of time: it was only when Miss Seeton (who had waited for someone to come for her sketches, not liking to worry people she knew were all so very busy) ventured at last out of her room and wandered to the main hall of the police station, there to discover its presiding genius, that the superintendent was reminded of his other case. The telephone on his desk rang desperately as Desk Sergeant Mutford (who had heard of Miss Seeton but never encountered her before, and now found the experience too exhausting for a man of his years) handed the entire imbroglio over to his chief with a heartfelt sigh of relief.

Brinton left Foxon and the rest of the team to carry on with what they were doing while he hurried to the rescue—although he wondered, as he strode down the corridor, which of the two it was, Mutford or Miss Seeton, who needed rescuing. He had a shrewd idea, though . . .

"There you are at last, sir!" Mutford's greeting told Brinton that his guess had been correct. The man looked as if he'd been tied upside-down in a sack and put on a roundabout running at full speed. "Here's Miss Seeton, sir—and here's Mr. Brinton, miss." Having said which, Mutford beat a hasty retreat into his little sanctum behind the reception desk, before his superior could say anything. Miss Seeton looked after him with a sympathetic smile.

"Poor Sergeant Mutford," she said, at which Brinton had to struggle with himself to show no reaction. "He has such a lot on his mind, it seems—as, of course, do you, Superintendent, and I apologise for disturbing you in this fashion, when you are so busy, but Mr. Mutford thought it best—"

"I'm sure he did," Brinton told her. "And I'm not in the least surprised. Still, never mind," he said as she turned an enquiring face towards him. "You've done the sketches, have you? I'm sorry not to have come back to you sooner, but . . . Anyway, we'll have a look at them now," and he led her over to one of the plastic-covered easy chairs which stood along one wall.

Having made her as comfortable as possible, Brinton sat beside Miss Seeton and accepted the drawings she held out to him. "I do hope that's what you wanted, Superintendent," she said earnestly as he began to study her handiwork.

The first picture showed a hotel dining room, hastily out-lined, with two small boys having a skirmish in front of one of the tables, and three adults—two men, one woman—gazing down on them with fond expressions. One man was white-haired, clearly older than the other, and on crutches, with distinguished features and a military moustache: the woman's similarity of feature seemed to bear out the Stan-dons' claim that these two were father and daughter.

"Which goes along with what the witnesses said," Brinton muttered to himself as he peered at the younger man, whose appearance was less well defined. His head was turned more to the side, looking farther away from his squabbling sons than his wife or father-in-law. "Almost as if," Brinton mused aloud, "he wasn't quite so keen on the tricks they're getting up to as the other two. Interesting . . ."

Miss Seeton's second sketch seemed to bear this theory out. The boys, upright now, had obviously just been stopped in the middle of another of their fights, for their clothes were dishevelled and their expressions either belligerent (the elder) or thankful (the younger). Their features were clearer than in the other sketch: and those of the man who had parted them, and who now kept them apart by the collar, were clearer, too. He looked far less doting and rather more annoyed than be-fore, though the blood tie was evident here, as well. "A family affair," muttered Brinton, turning back to the first drawing to study it more closely.

"Yes," he said, "a combination of these sketches and the PhotoFits everyone else came up with after looking at the mug shots, and at least we know what the blighters look like. And may I say, Miss Seeton, that I get a better idea of what they look like from your drawings than from the other stuff? Mind you, whether we'll catch 'em in the end's quite another matter. All we can do is circulate the likenesses round local hotels and issue a warning about what's happened. Ten to one, as the trick's worked once they'll try it again."

He had half expected Miss Seeton to chip in at this point with some remark about the regrettable effect of the parents' moral values upon the minds of innocent children and was surprised when she did not. He turned enquiringly to face her: to his continued surprise, she was looking uncomfortable. Surely she wasn't getting cold feet about having helped to make sure everyone knew what these characters looked like?

Or was it . . .

He remembered how his old friend, Chief Superintendent Delphick, usually dealt with Miss Seeton when she'd sketched something for him and looked guilty afterwards. He held out a coaxing hand and tried to sound encouraging as he said: "Miss Seeton, what about the other one? I'm sure you did more than two drawings, didn't you? You had time enough for ten, goodness knows."

"Oh dear," said Miss Seeton and sighed. "I'm afraid—that is, I feel rather foolish, because—I'm sure you don't wish to see this one, Superintendent. It has nothing to do with those deceitful Standons, I assure you—merely a reference to the conversation which Mr. Potter and I had in his car on the way over here. I imagine that, as it was the first picture I drew, it must have been still, well, lodged in my subconscious—the conversation, I mean—the others which I drew, the ones you wanted, bear absolutely no resemblance . . ."

She faltered to a halt as Brinton, still taking a leaf from his colleague's book, kept waiting and looking at her. She sighed and opened her handbag. From deep inside she withdrew a folded sheet of paper, which she passed to him as she murmured unhappily that she'd looked for a wastepaper basket, and not found one, and didn't care to leave it lying on the table for everyone to see how silly she'd been—and now she hoped that he wouldn't be cross with her for trying to remove official property from police premises . . .

And Brinton, who was used to her by now, said: "You've no need to worry about that at all. It's quite all right, Miss Seeton."

Chapter 20

Superintendent Brinton was on the telephone to his Scotland Yard colleague, Chief Superintendent Delphick.

"I couldn't make head or tail of it," he said, having first demanded the full story of Miss Seeton's arrest, then capping this with his own tale of woe. "She's drawn a load of heads—well, three of them, anyway, two men and a woman—mixed up with birds flying about—and the really daft thing is that it's all happening *indoors*, and old-fashioned-looking indoors, what's more. Sort of foreign, too," he added after a pause during which Delphick failed to find a suitable reply. "Well, she said I didn't really want to see it, and now that I have I agree with her."

"Don't be too hasty, Chris. When Miss Seeton starts to produce, well, drawings that don't seem quite right, we both know what it can mean: that her psychic ability, or whatever we want to call it, has gone into overdrive again." And the Oracle knew that Miss Seeton's possible status as a psychic—he'd never been able to make his mind up for certain—was what unnerved his old friend Brinton so badly. "Could you be a little more specific in your description?" he prompted, trying to take the superintendent's mind off his woes.

But Brinton was unable to do more than say that anybody who was happy to sit around indoors with a load of turtle-doves flapping about their heads must be as crazy as he was starting to think he'd gone himself, trying to interpret one of Miss Seeton's sketches.

"It needs someone who understands her," he said, "and we all know what that means—it means you, Oracle. And didn't you say you'd be here soon, anyway? You can interpret this sketch for me before we get stuck into the drugs murder."

"Yes, it's rather a pity someone's done for Sacombe—we had him earmarked as a likely lead to our end of the investigation. The evidence is pretty conclusive that he would have been worth keeping tabs on—"

"*We'd* been keeping tabs on him," Brinton reminded him in a gloomy tone, "and it got us absolutely nowhere."

"He was clever," acknowledged Delphick, "and that's what made him so dangerous—yet potentially so useful. If we'd only found out how the distribution system worked, we'd have made a definite connection with the London end, where the big money is—just that one vital link missing—we could have put a stop to at least part of this filthy trade. But, however it works, the system has so far proved too efficient for our liking. Which means," he added thoughtfully, "that it should be very easy for some-body else to take over . . . How I wish they'd tried it while he was still alive."

"What? You really fancy gun battles all over Kent, and heaven-knows-how-many corpses after the chummies've sent each other to kingdom come?"

Delphick cleared his throat. "Heretical it may sound, Chris, but if the chummies *did* clear one another out of the way, it would save the likes of us a great deal of work. So long as no innocent bystanders became involved—and, let's face it, how often . . ."

"Exactly," remarked Brinton dryly as Delphick drifted to an uneasy halt. "Miss Seeton again, you see. *Now* do you understand why I want you here to deal with her?" For they both remembered well Miss Seeton's first involvement with the police, after she prodded the notorious drug-runner and hoodlum, Cesar Lebel, in the back with her umbrella because she disapproved of the language he was using, and his attitude, to the young woman he was (unknown to Miss Seeton) in the process of knifing.

"Innocent bystander," muttered Brinton grimly. "Oracle, get down to Kent just as soon as you can. If she's getting herself mixed up in another drug murder . . ."

He paused, hoping that Delphick would reassure him that she wasn't. But the Oracle knew Miss Seeton of old. There was little reassurance he could give.

He altered tack, returning to an earlier thought. "Now, if only the takeover bid—if that's what it is—had come while Sacombe was still alive, we could have followed all the infighting from a safe distance and discovered, once somebody had come out on top, what I suppose we might call the new chain of command. Which would have been helpful. But as things stand, we're short one dealer at the distribution end, and overall not much farther forward . . ."

There was another thoughtful silence. Brinton broke it. "I suppose," he said grudgingly, "though I don't much care for the idea—but she *has* started drawing again . . ."

"I agree. Her gifts, such as they are—whatever they are—don't usually waste themselves on such a relatively minor matter as a bunch of people who scarper from a hotel without paying their—wait! Chris, just think about the timetable for a moment. They've scarpered *on the same day Sacombe's body was discovered.*"

And Brinton, after doing some quick calculations, found his voice shaking with excitement as he replied.

"Dickie," said Miss Popjoy in a thoughtful voice, "wouldn't you suppose Mentley must have had enough time to think it over by now?"

Mr. Nash favoured his lady with a mildly sardonic look over the top of his glass, which he almost drained before answering. "Well, with anyone reasonable, I'd have said yes, but he did strike me as an erratic sort of chap—hard for me to tell *how* his mind works, not knowing him that well—and to be honest, Juliana, just now I'm not particularly bothered. We came to these parts for a holiday, yet today's been less like a holiday than anything I've experienced since that ghastly cruise." He shuddered at the memory and helped himself to another drink.

Juliana frowned. "We may have been questioned by the police again, but on this occasion we've definitely got nothing to hide—and, in any case, we survived last time, so I really don't see the problem now."

"I suppose it's just that I feel a bit, well, haunted." He waved his hands in an expansive gesture which told her absolutely nothing. "I mean—the very next holiday we take, bingo! Questioned by the police again—it's enough to give anyone a persecution complex."

"Dickie, don't exaggerate. And don't have any more, if you're driving later on—"

"Am I?" Mr. Nash blinked at her. "Where to? Why? And who said so?"

"Yes," Juliana told him. "To see Mentley again, to find out about the pictures. And I did."

"Oh," said Dickie, subsiding. "I suppose, if you say so . . . We'd better order coffee straight away, then."

"But at least," Juliana pointed out, "this time we know where we're meant to be going, don't we?"

And fortunately (Miss Popjoy having mislaid the vicar's sister's instructions) both of them remembered how to get to Filkins Farm in Murreystone. Since their previous visit, an even greater air of dilapidation seemed to have settled over the whole place: another bar was missing from the gate, and the nameplate had fallen right off, to be propped up against a stone half buried by uncut grass. Anyone passing by in a hurry would have missed it altogether.

Taking his springs into account, Dickie did not rush up the rutted drive. He snorted when the car rounded the final bend, and remarked: "The vultures are still at it, I see. What a hole!"

"Miss Seeton said they were crows," Juliana reminded him rather sharply. She felt annoyed on Mentley's behalf. "Or I think she did, anyway. I can't imagine why you have to make such weak jokes sometimes. Oh, look, there he is now."

"And rather more lively than before," Dickie remarked, as this time the figure of Mentley Collier erupted round the corner of the farmhouse, waving its arms and apparently shouting. "He really doesn't like visitors, does he?"

"He's . . . touchy," Juliana said, sighing with relief as Mentley appeared to recognise the car, lowered his arms, and fell quiet, then began to walk towards them in a less agitated manner. "The artistic temperament," she explained as she opened the car door. "Hello, Mentley! You've probably been wondering where we'd got to."

Mentley Collier shrugged, thrusting his hands deep into the folds of his purple caftan. "Hello, Juliana." He nodded to Dickie as the latter climbed out of the driver's seat. "Hi, man." He turned back to Juliana again. "Did you want anything in particular?"

Juliana was a little nettled at this ungracious reception. "Suppose I told you we just happened to be passing and thought we'd drop in for a friendly chat?"

Collier scowled. "I wouldn't believe you. Nobody ever just happens to be passing—or, if they do, they pass right on down the road. Like, that suits me fine—this place is far out of the way, man. I told you that before."

"I remember." Juliana was trying not to let the ice in her tone become too apparent. "And do *you* remember that we had business to discuss, last time we called, and that's why we said we'd be back?"

"Oh," Mentley said. "The Old Masters—right on. Like, I didn't think you'd bother coming back . . ."

"Why ever not, for goodness' sake? I don't waste time when business is involved, Mentley. We'd have been here before, only we left a couple of days for sight-seeing while you thought it over, and then we got stuck with the police all this morning, and—"

"The police?" Mentley took two steps backwards, and his eyes darted to and fro. "You mean the fuzz, man? What have a straight pair like you got to say to the fuzz? You're all set to shop me, are you?"

As his hands, balled into fists, emerged from the purple folds, and his eyes flashed, Juliana uttered a little cry and took her own steps backwards. Dickie, ranging himself at his lady's side, became assertive.

"Don't be a fool, Collier. Why should Juliana or I—or for that matter, anyone—want to shop you to the police, as you put it? If you're referring to Juliana's earlier business

181

proposition, then since you haven't even agreed to it, I fail to see how it can worry you—and in any case, as she explained to you at the time, it's perfectly legal." Dickie glared at the startled Mentley Collier, and Juliana, no less startled by this show of force, squeezed his arm, then herself hurried into speech before either of the men could say anything in temper which they might later regret.

"Mentley, I don't know what you're so bothered about. Even the tax man has never heard anything about you from us, though goodness knows I've always had my doubts, but I kept quiet—and as for the police, honestly, you've no need to be worried. Provided you make it plain that they're only copies—"

"No," he said, interrupting her with a violent gesture. Then, as she looked taken aback, he added: "Thanks all the same, but no. I want to do my own thing, Juliana, not anyone else's, not any more—I need space, man, and copying isn't my scene now. You'd better find someone else." And he turned his back on his would-be associates and walked jerkily away without once looking back.

"Mentley," Juliana called after him, but he walked on. She turned to gaze at Dickie. "My goodness," she said and shook her head in amazement. "My goodness . . ."

"Come on, old girl," said Dickie, taking her arm. "The man's mad, didn't I say so all along? And, since he clearly wants nothing more to do with us . . ." He frowned, trying to recall the correct phrase to indicate departure. "We, er, we'll split," he announced, aping the undergraduates to make her smile.

So split, very much puzzled and disappointed, they did.

Miss Seeton was in her garden, diligently weeding the flower beds edging her short front path. The hot weather, coupled with the recent rain, had encouraged every lurking weed-seed to sprout at exactly the same time. The difference after a matter of only a few days was remarkable: strange, she mused as she stirred earth with her hand fork, that weeds always seemed so much more hardy than real plants—not, of course, that weeds weren't plants as well—but one always had to wonder why, if those that were to grow from Stan Bloomer's seedlings really were as hardy as those that grew from weed seedlings (if that was the correct term), why Stan always took such great pains to protect his plants before putting them in the garden. Why not leave them to grow unaided, as the weeds did, planting and seeding themselves every year with apparent success . . .

"The survival of the fittest, I suppose," Miss Seeton said, rising from her knees. How gratifying that *they* were so fit and had responded so well to the regime recommended in that most excellent handbook, *Yoga and Younger Every Day*! With a respectful sigh for the mysteries of nature, she dusted herself off and collected her tools.

"Ah," said an unexpected voice from the other side of Miss Seeton's new wrought-iron fence, "the weeds are shallow-rooted, Miss Seeton, are they not? Suffer them now," the voice continued as she turned to see who owned it, "and they'll o'ergrow the garden and choke the herbs for want of husbandry. Would you not agree? Not, of course," the vicar added hastily, "that I suppose either yourself or Stan to be wanting in husbandry, not wanting at all. Dear me, no. That would be an impertinence on my part, and indeed quite unjustified. Moreover," he went on, frowning, "I am not sure that the practice of growing herbs in one's front garden is something that Stan would approve."

Miss Seeton thought she recognised the quotation which the vicar had so aptly produced, for the senior class at her old

Hampstead school had once chosen *Henry VI* as the end-of-term play. She was not, however, able to cap it, so she merely greeted her visitor with a smile.

"Mr. Treeves, how nice to see you. I was just going in for a cup of tea—I do rather feel I've earned it for my efforts against the weeds this afternoon. Won't you join me? Martha," she added, in the voice of the temptress, "has made a fruitcake . . ."

The Reverend Arthur's eyes lit up, and he was about to speak when he hesitated, then sighed. "You are most kind, Miss Seeton, and indeed I would have welcomed a cup of tea—the sunshine, and one's pastoral cares, walking about the village—but in view of my dear sister Molly's remarks only this morning concerning my, ah, weight, I fear that I must refuse your invitation—with much regret, I do assure you." He sighed again: Martha's fruitcakes were renowned throughout Plummergen, but so was Molly, for having (as many thought) eyes in the back of her head. The Reverend Arthur wasn't exactly scared of his sister, but he was unable to remember a time when he wasn't being told by her what he should or should not do, and somehow he'd never managed to lose the habit of obedience. But—dear Molly! He smiled. She meant it all for the best: few brothers were cared for so assiduously. He rubbed a thoughtful hand across his tummy and beamed at Miss Seeton.

She was puzzled, though she knew the Reverend Arthur to be a man of some eccentricity. "You needn't take sugar, if you don't feel you should," she pointed out kindly. "Just a cup of tea—and no cake?" Molly, Miss Seeton believed, had a committee right now: the poor vicar would have to go thirsty until his sister returned, unless a neighbour such as herself took pity on him. The slightest suggestion that the Reverend

Arthur might ever be let loose in her kitchen was known to be a nightmare to Molly Treeves.

"I won't tell your sister," Miss Seeton added as Arthur Treeves glanced over his shoulder at the vicarage gate and sighed yet again. "Just a cup of tea," she promised, opening her new garden gate. "It won't take long to make—the kettle's already filled—and, if you feel you'd rather not risk temptation, I won't even put out any cake for myself."

"That is most kind of you, Miss Seeton, but—oh dear, you should not be permitted to make such a heroic sacrifice on my behalf." The vicar braced himself as he followed her up the front path and around the side of the cottage to the kitchen door. "Indeed, were I more sure of my own strength, you should not even think of it—but, as with all of us, I weaken when faced with temptation . . . yet what is the point, one might ask, of hiding temptation away? How, if it is not plainly seen, may we be sure that we can resist it? Bring out your cake, Miss Seeton, and place the plate beside me— or rather"—for he was an honest man—"within sight of me, anyway." His eyes met hers, twinkling. "Perhaps," he suggested—for Martha's cakes were unarguably delicious—"just out of arm's reach?"

Miss Seeton twinkled back at him but made no direct reply as she busied herself about the little kitchen. There was a thoughtful silence, broken only by the song of the kettle and the clatter of crockery. The Reverend Arthur was brooding on his own words.

"Temptation," he said at last as Miss Seeton finished setting things out on the tray. "Matter for a sermon, maybe— how far should one go, what efforts should one make, to render it easy for one to resist? It is the clear duty of us all to resist temptation . . . yet, if we know that temptation exists, do we not display prudence, rather than moral cowardice, in trying to avoid such circumstances as those in which temptation may lurk? And prudence is accounted a true virtue . . . So is it more virtuous," mused the vicar, courteously opening the door for Miss Seeton as she carried the tray through, "to face up to things—or to turn away for the sake of one's own conscience? For conscience must be our guide in all things, must it not . . ."

This struck a chord with Miss Seeton, whose own sense of duty and conscience had been troubling her ever since that unfortunate failure to reproduce, for Chief Superintendent Delphick, any likeness of the tomato ketchup man. She, in her turn, sighed as she poured the tea. The vicar took his cup with thanks and, in an absentminded moment, a slice of cake. The two people in Miss Seeton's little sitting room had a great deal to think about.

Chapter 21

DELPHICK AND RANGER arrived in good time at Ashford police station, where the desk sergeant welcomed them with a broad smile of relief and escorted them personally through the labyrinthine corridors to the door of Superintendent Brinton's office. "A pleasure, sir, a real pleasure, believe me," insisted the sergeant; which left the Scotland Yarders feeling rather surprised.

"What on earth's come over Sergeant Mutford?" demanded Delphick before Brinton had time to utter a syllable of greeting. "He was positively beaming at us, which is quite a change from his normal manner—not that he's ever rude, you understand, but he's never been so pleased to see us in his life. Not one murmur about the Met trying to steal all the Kent Constabulary thunder—what has happened to bring about this dramatic change?"

Brinton regarded his friend with a weary gaze. "Three guesses," he said, "if you need that many. You're supposed to be a detective, so it shouldn't be hard."

Delphick eyed Brinton briefly, then turned to wink at Bob Ranger. "Sergeant, do you recognise, as I believe I do, the look of one who has suffered at the unthinking hands of

MissEss, your dear adopted Aunt Em?" he remarked, settling himself cheerfully in the most comfortable chair. "Shall I deduce that Mutford, too, has been in the firing line?"

Brinton nodded glumly. "Don't ask what she said or did, because I don't know. Mutford was a nervous wreck after she'd gone—entirely my fault, of course. I shouldn't have left her alone to draw those sketches while I was busy catching up on all the Sacombe reports—I should have known a drugs murder was nothing like as important as keeping an eye on your—I mean our—favourite artist when she's starting on one of her little episodes . . ."

"You're sure?" asked Delphick as Brinton shuddered his shoulders in despair and sighed. The superintendent looked at him through haggard eyes: the question really didn't need any enlargement. Delphick nodded, smiling faintly. "Better let us see the evidence, then, Chris."

Without a word Brinton fumbled beneath the blotter on his desk and withdrew the three sketches made earlier that day by Miss Seeton. He passed the first two across for the chief superintendent to examine, and waited.

"So these," murmured Delphick as he studied the family groups, "are the Standons, who are known to have bilked the George and Dragon, and who might be suspected of a connection with the Sacombe murder because of the co-incidence of time—yes, I see. Excellent likenesses, I'd say, though I've never met any of them. Bob—take a look. And what's this?" as Brinton handed him a small sheaf of papers.

"PhotoFits and mug shots, courtesy of the other witnesses—*ordinary* witnesses—who saw the Standons at the George. Guests and waitresses and so on. Run 'em in tandem with the drawings, and . . ."

"And the Standons would be instantly recognisable, yes. Bob, would you . . . Thanks." Delphick received the sketches from his sergeant's eager hand and spread them side by side with the mug shots on Brinton's desk. "Oh, yes, definitely—but you know as well as I do, Chris, that the mug shots and PhotoFits on their own would have done almost as well. Miss Seeton has produced competent, indeed excellent, likenesses, as I said earlier—but a camera could do as much. What has she produced that a camera *couldn't* do—and why does it seem to cause you such concern?"

"I'm circulating copies of this lot," said Brinton with a wave of the hand to indicate the spread on his desk, "but *this*, now, I've saved just for you and Ranger, because I'd appreciate a translation. I tried asking MissEss, but of course, I couldn't understand most of her answer. I don't think she understood it herself, really."

"She never does," Delphick murmured, "not when she's on what we might call automatic pilot. She becomes a little embarrassed by her abilities, though she's been told more than once they're what we pay her for . . ." He fell silent, studying the third picture which Brinton had coaxed from Miss Seeton.

It was a pencil sketch, showing an interior which, as Brinton had previously informed his friend, was certainly not modern in style, though few details were clear. Light and shade, particularly light, were portrayed with few, but skilful, strokes: the room seemed to be at once both small and spacious, uncluttered by too much furniture, and such as there was heavy in appearance, with a definite foreign feel. "The Dutch influence, perhaps," Delphick said to himself in an absent tone, "though the costume's not as clearly drawn as they are . . ."

"They" were three heads—two male, one female—which were surrounded by an incongruous swirl of flying birds with strongly muscled wings and bright, black eyes. The eyes of one of the men were equally black, giving an appearance of blankness: but the eyes of the other man, and the woman, gave expression and obvious life to their faces.

Delphick sat up. "Great Scot, I know these people! Not all of them"—as both Brinton and Bob Ranger exclaimed—"but these two, certainly. I met them last year, when I went out to Greece when Miss Seeton had all that bother on the cruise ship. Jennifer—no, Juliana Popjoy . . . and Dickie Something."

"Nash," supplied Brinton. "Staying in Plummergen at the George and Dragon. The landlord had his suspicions of them, but with Miss Seeton to vouch for 'em, the suspicion didn't last long . . . Now, if *I* had a hotel, and MissEss recommended the guests, I'd say fifty to one there was something strange about 'em, believe me I would."

Delphick smiled but said nothing. He was still concentrating on the three faces. "Van Dyck," he said at last, "I think . . . Wasn't he the chap who painted that portrait of Charles the Second looking left, right, and straight ahead? And wasn't he Dutch?"

Brinton shook his head in a silent admission of ignorance; Bob rubbed the tip of his nose and murmured that it seemed to ring a bell with him, though he wouldn't care to swear to it. Delphick nodded.

"The more I think about it, the more likely it seems she somehow believes there's a foreign connection with the case. Whatever," he added dryly, "the case might be. I can't just at the moment recall anything to do with spies or national security that should concern her . . ."

Brinton looked blank. So did Bob. Delphick chuckled. "The Third Man," he explained. "But it isn't very likely—it would be too obscure, even for MissEss. We shall have to take a more serious look at what it might all mean—"

"That's what you're here for," Brinton reminded him with a nod in Bob's direction. "And young Ranger, too, of course. Any idea what your dear Aunt Em's trying to tell us, laddie? Take it nice and slow . . ."

Bob gazed dutifully at the Dutch interior with the three heads and the flying birds and rubbed the tip of his nose again. "Sorry, sir, the only thing that comes to mind is to ask about the other chap—the one who wasn't on the cruise, I mean." Adding, as Delphick stirred, "That is, I could be jumping to conclusions, sir, but as you recognised the other two, it seemed a fair assumption that he wasn't—sir."

"Very fair, Sergeant," Delphick assured him. "I've no doubt I should have thought of it myself in time, but you've beaten me to it—who exactly is this man, Chris? I'm sure he wasn't on the *Eurydice* last year—or, if he was, he had nothing to do with—oh. I do hope she hasn't muddled what happened the other day in London with your little affair of the vanishing Standons—or the stabbing of Gerald Sacombe, or both, or whatever it is. But I rather think this third face may be that of the man who stole that tourist's wallet by the tomato ketchup trick—she promised she'd try to draw him as soon as she calmed down after all the upset—"

Brinton, who had heard the story already, snorted a very meaningful snort. Bob cleared his throat defensively. The Oracle chuckled again.

"There's only one way to find out, which is to ask her—unless by some chance she said anything to you, Chris, about who he was. And I gather from your expression she didn't."

"She may have done. You know what she's like—I could hardly make sense of one word in three, I told you before." The superintendent rolled his eyes. "Me and Mutford—she's got us both thinking about early retirement . . ."

Delphick, studiously casual, picked up Miss Seeton's sketch. "I'll need this, of course, for her to identify the man, if she's able to," he said, and Bob hid a smile. Trust the Oracle not to miss a trick. He'd been saving MissEss's artistic efforts right from the start, never mind that the assistant commissioner himself always tried to pinch 'em for his private collection. The Oracle's regular answer to Sir Heavily's by-the-way-what-happened-to-the-drawing questions was to say that it was in a safe place—so safe, indeed, that even Bob didn't know where that might be.

"I'll give you a receipt for this," Delphick was saying, as if he might have caught a whiff of his sergeant's amusement and decided to become absolutely professional. "And if you wanted to take a photocopy before Ranger and I leave for Plummergen . . ."

Brinton grunted. "I'll fix something up—but we've got a few more matters to chew over before you go swanning off for tea and biscuits with Miss Seeton. This whole drugs business, for one thing, never mind Sacombe's murder—and a nastier mess . . . set of prints here somewhere . . ."

He delved into a heap of files and folders at one side of his desk and withdrew a sheaf of black-and-white photographs which he handed to Delphick. "You've been warned," he said, plunging back into the heap for the pad of lined paper on which he'd been writing when his London colleagues arrived. "Report summary," he said; and the three men abandoned, for the moment, the topic of Miss Seeton and set to work instead on the Sacombe case.

As the unmarked police car swept down The Street, Delphick said: "Since we're expected at the George, we won't bother checking in just yet—I'd like to try catching Miss Seeton before the tom-toms get going properly. This car may be, in theory, unnoticeable, but you, Bob, most definitely are not. The moment you're—we're—spotted anywhere in Plummergen, whether it's in the hotel car park or simply driving along the main road, the gossips will have a field day. But perhaps, just perhaps, if we can conclude our business with Miss Seeton in good time, the poor woman will be allowed a little relief from the constant speculation in which this village permanently seems to indulge."

"I doubt it, sir," replied Bob, six-foot-seven adopted villager, with a rueful grin. "I'll bet they've been having a field day from the moment Charley Mountfitchet took our booking, unfortunately. But at least MissEss never notices any of the, er, commotion—"

"We might go so far as to say that she causes it, Sergeant Ranger. An innocent commotion, I grant you, but caused by your Aunt Em none the less. Let us hope"—as Bob drove off the road into the George's car park—"the warnings of Superintendent Brinton are not about to be fulfilled . . ."

Miss Seeton was delighted to see her guests when they came knocking at her front door two minutes after Bob had parked the car at the hotel just across the road. She spoke of gingerbread with a twinkle in her eye and murmured that her kettle had boiled not ten minutes ago.

"Unless, of course, you wished to discuss the matter of my little adventure in London the other day," she added, the welcome fading from her eyes to be replaced by an anxious look. "Oh, dear, Chief Superintendent, I have tried so hard, and the vicar spoke such stirring words, but I regret that I still find it impossible to recall the face of that man who played such a—a despicable trick . . ."

"Don't think I'm doubting your word, Miss Seeton," said Delphick gently, "but are you absolutely sure you can't remember what he looked like? This drawing you did for Superintendent Brinton—I recognise Mr. Nash and Miss Popjoy, of course, but this other man, the stranger: might he be . . . ?"

Miss Seeton blinked at the drawing as Delphick held it out to her, then regarded him with a worried crease between her brows. "Oh, dear, yes, I do remember," and above his excited exclamation continued, in some embarrassment: "Miss Popjoy and Mr. Nash might have thought it a . . . an impertinence on my part, you see, his being a friend—not of mine, that is, for we only met for the first time the other afternoon, and he is such a talented artist I doubt if he would care to have his name coupled with mine—yet his knees, you know, for so comparatively young a man, click and creak far more than I believe mine do, though of course we did not discuss how long he has been practising, which could explain it. He called me," she said with a blush, "an adept—which I took as a compliment, although the book makes it very plain that there should be no spirit of vanity or competition in these matters—and I hardly felt it correct," she went on, "to, well, to poke fun, though that is not exactly what I mean, but one should perhaps not be too quick with one who might be considered a—a professional acquaintance rather than a friend, who might excuse the liberty. And Mr. Brinton never asked me who he was, so I thought that he must already know—because of Miss Popjoy and Mr. Nash, who had been looking at photographs with Maureen, you see."

Delphick didn't, but life was too short, he decided, to ask for the full translation: he'd make do with the digest, and fill in the gaps by guesswork inspired by what Brinton had already told him. "This man is known to you as a friend of Miss Popjoy and Mr. Nash, but he is not the man in London? Then"—as she nodded—"who, and where, is he?"

"Mentley Collier," she said at once. "Miss Treeves was a great help—so fortunate that the vicar's car is reliable—a Morris Minor, I believe, and, of course, he has done his best to discourage the emphasis placed by some parishioners on the foolish feud between the villages, with his pastoral duties spreading far beyond our own boundaries—and after the Best Kept Competition one would have hoped . . . yet they may, perhaps, grow out of it, and certainly Mr. Collier said he had noticed nothing, though, of course, he lives in rather an isolated spot—"

And as she drew breath, Delphick, in desperation, broke in: "Which is where, Miss Seeton? What is his address?"

Chapter 22

MISS SEETON LOOKED blank. "Mentley Collier's address?" the chief superintendent prompted her. "Where you went with Mr. Nash and Miss Popjoy the other day."

But Miss Seeton, sounding despondent, had to confess she had forgotten. It had been a farmhouse—sadly neglected, she feared—some local story of fire and an artist's thwarted ambition, she believed, but she regretted she could remember nothing more . . .

"Although Miss Treeves may know," she said, brightening. Miss Seeton disliked letting people down: Mr. Delphick, she knew, had been relying on her, just as he had done in London—when once before she had failed him . . . "And Miss Popjoy and Mr. Nash are sure to know," she said, smiling with relief even as Delphick was trying to work out where exactly the vicar, and his sister, fitted into all this.

At her final words the Oracle in his turn stared. "You mean that Miss Popjoy and Mr. Nash are still in Plummergen?" He tried not to catch Bob's eye: the strain was beginning to tell, and if either of them burst out laughing or began to tear their hair, Miss Seeton might never recover from the shock. "But of course, there's no reason why they shouldn't be. My fault,

Miss Seeton, for assuming they would have left after giving their statements to Ashford. If they're staying at the George, we're bound to bump into them sooner or later, so please don't worry about it any more."

She was still looking flustered. "You won't tell them, will you, that I drew my little likeness of them with their friend? Such a *vivid* face, almost unforgettable, although he looks less, well, distorted in the picture I did for Mr. Brinton, but that was after the storm had cleared the air, of course, and with a sensitive person thunder can be so very uncomfortable, as poor Martha knows to her cost—and Mr. Collier is obviously a man of *variable moods*, which would be accounted for by the weather and not just the artistic temperament, even if Mr. Nash did rather naughtily tease Miss Popjoy and insist he was mad—Mr. Collier, I mean, although he certainly did not seem so to me. I hardly know him, of course, which may explain it, yet he did not strike me as the sort of person to shoot a neighbour's cat, as Mr. Potter told me someone did this morning . . ."

After a pause, during which Delphick thought longingly of cold compresses and Bob tried not to groan aloud, she amended this. "As Mr. Potter told me this morning that someone did, although I don't remember his telling me when, or where, because he was, after all, merely passing the time of day. He told a most amusing story," she dutifully recalled, "about a motorist with a homing pigeon who ran out of oil, I think, on the motorway—the man's car, I mean, not the pigeon, although Mrs. Ongar tells me that in a cold spell one may feed birds a drop of oil, or fat, for the warmth. But in a summer such as this, of course, nothing of that nature would be required, would it? Even the pigeon which I found in my back garden, exhausted by the storm, poor thing, was fed on Chirrup, and nothing else—except fresh water, that is. Mrs. Ongar was most kind to say how well I had cared for the bird—not that I would accept a reward, of course," she said, turning slightly pink. "I understand that the owners of carrier pigeons pay quite large sums for the best flyers and insure them to win races, but I am glad to know that the poor thing is in good hands now and will soon be returned to its home—in Yorkshire, I believe Mrs. Ongar said."

Delphick had to know—he couldn't help it—probably it was nothing to do with the case: but he found himself asking who Mrs. Ongar might be, even though he dreaded the convolutions of Miss Seeton's reply. There was always the risk of missing, among all the detours and disorder of her speech, a vital hint (which she herself never noticed she'd given) to the case currently under investigation.

He asked; and Miss Seeton expanded on the theme of high winds and weary birds, and the splendid work Mrs. Ongar did at the Wounded Wings Bird Sanctuary. "I believe I shall become a life member," she said, "for I found what she told me most interesting—and after all, there are always my chickens."

Bob, who could see the Oracle struggling with his emotions, interposed hastily: "You mentioned something about gingerbread when we came in," contriving to look starved and neglected, a difficult task for one of his size. With a cry of hospitable horror Miss Seeton hurried off to the kitchen promising tea, and gingerbread, and whatever else she could find to assuage the hunger of her guests.

As the door closed behind her, Delphick sank back in his chair with a sigh, mopping his brow. "Well done, Bob, and thank you. I don't know how much more I could have taken—but be a good chap now, will you, and trot along after your Aunt Em to help warm the pot or something. I'd appreciate ten minutes or so before the next onslaught to think over what exactly she's been saying—just in case . . ."

And when the sitting room door opened again to admit a tray-carrying Bob and a beaming Miss Seeton, Delphick had indeed decided there were one or two matters arising from what she had said that warranted investigation.

"You mentioned, Miss Seeton, that Mentley Collier's face in the picture you drew for Mr. Brinton looked *less distorted*—with the implication, therefore, that it isn't the only picture you've drawn of him. Am I right?"

"Why, yes—you are," said Miss Seeton, and the teapot quivered in her hand. Bob, who was nearer than Delphick, reached across and guided the spout towards his waiting cup. Miss Seeton poured. "How very clever of you to know that, Chief Superintendent, though as a detective one must expect that you would, of course. I feel sure it was because of the storm—I was trying to remember the face of the man in London, you see, because I felt so ashamed at letting you and Inspector Youngsbury down, yet when I had completed my attempt to justify that most generous retainer, all I had managed, it seemed, was to portray the storm, which can be of no real use to you at all, especially with Mr. Collier's likeness in the middle . . ."

With some stern coaxing on the part of Delphick, she was soon hunting through her portfolio and produced at last the sketch she had drawn that thundery evening after Juliana and Dickie had taken her to meet Mentley Collier. "The storm, I thought," she said, indicating the strange shapes and images of fantasy which swooped and coiled about the blank-eyed face of the man staring out of the paper. "Quite nightmarish, just as poor Martha sometimes says."

"Maybe . . ." And Delphick held the sketch beside the one Brinton had given him, comparing the two likenesses of the artist as perceived by Miss Seeton, another artist: but an artist with, on occasion, extraordinary insight. "It takes one to know one," he murmured, trying to block out the sight of the other characters, the distraction of the weird forms around Collier's remarkable portrait.

"A moody man, you thought," he remarked to Miss Seeton, who nodded. He glanced at Bob as he passed the two sketches across for his inspection. Bob's own glance in return was as eloquent: once again, without knowing it, Miss Seeton might have pointed them in the right direction.

Tea and gingerbread had only taken the edge off their hunger—and in any case, Delphick wished to speak to Dickie and Juliana concerning the exact whereabouts of Mentley Collier.

"If we ask anyone else," he said as they crossed back to the George and Dragon from Sweetbriars, "the word will be round in ten seconds flat, and I don't want to let him know we're interested in him."

"Moody," muttered Bob, kicking a stone. "Nightmares and funny-looking shapes—drugs, d'you think, sir?"

"This could be the Sacombe connection," agreed Delphick. "Miss Seeton may believe the swooping birds and distorted trees signify the mental tumult of an approaching storm, but I beg to differ with her."

"Yes, sir. And did you get the impression from what she said that he knows about yoga? Not that everyone who knows about it is into drugs, sir," added Bob hastily, "but he's got that hippie feel to him—long hair, flowers—I could almost smell the incense, sir."

"And the smell of incense," murmured Delphick as they mounted the two low steps to the George's front door, "can cover a multitude of sins."

"Mr. Delphick! Hello there, young Bob—or should I be calling you Sergeant, if you're here on official business?" Charley Mountfitchet hailed the newcomers as he emerged from the swing door at the end of the hall. "You've been across the road to chat to Miss Seeton," he said in a lower voice as he drew near. "Spotted your car outside on the tarmac. Don't you fret, I've checked you in, and you've a good dinner ready and waiting—well, almost." He chuckled. "Truth to tell, I'd thought Miss Popjoy and Mr. Nash likely to stay in tonight, but no, they're off somewhere, so if the two of you can't help me out, it'll go to waste. Nothing fancy, mind"—the George was noted more for good, plain food and plenty of it rather than *cordon bleu*—"but you'll enjoy it, I reckon."

Since, without the help of Juliana and Dickie, the visit to Mentley Collier must be delayed, Delphick elected to find out more about the disappearing Standons instead. Charley, flattered to think that Scotland Yard itself had been set on the trail of the cheats, took great pains to serve in person the meal cooked with enthusiasm in the kitchen.

"Now, don't tell me as you're to work while you eat your dinner, Mr. Delphick, for I won't have my good food spoiled and the pair of you with indigestion," Charley said with a wink. He tapped the side of his nose. "I've looked out a bottle of something you'll find to your liking, I hope—on the house, of course, as an encouragement, you may say. And afterwards, you can ask me anything you want, I'll not be going anywhere. I want to see them Standons collared as much as either of you."

When dinner was over, he herded his two guests into the bar and poured three large whiskies, which he carried over to their chosen table. He pulled up a chair and sat down. "*Now* we can talk business," he said. "Cheers!"

"Yes, Mr. Mountfitchet, let's talk about the Standons." Delphick glanced at Bob. "No need for notes at this stage, but we'll report back to Ashford tomorrow, so if either of us has a brain wave we must, er, ensure that it is properly remembered." His eyes flicked to the whisky glasses, each of which held at least a quadruple measure.

Charley chuckled. "Bless me, Mr. Delphick, a drop or two like you've had won't fuddle your wits, I'm sure of that, so never you mind your jokes." He sighed. "I appreciate you aren't exactly on duty, but I'd rather thought to see young Bob here saying his piece with the caution, anything-I-say-will-be-taken-down-in-writing—still, if you don't see the need, you don't. I'd not tell you how best to go about your job any more than I'd let you tell me how to go about mine." He drained his glass, set it on the table with a decisive chink, and sat back with folded arms, his eyes bright. "Now then, fire away, gentlemen both, but one at a time, please."

It was a long time since they'd had a witness so eager to co-operate, and so able to do so. Miss Seeton was always willing, but co-operation involved communication, which was not (even Bob had to admit) her strongest point. Delphick and his sergeant listened with great interest to all that Charley had to say on the topic of the Standons.

"Not that I believe it was their true name, now I come to consider the point," he told them, "although when they first arrived I took 'em for regular bird-watchers, out and about the countryside and not too much luggage for dressing smart and visiting stately homes and so forth. Seemed a nice family, too, apart from the boys—mind you, the way the old man had 'em on the hop, I'd my doubts about what might not happen to him, some dark night."

The expressions on the faces of his audience urged him to continue: which he did, after offering another whisky all round and being the only one to accept the offer. Having wetted his whistle, he went on:

"Ah, yes, there's many a true word spoken in jest, but where there's money there's always someone to spend it, and Mr. Standon, *old* Mr. Standon, he acted careful with the cash, and his daughter and her husband currying regular favour with him, or trying to. Whatever he said, went—of course, I see now as it was an act, but when I first heard the tale of how he'd made the daughter's husband change his name to hers, I couldn't help but think *there's many men wouldn't take kindly to that, inheritance or no*—that's what was in my mind, I do assure you."

"Understandably so," said Delphick, who had encountered frequent examples of familial greed resulting in convenient death or disaster. Charley nodded sagely.

"Many men wouldn't take kindly to it," he repeated, "and I can't say as young Mr. Standon ever seemed like he did, for all we know now that he was playing a part. The old man was the one calling the tune—he'll have arranged the trick, mark my words. The boys, they were too young to do more'n what they were told; and the daughter, she fell in with whatever her father said, anyone could see. But the son-in-law, ah! He never did fool me—untrustworthy, I thought him, and not just in the way that's already been proved. Hardly ever looked you in the face, he didn't, and sometimes give the boys a clip round the ear even though he knew the old man didn't like it . . .

"Moody sort of bloke, that young Mr. Standon," the landlord of the George and Dragon summed up his erstwhile guest: and the two policemen exchanged meaningful glances.

Chapter 23

IT HAD BEEN a true pleasure, reflected Delphick when he woke up next morning, to deal with such an enthusiastic witness as Charley Mountfitchet; a witness who had, moreover, such a generous spirit—with (and Delphick smiled) spirits. The chief superintendent ignored the midget who was clog-dancing in slippers from his right temple to his left and back: more a soft-shoe shuffle than a raging hangover, and worth every throb. The whisky, which after the end of Charley's statement it would have been churlish to refuse, had been poured with a lavish hand; the company had been congenial; and the resulting sleep had been restful, refreshing, and dreamless.

Indeed, so refreshed did he feel that he took Miss Seeton's sketches out of their folder to study them again before heading downstairs for breakfast. She had been reluctant to hand over the drawing made at home, but he had persuaded her without too much trouble: an appeal to her sense of duty always worked, in the end. Despite the nightmare drugs association, he chuckled as he looked at the swooping birdlike forms among the animals and flowers, and remembered her talk of chickens . . .

"Wounded Wings," he murmured. "Life membership, oh, dear—oh." The chuckle vanished from his voice. He looked more closely at the pictures. Both had been quickly but clearly drawn: the faces were recognisable, no doubt of that—and so were the birds. "Vultures?" mused Delphick, "and, if I'm not mistaken, pigeons among the nightmare . . . She said something about Yorkshire . . . The setting looks foreign . . ."

Three minutes later he was talking to Babs Ongar of the Wounded Wings Bird Sanctuary; eight minutes after that he was thumping on Bob Ranger's door, waving the sketches under his sergeant's startled nose.

"Carrier pigeons," he said. "They can fly hundreds of miles without difficulty—the one Miss Seeton found was on its way home to Yorkshire, after being released near Dover. Bob, suppose someone used pigeons to carry the pure drug from the Continent to England—from, say, Amsterdam . . ."

Bob drew a deep breath. "Amsterdam's the centre for the European drug trade—and it's in the Netherlands, isn't it, sir? It's the capital of Holland—it's Dutch, sir!"

Delphick nodded. "Like the interior Miss Seeton drew— right from the start, Chris Brinton said it had a foreign look. Now, we know drugs are coming in from abroad, but we don't know what route is used, or what method, except that both have so far been undetectable. Something as small as a pigeon would never be noticed, and, once they arrived, who'd notice a few extra birds around the place? Especially if they were homing in to a house in the countryside . . ."

"Like Gerald Sacombe's," supplied Bob. "Although I don't believe Mr. Brinton mentioned a cage, or whatever, for any pigeons, sir," he added. "Er—did he?"

"He didn't but that doesn't signify. They could be flying to somewhere nearby but not on the immediate premises—in the country who'd notice a few extra birds flapping about in a wood, for example? If anyone noticed, Sacombe could have told them it was his new hobby . . .

"Mrs. Ongar tells me that birds can be bought as cheaply as twenty pounds each, although there are some really expensive prize specimens. But I somehow don't think the crowd we're after will be going in for prizes—not the cup-and-ribbon sort, anyway. Their birds are flying for a far nastier reward—preying on people, like vultures."

"Bring the pure stuff over from the Continent," said Bob thoughtfully, "adulterate it to a profitable street level, sell it, and wait for the next flight to arrive—that'll be the line we ought to follow next, sir. Baskets of pigeons crossing the Channel—where they've come from and where they're going . . ."

"Where they've come from has got to be somewhere in this area, Bob. Within easy distance of London but relatively rural—and the known incidents of drug abuse that we can tie into the network are all centred around here."

"Very roughly, sir," Sergeant Ranger was moved to point out. Delphick shook his head.

"Not so roughly that we didn't already suspect this was one of the places to look, and I don't believe Ashford would have been on the blower to the Yard quite so quickly if they hadn't thought so, too—even if"—with a grin—"part of our reason for coming here was to make sense of Miss Seeton, who as usual has come up trumps. Mr. Brinton may sometimes wish she was more the traditional, knitting-fluffy-garments spinster with a cat and a thatched cottage and roses round the door, but for my part I'm—"

"Cat!" burst out Bob, then choked out a quick apology as Delphick's jaw dropped. "I didn't mean to interrupt, sir, but the thought suddenly struck me, when you said about Miss Seeton—cats eat birds, don't they, sir? Even birds as big as pigeons? Potter's young Amelia's hoodlum of a Tibs has tackled larger birds than that—and didn't Miss Seeton say something about Potter having a story of some bloke who went berserk with a shotgun and did for the neighbours' moggy? I just wondered, sir . . ."

"Potter would know where Mentley Collier lives, too." An oracular gleam appeared in Delphick's eye. "And he might just have noticed if anywhere around here there was a flight pattern of pigeons that was a bit unusual. Bob, maybe we're building too much on this—"

"No, we're not, sir. Not if Miss Seeton's involved, you know we're not. It all ties in. She found that pigeon the night of the storm—and the following day friend Sacombe got his comeuppance, sir." Bob ventured a chuckle. "Maybe the disappearance of the Standons really was a coincidence, sir, and MissEss has been trying to tell us where to look right from the start. That storm would have blown more than Miss Seeton's bird off its course, so ten to one it was a junkie suffering from a missed fix, not a gangland takeover killing at all—it was certainly frenzied, judging by the photos. Any professional killer wouldn't have been so, er, haphazard in his methods, sir. Don't you think?"

The Oracle thought. Bob waited. The silence lengthened . . . to be broken by the rumble of somebody's insides.

"What I think," Delphick said, "is that we could do with a bite of breakfast before we hallucinate without the help of drugs. I can't think clearly on an empty stomach—and I know I suggested all this, but I'd still like to ponder it a little while longer . . ."

But Bob, who had every faith in Aunt Em, made a silent bet with himself that within the hour they'd be talking to PC Potter about pigeons, and cats, and Mentley Collier.

The two policemen had not been gone from the hotel more than ten minutes when the telephone rang. Maureen was flicking a languid duster around Reception and eventually answered.

"Hello, yes, this is the George and Dragon. Who's that? Oh." Maureen's voice changed. "Miss Seeton. Yes, and good morning to you likewise, I'm sure." She smothered a sniff and cocked her head for better concentration. "Mr. Delphick? Dunno. He *was* having breakfast, but . . . Well, I suppose I could go and see, if you want . . . You do want. All right." She plonked the receiver down beside Doris's iron spike, sniffed loudly, then dragged her weary bones the lengthy ten or twelve feet from Reception to the dining room door.

Having leaned in exhaustion against the doorframe while her eyes slowly scanned the room—in which only Juliana and Dickie, who had just come down, were sitting—Maureen shook her head, uttered a prodigious sigh, and ambled back to the telephone.

"He's not there," she informed Miss Seeton; listened for a while to the electrical chirrups coming down the line; and said, when they stopped, "Dunno. He's probably gone up to clean his teeth or summat . . . Go and look for him? Well, I dunno. I'm not the sort of girl as goes knocking at men's bedroom doors, Miss Seeton," and her eyes drifted with dismay towards the flight of stairs leading to the guest rooms. "Oh, all right," she said as the telephone chirruped some more. "Wait there—hey, no, hang about!" She was suddenly inspired. "If the car's gone, then *they* must've gone with it, right? Can you see it from your window?" The effort of walking to the front door and opening it was evidently too much for Maureen at this early hour. "You can't? Well, it must've gone then, and so's Mr. Delphick. Sorry. 'Bye."

Across the road in Sweetbriars Miss Seeton listened for a few bewildered seconds to the dialling tone, then herself hung up. And stood for a long time, thinking . . .

Mabel Potter told them that her husband had gone out earlier than usual that morning, making the most of the long summer days to patrol his beat twice daily, where possible. She believed they might catch up with him in the neighbourhood of Iverhurst—they knew where that was, didn't they?

"We do," Delphick assured her as Bob smothered a grin. It could hardly be considered Miss Seeton's fault that Iverhurst church had burned to the ground some years before, but it had certainly been one of her more spectacular cases. "Thanks, Mrs. Potter. If we should miss him, could you ask him to check with Ashford for messages, please? Come on, Sergeant Ranger." And they hurried back to the car.

Bob, on in-law visits with Anne, had explored the area around Plummergen in some depth and knew most of the back roads by now. He worked out which route Potter was likely to take, then drove carefully along it in the opposite direction. His gamble paid off. Within twenty minutes they spotted Potter's car bowling towards them, and hailed it.

"Cat? Oh, yes," said PC Potter, once his colleagues had explained what they wanted to know. "Funny thing, that was, this chap going berserk, but his neighbours said as he was a moody sort of bloke, though if they'd known he had a shotgun to hand they might not've been so quick to exchange words. Of course, living in the middle of nowhere like he does, you might think he'd want to stay on good terms with the few as lives nearby, but not him. Mother Bozen's pride and joy, that cat were, though there's many as say good riddance, it being as evil-tempered a beast as Tibs—almost," he added, mindful of his official duty to speak the truth at all times.

Delphick and Bob had exchanged significant glances when Potter mentioned the marksman as living in the middle of nowhere: suddenly, the chief superintendent's theory began to look promising again. "This cat killer's name, please, Potter," said Delphick. "And where exactly does he live?"

"Barkway, Owen Barkway—lives out the other side of Murreystone," came the prompt reply.

It was almost too good to be true. "Talking of Murreystone," said Delphick, "we understand there's an artist who lives there—a bit of a recluse, but we'd like to pay him a visit, nevertheless. Do you know him?"

A silly question to ask of a beat bobby with Potter's experience. "You mean Mentley Collier—daft beggar, hiding away all the time like he does—mind you, if I'd gone and made a spectacle of myself with hair as long as his, I'd not be keen for decent folk to see me till I'd got myself tidied up a bit. Whether or no his pictures are any good, I'd not care to venture an opinion, me not being what you might call artis—" He broke off. "Oh. Oh, ah." He eyed the Scotland Yarders knowingly. "At it again, is she, sir?" And he winked at Bob with the eye Delphick could not see.

Delphick knew Potter could be trusted. "She may be—we aren't really sure at this stage. Once we've spoken to Barkway and Collier, we may know a little more."

"As for speaking to," Potter said, "Collier's place, which is to say Filkins Farm, they lost the telephone when the farmhouse burned down, being overhead cables, and empty for months before he moved in, so they'd no reason to fix it and him as poor's a church mouse, or so he says. Barkway, now, he's got a phone, but whether he'll be in a mood to answer it's another matter."

"And he has a shotgun," said Delphick. "Not altogether a comfortable character to visit, I fear, but talk to him we must. He sounds more—interesting—with every word you say. Wouldn't you agree, Sergeant Ranger?"

Bob nodded. Potter looked gratified. "I'll show you to whichever you're wanting to visit first, sir, knowing the byways as I do—and should you want someone to stand guard on the back doors, I'm your man. Seems ages since we had a bit of excitement around here." He seemed not to count the recent intervillage punch-up in the middle of Plummergen over which he, Sir George, and Delphick himself might have been said to preside. "Which of 'em do you want, sir? Collier's place is nearer."

"Then to Filkins Farm we shall go," decided Delphick at once. "Lead on, Potter, but no siren, please. I'd like to catch Mr. Collier unawares . . ."

Potter proudly led the way, and Bob followed him at a reasonable distance, musing aloud on the convolutions of the Kent roads and hoping Potter would stay around long enough to help them find their way back to civilisation. Delphick passed various comments concerning his sergeant's adopted local status and spoke of maps, and bumps of location.

As it was, even Potter almost missed the entrance to Filkins Farm. He pulled up just beyond the three-barred gate and indicated the drive. "D'you want to go in front now, sir, or shall I carry on?"

"We'll go first," said Delphick, "and you can follow us, and keep watch in case he makes a run for it. Carry on, Sergeant. Drive with care."

"With potholes like these, you bet I will," muttered Bob as he changed down to the lowest gear, brooding about his suspension.

But all their caution was in vain. Though Potter stood guard over possible escape, and Bob's eyes never lost their vigilance, there came no answer to Delphick's official knock at the barn door; and when—checking that Mentley Collier hadn't met with some accident which rendered him unable to move—they opened the doors, and looked inside every building in the farmyard, they found nobody at home.

Chapter 24

"He'll have popped down to the shops," Potter suggested. "Nobody'll deliver to the farm, on account of their springs. The milkman says his bottles make a right racket in the crates, not to mention shattering with stones thrown up. Or he could be gone to post a letter . . ."

Delphick glanced at his watch. "Since we'd also like a few words with Owen Barkway, we could save time by leaving Collier for the return journey. At this stage I'm still not sure we need to start hunting for the man, although don't we have to go through Murreystone for Barkway's place? Would you recognise Collier's car if you saw it?"

"Doesn't have a car," Potter said knowledgeably. "Which is why he shops local instead of at the supermarket over in Brettenden—Murreystone folk don't go to Plummergen shops, 'specially after the Best Kept Village Competition." Potter so far forgot himself as to tap the side of his nose and wink at the chief superintendent.

Who (to Sergeant Ranger's surprise) winked gravely back before saying, "Then we certainly shan't bother looking for Mentley Collier, unless we happen to pass him en route—we shall make straight for Owen Barkway, Potter, with the same arrangements as before."

Once more they set off, Potter's car showing Scotland Yard the way; and once more they arrived at the home of someone who clearly did not relish the thought of company. It was another old house at the end of a drive, though in far better shape than Filkins Farm; but the massive gate was firmly closed, with barbed wire strung across its top and coiled around thinner parts of the hedge.

Delphick looked at the farmhouse roof, visible over the tops of screening trees. "No doubt the attic makes a splendid machine-gun post for Mr. Barkway—his neighbours may have been luckier than they realised." He indicated the two or three far smaller dwellings visible in the near distance. "I wonder how much they miss of what goes on here? And as we're talking of missing things, Potter, I doubt if you'll be able to lurk round the back of *this* house unnoticed. I suggest you drive up behind us and prepare to pursue any fleeing suspects if and when I give the word. You, too, Sergeant Ranger. Shall we go, gentlemen?"

Potter having unchained the gate, Bob drove through first, waiting on the other side to return the compliment. He led the way up the drive, and slowed the car to a halt on a gravelled area which was as good, remarked Delphick, as a burglar alarm.

"A nervous man, Owen Barkway, it seems. Shall I proceed to make him more nervous still? Bob, you stay outside with Potter, just in case. If Barkway should unleash his small arms, or you feel for any reason that I'm under threat, you are to use your initiative."

"Hadn't I better come in with you, sir? If you think he may turn nasty—"

"I neither think nor know. I *hope* that, after the unfortunate affair of the ginger cat, he may be rather more inclined to make some show of welcoming visitors, even if he would still much prefer to do without them. But cats, as we know, eat bats—and pigeons . . ."

Delphick's eyes flickered towards an airborne flurry of wings rising from the back of the house. "If Miss Seeton suspects it may be worth investigating," he remarked, "maybe we would be unwise to doubt her—so listen hard for sounds of gunfire, Sergeant Ranger. And both of you stay alert."

He opened the car door and climbed out, his feet falling with heavy crunches on the gravel. He signalled to Potter as Bob opened his own door, ready for action.

Before Delphick's hand reached the knocker, he spotted the twitch of a curtain and a startled eye. He knocked and waited. Nobody answered. He kept watching the curtain and knocked again. Still no reply. He called to Potter and Bob: "Better see about checking the back of the house," then motioned them quickly to ignore his words, knowing that the sound of the gravel would mask any sounds from within.

He knocked for a third time, impatiently. There came a clattering from inside, and at last the door creaked its slow, suspicious way open far enough to allow the head of a man to manifest itself through the opening. His eyes glared from the gloom at the tall, greying figure in tweeds, then moved beyond him to the two cars parked on the gravel, their vigilant drivers beside them.

"Mr. Barkway? I'm Chief Superintendent—"

"It *is* the fuzz!" Owen Barkway (if it was he) yelled this warning towards the back of the house, then slammed the door in Delphick's face. The yell and the slam alerted Bob and Potter before Delphick had time to speak. Without more than a quick look at each other the two policemen thundered across the gravel and around the house, Bob going clockwise, Potter running to meet him.

In fact, what he met first was the struggling form of a woman in a purple dress—no, a long-haired man, the backside was a completely different shape—attempting to disentangle itself from the trellis of climbing roses round the window through which (so Potter assumed) the man had just jumped. He seemed to be having so much difficulty in extricating himself that Potter ignored him and hurried on towards the sounds of combat which had arisen in those regions where he might expect Sergeant Ranger to be found . . .

And where, indeed, he was. But someone else had found him first: someone with eyes that were no longer slow and suspicious, but glittering and wild, set in a face belonging to a head belonging to a body with furious fists and flailing legs. "I'm coming, Sarge!" cried Potter; but Bob, six foot seven and seventeen stone, waved him away with one hand even as he shook his assailant by the collar with the other, though Barkway fought like two normal-size men.

"I can manage," called Bob. "You get his pal before he clears off to the—oof!" But Potter could see that, even with a desperate knee in his midriff, Bob Ranger needed no help. He left Delphick's gigantic sidekick to suppress Owen Barkway's futile attempts at nobbling and turned back to the trellis.

Where he discovered Delphick, standing just out of range and staring upwards. "He seems to have pulled it loose," remarked the chief superintendent as Potter joined him. "He couldn't get out by climbing forwards, so he must have decided to climb up instead. Logical, I suppose, but . . ."

"Ah," said Potter, "that's why he's swaying to and fro like that, is it? I was wondering." He coughed. "Reckon he'll fall, sir?"

"Help!" came a gasping cry from above their heads; a cry to which the delights of speculation rendered the speculators deaf.

"Gravity being what it is," mused Delphick, "I expect he will, Potter. Of course, if the trellis had been fastened more firmly to begin with, he might have managed it . . ."

"A chancy business, sir, playing hide-and-seek among a load of roses, wouldn't you say?"

"Some people enjoy taking chances, Potter." Delphick took no notice of the ominous creaking sounds coming from above as the arc of the trellis swayed wider and wider. "It is not unlike"—in a more carrying tone—"those who take, or who deal in, drugs—chancy. Quite apart from the risks to someone's health, the risk of arrest must be—"

"Help!" came the cry again, but a shriek this time, not a gasp; and the creaks evolved suddenly into a splintering, rending, catastrophic crash as the trellis yielded to the superiority of Newtonian forces and collapsed. The long-haired figure on the topmost bars screeched once—clawed vainly at the brickwork as it passed by—caught its feet somehow in the ruin, and tipped backwards—and finally fell headfirst into the riot of briars below.

And there was silence.

A breathless but cheerful voice broke it. "Here's one of them, sir," announced Sergeant Ranger, appearing with the dishevelled form of Owen Barkway held firmly by the arm. He blinked on beholding the devastation and enquired:

"A spot of pruning, sir? Rather drastic, if you don't mind my saying so. I doubt if you'll be offered the job on a permanent basis."

"I doubt it, too," replied his superior, "although it is hardly my place to say, with Mr. Barkway among us. What have *you* got to say, Mr. Barkway? Assuming, of course, that you are indeed the owner of this establishment."

"That's him, all right," confirmed PC Potter as Barkway merely glowered. "Not a week since I was talking to him on this very spot, sir, matter of civil proceedings likely to arise from wilful damage to valuable property, to wit, one ginger tom, sir."

"Good," replied Delphick as he headed for the wreck of the trellis. "So, now that the introductions are complete—a hand here, Potter, if you please—I repeat my question, Mr. Barkway. What have you to say for yourself?"

"I want my solicitor," said Owen Barkway and clamped his lips together.

Bob stood guard over him as Delphick and Potter strove to extricate the body from the briars. "Reckon he's knocked himself out, sir?" asked Potter as the long-haired figure lay still and silent among the thorns, despite all attempts to rouse it. "Concussion, d'you think? He packed a fair old wallop when he come down—mind you, he'd've been splattered to kingdom come if he'd fell on the flagstones, so it could've been worse," he added, sounding more cheerful.

"Oh, I believe he'll live," Delphick said dryly as he spotted the unconscious man wince at Potter's mention of the flagstones. "I have no doubt he'll astonish us all by the speed of his recovery—won't you, Mr. Collier?"

But the long-haired man was too canny to respond this time, not realising he'd already given himself away. Bob, a keen observer nearby, called out:

"Is it really Collier, sir? What does Potter say?"

"There can be absolutely no doubt, Sergeant Ranger, even without Potter's identification. This man is the image of Miss Seeton's two drawings—" Delphick broke off as, on hearing Miss Seeton's name, the face of Mentley Collier was convulsed by another spasm. "And I'm quite sure," remarked the chief superintendent as he motioned Potter to one side, "that he'll live—but don't take my word for it, Sergeant Ranger. After all, I'm no doctor . . ."

Whereupon he suddenly released the prickly tangle which he and Potter had laboured to remove from Mentley's flowing locks, to let it fall again on the folds of his purple caftan.

"Hey, man—what's the big deal!" Mentley Collier tried to leap to his feet, failed, cursed, and collapsed, with a groan. Delphick looked grimly at Potter.

"I told you he'd live, Constable. I suppose we'd better set him loose—but have your handcuffs ready."

"Don't give me that handcuffs hassle, man," said Mentley at once. "I've done nothing—"

"And neither have I," broke in Owen Barkway at once, and at volume. "This is unwarranted police brutality! I demand to speak to my solicitor! And that man there"—as Delphick and Potter at last freed Mentley from the thorny toils—"is injured. He ought to be in hospital—because," he said, in a meaningful voice, "with head injuries you can never be too careful. It wouldn't surprise me if he'd hurt himself badly—and developed amnesia . . ."

Superintendent Brinton soon had Barkway cooling his heels in an Ashford interview room while the police doctor examined Mentley Collier for signs of shock. Barkway had demanded the presence of his solicitor; Mentley had demanded to be taken to hospital, claiming concussion.

However, once Owen Barkway's encouraging presence had been removed, he quickly wilted beneath the brisk, knowing treatment of one who'd seen it all a hundred times—and seen it far better acted, Dr. Wyddial pointed out as she packed her instruments away.

"Nothing much wrong with this chap here except bumps and bruises," she said to Delphick, who had come in to hear her official verdict. "Quite a few scratches, of course, but I assure you he'll live."

Mentley glowered at her. "What do you mean, man, a few scratches? I could die of blood poisoning—lockjaw!"

"I'll give you a tetanus jab with pleasure," replied the doctor promptly. Her eyes glittered. "Drop your trousers and bend over—man," she commanded. Delphick hid a grin.

Mentley turned pale. "No way," he spluttered as with a gleeful relish she selected the largest syringe in her bag and fitted an enormous needle. "Keep her off, man!" And he backed into a corner of the room. "I'll talk—though I don't have any idea what you want me to say—I'm just an artist, doing my own thing, right? Never hurt anybody, not my style—don't you let her hurt me, okay?"

Dr. Wyddial glanced across at Delphick, nodded, and began to dismantle the syringe. "A great pity," she said with a sigh and a lingering look in Mentley's direction. The artist's forehead was beaded with sweat. Dr. Wyddial smiled, snapped her bag shut, and left without another word.

Mentley sank down on a chair with a shudder. "Man, that is one tough lady," he murmured, wiping the back of his hand across his brow. "Nerves of solid steel."

"Unlike yours, evidently," Delphick said as he took the opposite chair. Bob stationed himself in a corner and began to make notes. "If your conscience is as clear as you would have us believe, why did you bolt out of Owen Barkway's window and climb up the trellis?"

Mentley stared and gulped. His legs squirmed under the table, and he breathed in deeply. He muttered something the chief superintendent didn't quite catch.

"Did I hear you say 'spies,' Mr. Collier?" Surely that weak joke he'd made about the Third Man couldn't be starting to bear genuine fruit.

Mentley squirmed again. Delphick could see his brain going into overdrive. At last: "There's like altogether too much hassle, man," he said. "I get nervous—my artistic temperament, not that I'd expect the fuzz to understand, of course—but they arrive out of the blue, they follow me around. Friends I've not seen in years, old women making like they don't know the time of day, doing the fuzz's dirty work for them—so that's who I thought it was, and I didn't want any more of it," he concluded in a rush. It seemed unlikely that he expected them to believe his story for long.

Delphick didn't believe it at all. The reference to the visit by Dickie Nash, Juliana Popjoy, and Miss Seeton to Filkins Farm tied in with the pictures MissEss had produced: he wasn't sure exactly how, but she'd hinted at a connection between Collier and drugs—and they'd found one.

"We have reason to believe that Owen Barkway is a drug dealer," he said. "If *he* is the friend you haven't seen for years, you picked an unfortunate time to visit him."

"Not him, not Owen—no way! Juliana Popjoy, that's who I mean, keeping on with questions about my pictures, letting that old woman snoop about—" He snapped his mouth tightly shut.

Delphick said: "Then, if Barkway is not a friend, from what you say I must infer that he must be an associate—in a filthy business, in which I suspect that you have a part to play: the supplying of drugs, Mr. Collier. Am I right"—loudly, over Mentley's splutter of protest—"to infer that you walked to his house this morning, in the heat, to warn him that you suspected the game might be up—or was it"—as Mentley squirmed again—"to ask him for another fix?"

Chapter 25

"AND NOW," SAID Delphick as once more Bob drove back to the George and Dragon, "we consult with Miss Seeton. I should very much like her second opinion of these sketches . . ."

But, though they knocked and rang at both the front and back doors of Sweetbriars, Miss Seeton was not to be found. "Gone shopping, I expect, sir," said Bob. Delphick glanced across the road to the hotel.

"Then we won't hang around waiting for her, when there are, if we're in luck, two more people who might be able to help us not a minute's walk away. Failing Miss Seeton, Mr. Nash or Miss Popjoy could well come up with something—they seem to be peripherally involved in the case anyway, and if they *are* friends of Collier's, I can't see either of them sympathising with drugs." He recalled the splendour of Miss Popjoy's eyes and her melodious voice. "We don't want to upset them more than necessary, though. I won't go into too much detail—just show them the sketches and wait for them to comment. They're both art experts, one way or another."

"Barkway's an old hand at this game, stands out a mile, doesn't it, sir," muttered Bob as they shut Miss Seeton's gate and made for the hotel. "The way all he does is yell for Proctor . . . if that man manages to get him off the way he's done with so many other villains . . ."

"Quite apart from the fact that Collier was talking more than he should have done, there was far too much evidence at Barkway's house for him to get off, no matter how good his defending counsel. The one argument I can see him trying is that the stuff was planted on him—if Collier turns Queen's Evidence, he'll suggest by him—but it won't work. There's the business of the ginger cat, and the pigeon loft, and the excessive amounts of baking powder—fly in the pure stuff by pigeon post, cut it by twenty or fifty or eighty times, and bingo! Barkway is on to a winner, just so long as he doesn't get caught. Only this time he did . . .

"And we're going to sew up half the network, Bob, thanks to Miss Seeton. Before they're much older, we'll have the distributors behind bars where they belong—but I'd dearly like to collar the lot. The big boys, the money end of the chain, that's what we're after now. If Collier hadn't gone silent on us in the end, we might have had something to go on, rather than leaving him and Barkway to Superintendent Brinton's tender care . . ."

They found Dickie and Juliana chatting over coffee with Charley Mountfitchet, who had been much smitten by the ripe charms of Miss Popjoy. After the episode of the wallpaper—to the cost of replacing which Dickie, at Juliana's urging, had insisted on contributing—the landlord had taken to joining his erstwhile suspects at mutually convenient moments for a chat, or a drink, or both.

When Delphick and Bob joined the little group, Charley reluctantly dragged himself away to supervise the decorating of the Blue Riband Suite which an assortment of his family and friends had arrived to undertake. Delphick excused himself for having interrupted, declined coffee, and produced Miss Seeton's sketches from their folder.

"I'd be interested in your views on these," he said, "if you'd study them for a while—don't worry if you can't make proper sense of them"—hiding a smile—"but if anything at all comes to mind, please tell me." And he waited.

Dickie glanced at the first sketch and said at once: "What powers of persuasion the police have! I'm impressed. Here's poor Juliana, known the chap for years, yet would he accept her kind offer of payment for knocking off a few Old Master copies for the shop? From the way he responded, you'd have said the last thing in the world he wanted to do was work at anything ever again. Then you drop in to see him, and bingo! He runs up a self portrait for you, and I bet—that is, I'm pretty sure he won't even have charged you."

"I wouldn't want that—that nightmare hanging on the walls anyway, Dickie," Juliana said, pulling a face. "What a horrid imagination he must have, and for all those years I never suspected it—and now it's finally broken out. Maybe that's why he refused the commission. How tragic—he knows he can't do it any more, and he doesn't want to admit it."

"Especially to an old friend," agreed Dickie. "I'm only going by what you said about him, but if he's lost his gifts to this extent, then I agree, even though I didn't think much of the chap to begin with—it's a tragedy. I wonder what happened?"

"Goodness knows," said Juliana sadly. "Poor Mentley . . . Oh, I'm sorry, Mr. Delphick. I don't know if he—if Mentley told you I'm a friend of his from years back—when we were all young and enthusiastic and bursting with ideas . . ."

As she shook her head and sighed, Delphick said: "You're sure this is a picture of Mr. Collier, Miss Popjoy? Not some imaginary portrait?"

She frowned. "Certainly, at first sight I was sure, but now I look again, I suppose—"

"*I'm* still sure," Dickie broke in. "It's not just the long hair and that weird dead-eyed way he has of looking at you, it's—well, the flora and fauna *are* pretty weird, too, though I suppose that'll just be a bad dream or something—but the face . . . it—it really is him." He blinked. "I'm surprised, because when you look closely at it . . . but even if I can't tell you why, I simply know it is."

Delphick nodded. Not a bad dream, he suspected, not the nightmare Miss Popjoy had referred to—not literally. But the nightmare of drugs, the distortion and horror they could impart to the mind: *that* was why Mentley Collier must have lost the skill and talent she remembered . . .

"The other drawing," he said and slipped the nightmare head to one side, leaving the interior scene which had so puzzled Chris Brinton clearly in view. Dickie and Juliana leaned over to look.

"Why, isn't that us?" Miss Popjoy turned to Mr. Nash and smiled. "Even if all we can see of you is the back of your head—but it looks just like you, Dickie . . . though I'm not sure I could say why, any more than you could with the other . . . perhaps it's the way you're standing beside me. You look so very protective and possessive! And I love," she added as he turned red, "the long dress he's given me, and my hair—a bun's so unusual, and the little ringlets and the ribbon—how nice to know that he sees me as being unusual. After all these years when I never suspected that he saw me as an exotic—as a *femme fatale* . . ."

227

"You said yourself," Dickie remarked with a halfhearted scowl, "the chap's developed a warped imagination since you knew him . . ." He was concentrating on the sketch and did not notice the darkling look Juliana cast at him. Frowning, he scratched his head.

"Foreign," he corrected her, "not exotic—and it's old-fashioned foreign, as well as mad, with all those birds fluttering about the place. But even if it *is* mad, for some reason this reminds me of something—some painting . . . the tiled floor, and the Persian carpet or whatever it is used as a tablecloth, and the pictures on the walls . . ."

"Now you mention it," said Juliana, "it reminds me, too. The leaded lights on the window, and the way the shadows are dark without being black—which is ridiculous, because he's drawn it in pencil, but I'm sure you know what I mean—it's not *black* black, there's still light in the darkness . . . And he's put himself in," she added, "gazing at me—in admiration, probably." She chuckled. "But don't start brooding, Dickie. After all, he has drawn you protecting me from his wicked wiles—you needn't be jealous."

"I never was." The audacity of this remark made Juliana catch her breath, and while she was still struggling to find some cutting remark, he added: "It's obvious the chap is off his head. Look at this picture: talk about a split personality. Those huge birds swooping in through the window, and flying round the room—despite which, the room itself and the people in it seem so very quiet, somehow, very peaceful— even Collier, oddly enough. With his long hair he looks like a cavalier—or rather no, he doesn't. There's that foreign look again . . ."

"Vermeer," Juliana said after a pause. "Which of them does it remind me of? *The Music Lesson* or *The Concert*? One or other, I'm sure, but I always muddle them. Dutch paintings aren't my speciality."

Dickie slapped his forehead. "You're right—Vermeer," he said as Delphick asked:

"Vermeer? I beg your pardon, Mr. Nash, but—I recognise the name, of course, but my knowledge of the artist is not extensive. If you could enlarge, Miss Popjoy, please?"

"Johannes Vermeer," she obliged. "Familiarly, Jan. Born in Holland in the seventeenth century, twenty years or so after Rembrandt. Noted for capturing light on canvas better than anyone ever did before—modern authorities say he probably made use of something like a camera obscura to help him with perspective and the use of colour, because his eye was remarkable, even by today's standards. Almost like a photograph, only, well, more *real,* somehow. But as I told you, I'm no expert."

Dickie grinned. "Experts aren't always right, remember. Wasn't it Abraham Bredius who said Vermeer conquered reality as a bird conquers gravity? Which is a high-falutin' but marvellous simile for the way the chap, well, makes one particular moment more real than reality, just as Juliana said—a sort of super-photograph, as it were. But even Bredius was fooled by Van Meegeren, so you shouldn't—"

"What!" yelped Bob, who had been sitting so quietly that they'd almost forgotten him. He turned red, then looked at Delphick in apology. "I'm sorry, sir, but—Van Meegeren—I couldn't help thinking . . ."

"Yes," Delphick said thoughtfully. "Van Meegeren. How do you happen to know about that business, Mr. Nash?" Then, before Dickie had time to reply, he added: "Of course, Miss Seeton will have told you when you had lunch together. Daft of us not to remember. My apologies."

Dickie and Juliana regarded each other doubtfully. Miss Popjoy motioned for Mr. Nash to speak. He said, puzzled:

"The topic never came up, Mr. Delphick—no real reason why it should. Is Miss Seeton interested in forgery? When Juliana mentioned she was going to ask—"

"Forgery!" Now it was Delphick who was startled into interrupting a witness, although Bob's yelp didn't come far behind. The chief superintendent drew a deep breath. "We'd better take this more slowly, Mr. Nash. Did Miss Seeton tell you of her, ah, little adventure in Town the other day, when she was coming out of an art gallery and spotted someone, as she thought, who'd been stabbed in the back ? Or do you mean the chap who faked some paintings during the last war, or whenever it was?"

Their looks and little exclamations had convinced him, before he finished, that they'd heard nothing of what had happened in London. In which case he knew he had to make sense of it all, and quickly. The connection was loose, in places, but it was there: drugs, Mentley Collier, his copying skills . . . was his reaction to the thought of Miss Seeton due, perhaps, to an interest she'd shown in some work he would rather not let anyone see?

"I don't know anything about Miss Seeton," Dickie said as Delphick looked to him for a reply. "About Van Meegeren, though, I suppose I know as much as the average art historian, even if my speciality's the Byzantine era—but don't ask me, ask Juliana. Remember, she's a dealer."

"Goodness, yes," said Juliana as Delphick turned an enquiring face towards her. "Every dealer in the world must keep the Van Meegeren story carved on tablets of stone as a ghastly warning, though I doubt if anyone could manage fraud on such a scale nowadays. Imagine if somebody tried it with—oh, I don't know—say Samuel Palmer." She chuckled. "Is anyone going to risk it, with all the expertise the critics have accumulated over the past few years? And Van Meegeren, you could say, really started them off . . ."

"My sergeant and I," Delphick said, "would be grateful for your summary of the case. In plain language, please."

Juliana's noble forehead creased in a frown. "Dickie's sure to correct me if I get it wrong, so—Han Van Meegeren was a Dutch artist, between the wars. Reasonably successful, but he thought he ought to be more appreciated than he was—so he decided to make asses of the critics by, well, creating a masterpiece and having them all claim it rapturously as genuine . . . and he did. And they did—most of them, anyway, though right from the start there were one or two dissenting voices."

"Who were ignored," put in Dickie. "Not surprising, if you think about it—even now, nobody's absolutely certain how many paintings Vermeer left. Somewhere under forty, though. When Van Meegeren produced *Christ and the Disciples at Emmaeus* he could be pretty confident it would be given the benefit of the doubt, if he'd got the obvious technical aspects correct—and he had, more or less, so it was. As Juliana told you."

Chimes were starting to ring in Delphick's head as the links in the connective chain were hammered close. Van Meegeren—forgery—Mentley Collier—Miss Seeton's nightmare sketch—drugs . . . "Go on," was all he said, but it was enough.

Juliana and Dickie looked at each other. Juliana smiled modestly. "Dickie's bound to know the details better than I do—tell Mr. Delphick what happened after the war, Dickie."

Dickie nodded. "That's how he was caught—when he was charged with collaboration, for selling a Vermeer to Hermann Goering. He was imprisoned on a charge of treason, and of course his obvious defence was that he could hardly be sent down for selling a Dutch national treasure to the Nazis when he'd painted it himself—only, he'd done too good a job, and at first they wouldn't believe him, because he told them he'd faked four or five other Vermeers, as well as a couple of, oh, De Hooghs, I think—and they'd been accepted as the real thing, too. So in the end he offered to paint another Vermeer as proof, in prison—and he actually began it, only then he heard they were changing the charge to forgery. You know, I can't help feeling that was a bit sneaky . . ."

Despite their position as upholders of the law, Delphick and Bob found themselves nodding in sympathy as Dickie drew breath, and Juliana took over.

"They found the poor chap guilty and sent him to prison for a year, but he died—a heart attack, I think—before he began the sentence. I must admit, though of course it's a real horror story, there's something about Van Meegeren which does rather appeal to the maverick in me, or"—with a laugh— "the masochist. I'd hate to be taken in as those other dealers were—Goering always excepted, of course." She looked at Delphick in some curiosity. "I don't quite see, though, what all this has to do with Miss Seeton—or with my friend Mentley Collier, either," and she tapped the "self-portrait" with an elegant finger.

Delphick shook his head. "I'm afraid I can't say, just at present. But what you've told us has been most helpful, thank you, and our next step has to be to take these back to Miss Seeton and ask if she'd venture a second opinion on her work. Oh, yes," he added as Juliana and Dickie exclaimed,

"I'm afraid you may both have been misled. Quite by accident, of course—but it wasn't your friend Collier who did these drawings, it was Miss Seeton. And, taking various matters into consideration, I'd like to know why she did . . ."

Chapter 26

THREE MINUTES LATER they were knocking again at the door of Sweetbriars. With relief they heard footsteps approaching.

The door opened. Martha Bloomer stood there. "Well, if it isn't you, Mr. Delphick, and young Anne's hubbie, too, talk about coincidence. I was only thinking of you just now, on account of Miss Emily, you see—"

"Why?" demanded Delphick. "What's happened to Miss Seeton? Where is she?"

"Gone looking for you, so far's I could make out, but it wasn't a very good line. She was in a hurry because of the train, she said—"

"Train? What train? Where?"

Martha began to look a little anxious. "Brettenden, I suppose, but she didn't have time to say much—the train was just leaving, it was the one before running late, so she said, and she'd only rung to catch me when she knew I'd be here doing for her. One of my days, today. Most times she puts a note in the kitchen to say don't bother about dinner, only she left in a bit of a hurry for the bus and forgot—I'd been thinking she'd popped out to the shops when I come in and she wasn't here, you see."

"We thought so, too, when we came round earlier to talk to her. After she, it seems, must have been out looking for us—while we were busy over at Murreystone," he added aside to Bob, who nodded grimly. Delphick turned back to Martha. "Did she explain why she wanted to see me—us?"

But Martha, who had known Miss Seeton for many years and was seldom surprised by anything she did, said that all she could recall of her employer's hasty message was something to do with Mr. Delphick, and pictures—oh, and a gallery . . . She hadn't paid too much attention at the time, thinking it to be no more than one of Miss Emily's starts, and Mr. Delphick knew what *they* could be like, if anyone did. But—the look of anxiety was deepening now—he wasn't really worried about Miss Emily, was he?

To which the chief superintendent had to reply that he didn't know whether to be worried or not, but that if Martha could tell him as soon as she heard anything more from Miss Seeton, he would be obliged to her. Superintendent Brinton at Ashford would pass on any messages . . .

From his room at the George and Dragon, Delphick took his own advice and telephoned Ashford, demanding to speak to Brinton. There came an agonising wait, during which Bob ground his teeth and Delphick muttered. At long last—it felt too long—Brinton's familiar boom crackled its way across the wires.

"Chris, have you heard anything from Miss Seeton?" asked Delphick, without bothering to announce who or where he was. "And have you got anything more out of Barkway or Collier?"

"Oracle, if that's you, then for goodness' sake don't give me heart failure like that. I haven't heard a sausage from Miss Seeton, which is nice and peaceful and how I'd like it to st— What?"

Delphick didn't repeat the oath. "Barkway and Collier, Chris. What about them?"

"Collier's keeping his lip buttoned all right—better late than never, I suppose he thinks. As for Barkway, he's a bright lad, more's the pity. Parrot's the word for him. All *he'll* say is 'Where's my solicitor?' There's still no sign of Proctor. A fast train'd do it in an hour, but since Barkway made his first call to the blighter's clerk . . ."

Delphick did calculations in his head. "She ought to be there by now, if she was coming to you. Chris, if she shows up, grab her and keep hold of her, will you? But I have the nasty suspicion she may not."

"Suits me fine," Brinton couldn't help saying, though he sobered quickly. "Why the panic? What's MissEss getting up to now?"

"Taking time to consult with the bosses," Delphick said, sounding anxious. "Barkway's brief, I mean. And I suspect that Miss Seeton could be among the topics of conversation, because if the word's been passed to the gang that they're now short two members—and that she happened to be indirectly responsible for creating that shortage . . ."

"You've lost me," said Brinton. "Why should—?"

"Sorry, Chris, no time for that. I've got to ring the Yard. If she turns up, tell them—they'll see that I hear about it. Sergeant Ranger and I are heading back to Town in two minutes flat. We'll be in touch."

Delphick depressed the cradle twice, heard a fresh tone, and dialled Whitehall 1212, as it would always be to him.

"Fraud, please—Inspector Borden . . ." He drummed impatient fingers on the table while Bob groped in his trouser pocket to make sure the car keys were ready and waiting.

"Sir," he ventured, "shouldn't we check with Brettenden station for which trains were running late? Then at least we'd have some idea of—"

Delphick cursed, broke the connection, and groped for the directory in the bedside table. "I should have thought of that, Bob. No sense in going off half-cocked."

Nine minutes later he was dialling Scotland Yard again. British Rail (Brettenden) had answered the telephone after what seemed like an age, saying gleefully in reply to Delphick's urgent questions that *all* trains were subject to delay, and they really couldn't say when things would be back to normal. Delphick claimed rank and demanded to know more. At last the station-master was dragged to the telephone, to admit that yesterday had apparently been Signalman Chipping's birthday. Signalman Chipping had visited every pub in Tonbridge before coming on duty. The knock-on effect of Signalman Chipping's spree had already lasted some hours, and nobody knew how long it would take to clear the backlog.

"Borden? Delphick here. Sorry—that was me on the line ten minutes ago, but we, er, got cut off. What do you know about the Van Meegeren art gallery in the Haymarket?"

"Van Meegeren? Nothing much, sir, in the sense I understand you to mean—they like to keep rather a low profile, in some respects. A leg-pull, of course, the name, but all good fun for the in-crowd—er, you do know what I'm talking about, sir?" he added, cautiously tactful.

"I've just had a ten-minute lecture on Vermeer, thanks. Now I want to know about Van Meegeren the gallery as opposed to Van Meegeren the forger. And fast."

"As I said, sir, there doesn't seem much to know. Some of the paintings are genuine—no Vermeers, of course—but plenty of copies as well. Not forgeries, though. Quite a reputation for honest dealing, they've got: yellow price tags instead of red, as I recall, and the name itself is a dead give-away, in any case. A couple of our lads weaseled into the opening party to give 'em the once-over. They said everyone was nudge-nudge enjoying it as one great unspoken joke."

"Unspoken, therefore perhaps not properly understood by everyone—and nobody liking to admit their ignorance for fear of being thought untrendy. Very clever," Delphick said grudgingly. "There's a subtle mind behind all this, if I'm not mistaken. Whose?"

"The owners, sir? That's what I meant about sometimes keeping a low profile. Nobody seems to know who put up the cash, but nobody seems to care, either. A hint of mystery doesn't do their publicity any harm—"

"So everyone's talking about the place—people go there a lot? It's busy?" And Miss Seeton, if she popped in as he feared she intended, ought to be safe among a crowd . . .

"Busy enough, I suppose. I've looked in a few times, and there's usually a couple of people wandering around—"

"Then they know you. As a copper?"

"I couldn't say, sir. Probably. I've been in this job a few years now, not that I'm exactly a household name like you, sir, but—"

"Then it's no use asking you. We don't want them scared off before we can get there. Borden, I want you to dig out someone who can spend the next hour or so looking like an aesthete and send 'em along to Van Meegeren to watch for signs of trouble. To watch out for Miss Seeton, in fact—"

"Not the Battling Brolly, sir?" Borden's voice sounded anguished and pleading. "You don't mean MissEss!"

"I'm afraid I do. I suspect she may be on her way to the gallery because she's rumbled them—quite by accident, of course—as the money-laundering base for that drugs operation I've spent the last few months trying to nail. And I don't want her involved in any more accidents, Borden. You know what she's like. She'll rush in all innocence and tut-tut-tut, such debasement of art is hardly ethical, and if we can't stop them they'll be stuffing her in a sack and chucking her in the Thames to shut her up."

There came an audible groan down the telephone wires, as Borden said weakly, "Someone to be sent to the gallery, sir. Will do. Right away . . ."

"Have warrants sworn out, and we'll raid the place when Ranger and I arrive back in Town. Tell your man not to try anything unless he hears the sound of picture frames falling from the walls, or shouts for help, or a small riot. Where Miss Seeton goes, chaos generally goes with her . . . She could be there already, by the way. Nobody knows when her train was due in. If he sees her wandering about, tell him to fasten on her like a porous plaster and stop her doing anything at all—if he can," he felt obliged to add. "We'll be with you just as soon as possible. Within the hour, if we're lucky on the road."

Inspector Borden had finally gathered his scattered wits together. "But, sir—I know that where MissEss is concerned the only one who understands the way she works is you, but—the gallery's legit, sir, from all we know about it. How could anyone launder drug money without us having our suspicions, at least—never mind Miss Seeton finding out by remote control." He sounded almost aggrieved about it.

"*I* had strong suspicions before I spoke to you, but you clinched it with your talk of a two-colour pricing system. I'm willing to bet the yellow labels—forgeries, copies, call them what you will—are very attractively priced, to pull in the less discriminating punter. The sort who'll buy a picture because of what other people say about it, rather than because he knows the intrinsic value. He pays for it by cheque, the gallery pops the cheque straight in the bank, and everything's sweetness and light until somebody drops by and says, 'Where did you find that clever copy of . . .' of whatever they'd thought it was.

"Whereupon he goes storming back to the gallery and asks to speak to the manager—who says, 'So sorry, didn't realise you didn't realise the yellow labels were copies,' and gives him his money back. In used notes—notes which have been paid to suppliers by junkies wanting a fix . . . The cheque's been cleared, the money's clean. Which is why the paintings have to be fakes, of course—if they weren't, nobody would ask for their money back. Hence Van Meegeren's reputation for shining honesty . . ."

"It might work, sir," admitted Borden, after a pause.

"I'm betting on Miss Seeton that it *does* work—and that she knows it, too. Which is why I want someone round there to keep his eyes skinned—someone who knows Miss Seeton by sight, for preference."

"I'll say to watch for the brolly, sir," Borden said. "On a day like this nobody but MissEss is going to cart an umbrella all the way from Kent, are they?"

"Probably not, Inspector. Which is why I want someone in that gallery before she gets there, because if Barkway—I'll explain about him later—has told them everything he must have been told by Collier—I'll explain about him, too—then the Van Meegeren crowd will know what to look out for, as well . . ."

Miss Seeton, like so many of her generation, is not given to extravagance. Art teachers receive salaries no more generous than any others on the Burnham Scale: their pensions are commensurate with his. Moreover, a child of parents raised according to the Victorian ethic will herself have learned that self-indulgence and laziness are venial sins, to be frowned upon at all times.

It was with a slight feeling of guilt, therefore, that Miss Seeton, on her eventual arrival at Charing Cross, made for the taxi rank and joined the queue. When at last she climbed into a black cab, she gave the breathless instruction to the driver that he should head for Scotland Yard. The expense, Miss Seeton told herself, was more than justified by the lateness of the train, as well as by the handsome retainer paid her by the police; the time she would save by not taking the Tube was surely a good excuse. Mr. Delphick had wished her to produce a likeness of the tomato ketchup man for Inspector—Youngsbury, was his name?—and she had made so many useless attempts to draw one: and then, following his visit with dear Bob, she had found she could remember the man's face, after all. It was her obvious duty to show the results of her work to the chief superintendent, and as soon as possible—he had been, not insistent, but certainly encouraging her in her efforts—and when he could not be found, professional etiquette demanded that she must hand the drawing over to his Scotland Yard colleague. Her colleague, too, she supposed and blushed.

"I thought, you see, that it must be the correct thing to do," she explained to Inspector Youngsbury, "when Maureen told me he was no longer in bed. To bring it to you. Chief Superintendent Delphick, that is. One hesitates to criticise the young, but I remembered that it was on your behalf he asked me to do it the other day, and she said the car had gone, too. So I supposed you would be glad to have it, even though we were not properly introduced on that occasion and would excuse the liberty of my bringing it directly to you without going through the correct channels, as I believe Sir George would say. I understand that police officers are as particular about matters of rank and regiment as serving members of the other forces, except that you are not soldiers, of course. And strictly speaking, I know I should have given it to him. Or sailors, or airmen. To Mr. Delphick, I mean. But she seemed to know nothing of where he was, or Sergeant Ranger, either, although I am quite sure they would never have left without paying."

Inspector Youngsbury's head was spinning. Miss Seeton seemed to be telling him that the Oracle, of all people, had picked up some tart down in Kent and not only gone shares in her with young Bob Ranger—and where did the mysterious Sir George come into all this? The imagination boggled—but could well have skipped before she'd had time to collect her fee. Which he knew couldn't possibly be right, but unless he wrapped a wet towel round his head and concentrated, he'd never make sense of it all . . .

He took a very deep breath and closed his eyes.

A click and a rustle made him open them again. What was she getting out of her handbag—incriminating pictures?

Pictures, certainly—or rather, one picture. The head of a man, sketched in great detail, handed to him with a nod and a smile by Miss Seeton, who snapped her handbag shut and rose to her feet.

"It is such a beautiful day, Inspector, that I believe I will take a little stroll through St. James's Park. There is plenty of time before the gallery closes, I imagine, and the sunshine is so pleasant . . ."

But he wasn't listening to her. He was staring at the neatly sketched head and frowning. Suddenly he smiled.

"It's the bloke who pulled the ketchup scam the other day," he said, and she beamed, proud of having done her duty at last. "It's a hundred times better than all the PhotoFits put together. Thank you very much, Miss Seeton . . ."

But, grateful as he was, after Miss Seeton's departure he took the lift straight to the canteen and drank three large cups of strong black coffee one after the other, and answered all questions absently, with a glazed look on his face.

Chapter 27

MISS SEETON HAD thoroughly dismissed from her memory any hint of having been accused of complicity in the ketchup crime, and of having made her last visit to Scotland Yard under arrest. Gentlewomen do not, in Miss Seeton's eyes, undergo adventures of such a nature, and therefore she herself does not undergo them: particularly as this adventure had been a mistake. The sole reason for her failure to complete her programme of visits to various art galleries had been the rain, which had driven her from the London streets to seek shelter, which had delayed her . . .

But today she had no need of shelter. The sky was blue, the few clouds dancing above were merry fleeces without a thought of rain, the sun shone, and above the traffic the occasional brave bird might be heard to sing. Miss Seeton emerged from Scotland Yard with a smile on her lips, her umbrella on her arm, and sensible walking shoes on her feet. Her conscience was clear: she had delivered the sketch to Mr. Youngsbury, and the remainder of the day was hers to enjoy. There could be no excuse now to take a taxi. She would walk along to St. James's Park, watch the ducks, perhaps sit in the sunshine for a while, then stroll through St. James's to Piccadilly, and thence to the gallery, to resume her interrupted little tour.

She had no idea of how much time passed before she was hovering outside Fortnum & Mason, still unable to make up her mind whether it would be self-indulgent to treat herself to a round of their most excellent sandwiches and a pot of tea. She had thought about it right the way through the Park, although afterwards crossing the streets her concentration had been needed for the traffic. The decision had been put off, and put off; but now she had to decide. Were the attractions of Burlington House sufficiently strong to outweigh the delights of fine bone china, white damask, and paper-thin, crustless triangles spread with unsalted butter?

As she gazed thoughtfully across Piccadilly at the Royal Academy, her eye was caught by a slight commotion farther along, near the entrance to the Burlington Arcade: a commotion which reminded her of something, though the traffic island dividing the bus lane from the rest of Piccadilly's one-way system rendered her view not altogether clear . . . Without thinking, Miss Seeton, still peering between passing cars to make out what was happening, stepped forward to the edge of the pavement.

The Royal Academy is a fine specimen of architecture, so large that it is best appreciated from the Fortnum's side of Piccadilly, that busy thoroughfare. People with cameras are forever stepping backwards unexpectedly, to fit a slightly different angle into their viewfinders.

And it was just such an unexpected backstepper who now blocked Miss Seeton's path—that abstracted path as her attention remained fixed on the far side of the street.

"Oh!" gasped Miss Seeton, throwing out her hands to ward off the solid body whose heavy heel missed her toes by less than an inch.

"Ugh!" exclaimed the photographer as her upflung hands brought her umbrella swinging forward, and its momentum sent it thumping into the base of his spine, knocking him off balance. The camera, a heavy, long-lensed affair, dropped from his grasp on the end of its strap; automatically he tried to catch it, but it tangled in his collar and twisted his jacket to one side. Dishevelled and annoyed, he swung round to face his assailant. "Watch where you're going, can't you!"

"Oh, I do beg your par—" But then Miss Seeton, that stickler for the courtesies, stopped. Suddenly it had come back to her. The face of an angry man—his jacket slipping from his shoulders . . . "Oh, do excuse me," said Miss Seeton breathlessly and scuttled across the road.

"Hey!" he shouted after her. "Hey, just a minute—you might have broken—"

But above the screech of brakes as a bus driver brought his Number 38 to a horrified halt, his protest went unheard.

Miss Seeton, a little shaken by her foolishness but sure duty had demanded it, stood on the traffic island and gazed towards the nearest set of lights, wondering when they would change to red and she might complete her Piccadilly crossing. The man with that scarlet splodge on the back of his jacket was now alone, looking puzzled, staring after the so helpful stranger . . . who was walking eastwards along Piccadilly, trying to melt into the tourist crowds. But the eye of the artist is not easily deceived. Miss Seeton recognised the walk, the carriage, even the clothes of the man she had encountered outside the Van Meegeren Gallery . . .

A Number 19 bus came trundling down from the lights. Miss Seeton had an awful premonition. She set her teeth, raised her umbrella like a baton, and plunged into the slow-moving vehicle stream with a prayer on her lips. Drivers braked, tyres squealed, horns blared—but Miss Seeton was over the road and on the north side of Piccadilly just as the Number 19 went past . . .

And the tomato ketchup man put out an arm, swung himself on to the platform—and was gone.

Miss Seeton let out a little cry of vexation. Take his number! The memorandum page of her diary—open her handbag to look for her pencil—a clatter as her umbrella slipped from her arm and fell to the ground. Bother. She bent to pick it up—the handbag slipped down her arm—she clutched and fumbled as she rose, trying to keep the vanishing Number 19 in view even as she strove to stop everything falling out of her bag—the end of her umbrella waved wildly, in a gesture of beckoning . . .

"Where to, luv?" came a sudden, throaty voice. A taxi rolled towards Miss Seeton, its flag up. "Whatcher want?"

And Miss Seeton, busy sorting out herself and her bits and pieces into their habitual order, knew him at once for her champion—the champion of law and order, indeed. With a brisk snap of her handbag, tucking her brolly for convenience under her arm, she opened the door of the cab and climbed in. She took a deep breath.

"Follow that bus," said Miss Seeton.

The driver looked at her. "You having me on?"

"Indeed I am not. There is a—a person on that bus in whom the police have . . . expressed an interest, and—"

"You *are* having me on. Look, luv—"

Miss Seeton raised her voice, to which years of teaching had given authority in moments of crisis. "As soon as we find an officer of the law, the whole matter may be handed over to him. But, until then, you are wasting time."

The driver took one look in the mirror, met her gaze, and without another word dropped his flag. The taxi moved off into the traffic, the Number 19 still just in view.

After a while the cabbie asked: "Want me to get a bit closer, luv? Then you'll see if he hops off before a stop."

"That is a sensible idea, although he has no idea we are in pursuit, and might reasonably expect the other poor man to be cleaning his jacket, so he is likely to feel confident—the man with the tomato ketchup, I mean." The driver was about to say something, then didn't. "But if," Miss Seeton continued, "it is not too difficult for you to drive rather nearer than at present, please do so."

"Hold tight, then." He jerked the wheel, pressed his foot hard on the accelerator, and darted between two lanes of vehicles so startled that they moved aside to let him pass. "All in the name of the law," he muttered to himself as drivers shook their fists at him. He chuckled.

"Never done this in me life, luv," he told Miss Seeton and cut gleefully in front of a grey Rolls-Royce. "Not with a good reason, anyhow. Hold on—with luck, this time . . ."

The bus had swept round into Piccadilly Circus, the taxi almost on its tail. "Whatcher want doing now?" the cabbie enquired. "Get any closer, he might see you. Not planning to go after him on foot, are you?"

Miss Seeton bridled. "You need have no fears that I intend to leave without paying my fare," she remarked, sitting even more upright on the squashy leather seat, frowning.

"I didn't mean that, luv. But you're hardly the type to go chasing some bloke who for all I know could be twice your size . . ." He eyed Miss Seeton in the mirror again. "Three times, more like." Then he shrugged. "If he spots us, and there's no copper handy, then *I'd* better nobble him for you, luv. I don't like to think of something nasty happening to any fare of mine, I tell you straight."

"That is most kind of you," said Miss Seeton, thinking, as Eros beckoned to them from his pedestal as they passed, that Lord Shaftesbury would have approved this gallantry. "I trust it will not prove necessary, however, and that we encounter a policeman before much longer."

"Never around when you want one," remarked the cabbie, signalling the turn into the Haymarket. "When you don't, mind, they're all over the—"

"Stop!" cried Miss Seeton suddenly. He slammed his foot on the brake. "I mean—no, go on—we must keep the bus in sight—my umbrella," she babbled, groping on the floor with one hand for her brolly, which had shot from her knees as he braked, while with the other struggling to open the side window.

"Go on? You're sure, now?" But the driver, still shuddering from the close shave to his rear bumper, was already responding to the furious hoots of the traffic behind him. "Going on," he said.

On the pavement outside the Van Meegeren Gallery, having emerged on foot from Panton Street with the extra officers requested from the Yard, Delphick and Ranger stood making final plans for the proposed raid. Inspector Borden confirmed that the warrants, duly sworn, were in his pocket ready to brandish at the appropriate time. The Oracle opened his mouth to give the command.

Bob let out a yell and grabbed his superior by the arm. "Look, sir—it can't be—that taxi, quick!"

Delphick winced as he turned to stare after the pointing finger. The taxi accelerated down the Haymarket, hurling Miss Seeton back on the seat, out of sight. Delphick continued to stare as he asked: "That taxi, Sergeant Ranger? What about it?"

"She was signalling for help through the window, sir—she saw us, but they dragged her away—if we don't go after them right now, heaven knows what they might do to her!" Bob was shaking the chief superintendent as a dog shakes a bone. "Sir, we must hurry! You said they'd try to get rid of her, but this is right under our noses—"

Delphick wrenched himself free from the frenzied grasp and gave him one quick look. "You're telling me Miss Seeton is in that taxi?"

"We've only got one chance—she's relying on us, we've already let her down by being late! Come on, sir!"

Borden was squinting down the street. "Which taxi? Did you get the number? There's two or three to choose from."

"It all happened so fast—one of those just behind that Number nineteen, but—"

Borden turned to his henchmen. "You heard the sergeant, lads. Get after them! Taxi following the Number nineteen, one elderly woman passenger, probably a man as well— wouldn't take more than one to keep her quiet, would it?" he added, aside to Delphick. Bob heard him and grew pale. Delphick, too, looked worried.

"Not more than one, no. Your car's round in Oxenden Street, isn't it?"

"All one way," said Borden, preparing to run. "We'll try heading 'em off if they get as far as Pall Mall—leave it to you to chase 'em down the Haymarket, sir," and he was gone. Bob danced from foot to foot, grinding his teeth.

"Orange Street, sir—come on!" And bolted southwards, elbowing unwary pedestrians out of his anguished way.

Delphick sprinted after him, one eye still on what was happening to the taxi—all the taxis—too many taxis, in too heavy a flow of traffic. They might almost try catching up with 'em on foot, he supposed as he panted in Bob's blundering wake, but what if they did? How many heavies had the Van Meegeren gang thought necessary to silence Miss Seeton? Could he and Bob tackle them alone? Borden and his crew would do their best to reach them, but there were those damned one-way streets to contend with . . .

Bob pounded along Orange Street ready to massacre anyone double-parked and blocking his route. A traffic warden took three steps backwards at his approach and tumbled into the gutter. She was just hauling herself out as the slipstream from Delphick's passing tumbled her down again. A gleeful delivery van put paid to her notebook and pencil as she lost her grip on them; she was memorising number plates in fury as the unmarked police car pulled out from the kerb, did a savage U-turn, and hurtled off against the flow of traffic, a huge hand slapping a flashing blue light on the roof.

Miss Seeton had collected herself once more and leaned forward eagerly on the squashy leather seat, eyes fixed upon the Number 19 ahead. The cabbie remarked:

"Sorry about the shake-up, luv, but you did rather catch me on the hop. No bones broken?"

"Thank you, no, a trifle dusty, that is all, and fortunately my umbrella is also undamaged, although of course that is of small importance compared to the need for maintaining our watch on that bus until Chief Superintendent Delphick comes, as I trust he will." She sighed. "I do hope that he understood what I was trying to tell him, for there was really no time to lose if we wanted to keep the bus in sight, and it was somewhat hurried, was it not? My message, I mean, not the bus, for he has no idea that we are following him, and in any case I doubt if he could persuade the driver to go faster in such a heavy flow of traffic. Or, indeed, if anyone could, since I am sure it must be inadvisable to distract the driver of a vehicle when it is in motion. Yet if anyone were to leave it now—the bus, I mean—unobserved . . ."

The cabbie said that, speaking for himself, he hadn't observed anyone getting off, though of course there'd been a tidy bit to think about all at once, what with her sent flying when he jammed on the brakes, and so on; but yes, she'd got the right idea, not much chance of anybody going fast in traffic like this, so if they could only keep close behind the bus, he supposed the bloke she was after stood no chance of getting away, with her being so sure he didn't even know she was after him in the first place . . .

And Miss Seeton instructed him to drive on.

"Get on with it, Bob," urged Delphick as the police car lurched at last into the Haymarket leaving the one-way traffic in Orange Street breathless behind it. "Get weaving, for heaven's sake!"

Bob proceeded to do just that. Vehicles heading south from Piccadilly Circus screeched to an astonished halt at the emergence of the police car from a street they were only permitted to enter; Bob seized his chance, darting into the gap and twisting the steering wheel to force a way through the metallic ranks which recognised his coming and moved aside as far as they were able.

Which was not far enough. The Number 19 bus had passed Charles II Street on the right, Suffolk Place on the left, and was fast approaching New Zealand House on the corner of Pall Mall. All three taxis followed close in its wake—and any one of them could have turned off at any moment.

"Go faster, Bob!" said Delphick, straining to catch any glimpse of untoward activity inside the distant black cabs: flailing arms, a brandished umbrella, perhaps the smashing of a window, the desperate opening of a door. "Faster!"

Miss Seeton, peering forward, did not notice the faraway flash of the blue light; the cabbie did. "Looks like your friends've got the message okay," he said, glancing back in his mirror. "Let's hope they catch us up before Trafalgar Square—gets even busier there."

"Mr. Delphick," Miss Seeton said, "will do his best, I'm sure, and I confess it will be a relief to me to—oh, dear, the lights are changing! Oh, no!" For the Number 19 had been too close to the amber to stop, and lumbered round the corner and into Pall Mall East just as the signal went red. Miss Seeton, staunch upholder of the law, realised she was beaten.

The blue light came swooping at a great rate, its siren wailing; vehicles moved out of the way at its approach, and the cabbie uttered a sigh of relief. "You can tell 'em the tale now, luv," he said as he pulled over to let Bob drive up beside him. "Want me to—hey!"

As Bob drove, Delphick had been examining the passengers in each taxi they passed. A courting couple, oblivious even to the siren, whose activities warranted a red light rather than a blue; a briefcase-toting businessman—unless she'd been wrestled to the floor and rendered unconscious, no sign yet of MissEss. "That taxi—it must be!" he told Bob, and prepared to leap from the car as it slowed.

It slowed. He leaped: flinging open the door and covering the few yards to Miss Seeton's taxi with giant strides. Bob was just behind him, rushing round from the driver's side to grapple with the cabbie while Delphick wrenched the the taxi door almost off its hinges as he saw Miss Seeton's frantic gestures for help.

"Miss Seeton, are you all right?" Then he blinked; she was alone. "What's happened? Where did he go?"

"Why, on the bus, of course," she replied, waving her hands in the same frantic gesture, "as I was trying to tell you—and although, naturally, I am pleased to see you both, would it not be more sensible—not that I would presume to teach you how to do your job, as you know, but suppose he should escape again? Which would be such a waste of all our efforts, I cannot help but feel. You see, when the lights changed . . ."

She waved her hands again, and the gesture seemed just as frantic as before. Her eyes were anxious. "The Number nineteen," she said, "and now the lights are green again, perhaps you will be able to follow it? It would be such a pity, one cannot help thinking, not to do so."

Delphick had to make a quick decision. MissEss's abductor was getting away—unlikely they'd try anything else now the police were there, but in any case she seemed less upset about it all than either himself or Bob, who was still—

"Sergeant Ranger!" Delphick pushed back the sliding glass partition. "Blue-faced cabbies are hardly required at this stage in the proceedings, I think. You'd better let him go and return to the car so that you can escort us in this taxi. Oh, yes"—as Miss Seeton exclaimed and the driver spluttered—"I'm staying right here—we'll have all the explanations later. But, for now, cabbie . . ."

Delphick looked at the traffic lights, and the crawling progress of cars and buses, and listened to the angry hoots of vehicles trying to persuade him to move on. He looked ahead into Pall Mall, and wondered how far along the Number 19 had gone, and whether it would have met Inspector Borden and his team just yet . . . He took a deep breath.

"Follow that bus," said Chief Superintendent Delphick.

Chapter 28

"COME OFF IT, Oracle," said Superintendent Brinton. "I told you when you rang from Town that I didn't believe it—and I still don't. What's more, I think you ought to show some consideration for a man with blood pressure like mine . . ."

Delphick had returned, at long last, to Ashford police station, and now sat regarding his old friend with a smile. "I'm hurt that you should doubt my word, Chris. I assure you that I'm speaking the absolute truth. Ring the Yard—anyone you like: Inspector Borden of Fraud, Youngsbury, even those lunatics who pretend to run Traffic Division—every one of them will tell you the same."

Brinton scratched his head and sighed. "Miss Seeton—Miss Emily Dorothea Seeton—your perishing MissEss, that *is* who we're talking about?"

Delphick shrugged. "Naturally."

"And you're seriously expecting me to believe that she hopped into a London taxi and went chasing after a chummie on a bus—and you and your young giant roared after her in an unmarked car—and Borden had to go the wrong way round the one-way system and didn't meet up with the whole kit and caboodle until you were halfway round Trafalgar Square—and—and . . ."

He spluttered and clutched at his hair and closed his eyes. "I still can't believe it," he moaned. "But you keep telling me it's true—that MissEss was let loose on the streets of London and *nothing happened*. It's—it's . . ."

"Incredible?" supplied Delphick with a smile. "I know. I find it hard to credit, myself, and I was there. But let me repeat, Chris, there wasn't a dented bumper, or smashed headlight, or damaged wing to be found from Piccadilly Circus to St.-Martin-in-the-Fields—not due to Miss Seeton, anyway. A thorough-going triumph, in my opinion."

"You stopped the bus without hitting it," Brinton said in a hollow tone.

"Between us, we did—Borden's crowd, Bob, and myself in Miss Seeton's cab. Bob radioed ahead and told Borden what we were really supposed to be doing."

"Chummie was still on board the perishing bus, and he didn't make a run for it."

"He was, and he didn't: he had sense enough to know when the game was up. Besides which, Miss Seeton's verbal identification was positive. It hardly needed the confirmation by PhotoFit, or her sketch—"

"No!" cried Brinton, slapping his hand on the top of his desk. "Don't tell me any more! Giving us all forty fits, making you gallop up to Town to rescue her, and all she was doing was delivering some damned drawing everybody'd forgotten you'd asked her for . . ."

"Everybody except Miss Seeton." Delphick grinned. "And you should know by now how strong her sense of duty is.

She thought it was obvious that, in my absence, she should take it to Inspector Youngsbury at the Yard—"

"And I suppose he was thrilled," Brinton broke in with a glower for the smiling face opposite. "You're going to tell me he thanked her for making it all clear to him, and handed her a medal, and never thought to mention she'd been there when we all started looking for her."

"That's true, more or less. Youngsbury was grateful for the sketch, although it wasn't one of her inspired efforts, more the routine stuff almost anyone could turn out—but be fair, Chris, he didn't know we were looking for her. Nobody thought to tell him. Why should they? He certainly doesn't blame Miss Seeton for anything—thinks she's the best thing since sliced bread, in fact. You should have seen his face when we bowled into the Yard with the tomato ketchup chummie in tow—his name's Mickey Newsell, incidentally. And he's by no means the strong, silent type. Once he realised we'd got him bang to rights, he started singing like a whole symphony of canaries."

Delphick chuckled. "It didn't help his defence, feeble as it was to start with, that he hadn't yet had the sense to lose the day's collection of wallets. Anyone carrying five of the things, all with different names and addresses, needs a pretty good cover story—which, when faced with Miss Seeton's insistence that she recognised him, he simply couldn't produce."

Brinton grunted. "So the tomato ketchup crowd is sewn up nicely—but what about the Van Meegerens? They'll have done a bunk when they realised the game was up, won't they? Owen Barkway's brief took an eternity to get here—time enough to warn the lot, I'm sure."

Delphick shook his head. "I was sure, too. I honestly thought there'd be little evidence left when we eventually reached the gallery, but I was wrong. There *had* been time, only Proctor didn't make sensible use of it. I imagine his reputation as one of the brightest stars in the criminal fraternity's sky will suffer badly as a result of his tardy response to Barkway's telephone call."

"A day at the Oval," marvelled Brinton. "Who'd ever dream of a crook like him enjoying cricket?"

"Patriotism," pointed out Delphick, "is not enough. Our friend Proctor may well have been worrying about the Ashes, but I hardly think that particular argument will wash with his clients—and you'd better be careful about calling him a crook. He's just the type to sue for slander, especially now. The Van Meegerens look set to be the first of a long line of client losses, and he'll miss the income."

Brinton grunted. "Collier seems to be sticking to him, for some crazy reason, though I suppose most artists are a bit crazy. And I'd be grateful if you didn't mention Miss Seeton, thanks. Not that I'd call her crazy, but . . ."

Delphick refused to rise to the bait. "Collier was certainly a very small fish in an ocean of sharks—sharks who are happy to abandon him to his fate, it seems. While they agree he faked pictures for them—only they insist that it was legitimate copying, nothing more—they claim not to be aware that it was to support his drug habit—nor are they aware of the existence of the pigeon post from Amsterdam, or the recently terminated existence of Gerald Sacombe—"

"What d'you reckon," Brinton broke in, "that it wasn't a frenzied junkie missing his fix who did for Sacombe, after all. Owen Barkway's quite slimy enough to have bumped the blighter off so's he could run both supply areas together. Maybe on instructions from the Van Meegeren lot—they're letting him go shares in this new character they've produced to defend 'em, remember. Barkway must know something they don't want known, or they'd have let him go, the way they've done with Collier."

"He knows the supply route from the Netherlands, for a start. Somebody had to train those homing pigeons to come back with two or three grammes of pure cocaine in their leg canisters, ready for adultera—"

"Grammes be damned!" snorted Brinton, who still resented the introduction of decimal currency. "Tell me in good old ounces, and I might start to understand you."

"A gramme," said Delphick, who had boned up on the mysteries of division by ten, "is one-twenty-eighth of an ounce. A dozen pigeons, therefore, can carry around one ounce of cocaine—over a thousand pounds' worth. And I haven't just taken Babs Ongar's word for it," he added as Brinton opened his mouth. "I asked the real experts to check the figures for me . . ." He chuckled. "It took a little time, though. I was given a decided brush-off from the Royal Pigeon Racing Association when I rang to ask them to confirm the Wounded Wings idea of how much weight one bird can carry—canister included, of course. An agitated young woman stuttered that she really didn't know, then handed me over to a chap who virtually hung up on me. I think they feared I wanted to run, or should I say fly, the drugs on my own behalf."

"Can't blame 'em for being suspicious," Brinton growled, "the number of crooks there are on the loose. A handful fewer than yesterday, of course, but still too many."

"We'll try to reduce the numbers even further. We're making full enquiries about shipments of birds to Holland, and with luck we'll be able to follow the trail through. If Barkway turned Queen's Evidence, though, it would be very helpful."

"He won't," Brinton said. "If it wasn't a junkie who did for Sacombe, then it was Barkway, as I said, without even the excuse of withdrawal symptoms. He's the sort of creep who'd be only too glad to do the dirty on a pal—well, business associate"—he pulled an expressive face—"for the money, instructions from above or not. Suppose Sacombe came up with a good swindle and refused to bring Barkway in on it—or suppose Barkway just invented some tale of a swindle as an excuse to get rid of him . . ." He yawned hugely. "If you ask me, the whole boiling lot are as bad as each other, and the more we get rid of, the better. I can't say I really care who does the getting rid. Every time even one link in the chain's busted, it makes our job just that little bit easier . . ."

His yawn was infectious: Delphick found himself stretching and rubbing his eyes. "It's been an exciting day," he said. "Satisfying, too. Miss Seeton has helped to sort out the Tomato Ketchup Gang, which has made Inspector Youngsbury very happy; she and her drawings have been responsible for the partial breaking of an international drug ring, and if all goes well, we'll be able to finish the job she began; we can't yet be sure who killed Gerald Sacombe, but everything suggests he was tied in with the Van Meegeren operation—as they seem to have controlled a sizable chunk of this area, I can't believe they would have allowed an outsider to share even a small part of their territory. Collier will give us the answers before long, I fancy.

If, indeed, as you said yourself, it really matters who removed a blot like Sacombe from the landscape. He was only a small blot, and we aim to mop up the big ones—which, with the help of Miss Seeton, I rather think we've done."

"And all," marvelled Brinton, "without anything happening. Just a car chase—uneventful, at that. Which must be a record for one of MissEss's cases. Nobody hurt, nothing smashed. A red-letter day, this is, Oracle, a red-letter day and no mistake. The only time that woman has pulled it off without some sort of chaos ensuing." He rubbed the tip of a thoughtful nose. "What have you done with her, by the way? You surely never left her to make her way back from Town by herself. Things were bad enough on the railways this morning without the risk of her making it worse in the afternoon."

"She was slightly bothered at first about wasting the unused half of her cheap day return ticket, but we persuaded her to come back with us by car after she'd given her statement to Inspector Youngsbury. We, er, thought it safer not to risk it." Delphick hid a smile. "Of course, she had to wait at the Yard while we began enquiries into the Van Meegeren case, but she saw it as her duty, so she didn't mind. Our canteen cook did her proud with tea and buns, poor chap, but she said she wasn't really hungry after all the excitement and turned out rather a jolly sketch of him by way of apology for not eating anything. He's thrilled. And talking of tea, that's where she's gone. I spotted her looking a little wistful as we drove down the main street with all the tea shops shut, and knowing what the Ashford police canteen is like, I told Bob Ranger to take her to—"

The telephone shrilled on Brinton's desk just as there came a tap on his office door. He called out: "Come in!" and picked up the receiver; then dropped it again, his mouth agape, as the door opened and four battered figures appeared—three large men, one far larger than the others, and . . .

"Miss Seeton!" gasped Delphick while all Brinton could do was stare. "Foxon! Ranger! What on earth . . ."

The men merely gazed at him. Bob risked a quick grimace in Miss Seeton's direction. Foxon, his kipper tie hanging by a thread from his neck, looked resigned; the third, unknown man looked stunned. Miss Seeton trotted forward.

"Oh, dear, Chief Superintendent, I am so sorry—and of course I must also direct my apologies to you, Mr. Brinton, as it was one of your police cars involved. Yours, too, Mr. Delphick, naturally—"

"Naturally," echoed Delphick as Brinton groaned.

"Because dear B—er, Sergeant Ranger was driving it, you see, and when I recognised them as we were leaving the hotel—such a delicious tea, most generous—they took one look at us and jumped into the car. And drove away. Rather too fast," she said, "if one is going down a one-way street, I fancy, and then there was the red light as well . . ."

"Red light," moaned Brinton. "One-way street—didn't you put your sirens on, you idiots? And in any case, just why were you in such a hurry to get away after you saw . . ." His eye turned to Miss Seeton standing innocent and bedraggled before him. He choked and fell silent.

"Beg pardon, sir," said Foxon as his unknown companion struggled for words, and Bob Ranger cleared his throat with unusual thoroughness. "It wasn't us, sir, that jumped the light—we were coming the other way, minding our own business, and they went slap into us—"

"Don't tell me any more," Brinton begged, his face going purple. "Please, just keep quiet while I—and *you* can shut up, as well!" to the telephone, which was swinging from its cord emitting urgent little squawks. He banged it down on the cradle, then took it off again. "Let's get one thing at a time sorted out," he said. "As if I couldn't guess."

"Well, sir, we got them," Foxon pointed out cheerfully. He was a better judge than the rest of Brinton's ability to survive apoplexy. "The Standons—the hotel fraudsters. They were coming in to register as Miss Seeton and Sergeant Ranger were on their way out: grandfather, parents, two kids all nice and tidy. They recognised Miss Seeton just as she recognised them . . ."

"He was walking without his sticks and had dyed his hair," said Miss Seeton, "but the bones were unmistakable—the older man, that is, even though he had shaved off his moustache. For disguise in perpetrating another fraud, I suppose, but the children have inherited the same structure, from his daughter, that is. Such a pity. That they have not been taught right from wrong, which is what fraud is, is it not? For which, I fear, one must blame their elders. So foolish, that they tried to deny knowing me—the parents, I mean, because I spoke to them for some time only yesterday, and they are not usually as good at concealing their feelings, are they? As adults. And I do have some experience of them, after all. Children, I mean. And perhaps I am flattering myself," said Miss Seeton modestly, "but I was rather of the opinion that they were pleased to see me again, even if their parents and grandfather were not, for had they been they would hardly have turned round and run back to their car and driven away in such a hurry."

"The wrong way down a one-way street," supplied Foxon in a tone he struggled to keep calm, "because they didn't know Ashford at all—but of course, Sergeant Ranger does, after the number of times he's been here. He knew where to go to head them off at the pass, as you might say, sir, only . . ."

He gave up the struggle and began to snort with glee as he motioned to Bob to take over the story. With shaking shoulders Bob did so. "Only I'm afraid, sir"—carefully looking directly between Brinton and Delphick, dividing the wrath to come— "that we weren't the only ones at the pass, or rather the traffic lights. Which were, well, which were red when the Standons went through them—with me and Miss Seeton right behind—and . . . and . . ."

"And me and Buckland," Foxon took over as Bob succumbed, "coming in from the side. A lovely mess we made of their car, sir—the Standons', I mean. Took Traffic half an hour to sort it all out and get things moving again, and I think Highways is going to hit us for the cost of a new bollard—plus the 1-lamp standard that sort of got m-mixed up in . . ."

As Foxon once more gave way to his mirth, Delphick, who had been listening with growing amusement while he observed Miss Seeton's reaction to her friends' hysteria, struggled to keep his voice calm. He regarded Brinton's purple face with pity.

"Just a car chase," he reminded the superintendent in a shaking voice. "Un-uneventful, at that . . ."

"Hardly *uneventful*, sir," said Bob without thinking and indicated the dishevelment of his companions. "I wouldn't exactly call it that."

Delphick looked at Brinton. "I don't think the superintendent would call it that, either. I somehow think he'd prefer the term *red-letter day* . . ."

And gave himself up to laughter.

Preview

Lucky Miss Seeton! A modest Premium Bond win means a whole week in magical Glastonbury. She can draw and drink in the surroundings, just what she needs for her scene-painting role in the village production of 'Camelot'.

By coincidence, the kidnapped Heir to an industrial family may be hidden around there and Chief Superintendent Delphick has asked the ex-art teacher to create some of her famous, insightful sketches. Even he is nonplussed by the resulting images of capering sheep in straitjackets, flashing false teeth!

But the Heir is in danger, a murderer is lurking, and the first victim may not be the last. Then fortune favors Miss S again, her raffle ticket winning her a hot air balloon flight, and well, it's just amazing what you can see from above . . .

The new Miss Seeton mystery

COMING SOON!

About the Miss Seeton series

Retired art teacher Miss Seeton steps in where Scotland Yard stumbles. Armed with only her sketch pad and umbrella, she is every inch an eccentric English spinster and at every turn the most lovable and unlikely master of detection.

Further titles in the series—

Picture Miss Seeton
A night at the opera strikes a chord of danger
when Miss Seeton witnesses a murder . . . and paints
a portrait of the killer.

Miss Seeton Draws the Line
Miss Seeton is enlisted by Scotland Yard when her
paintings of a little girl turn the young subject into a
model for murder.

Witch Miss Seeton
Double, double, toil and trouble sweep through
the village when Miss Seeton goes undercover . . .
to investigate a local witches' coven!

Miss Seeton Sings
Miss Seeton boards the wrong plane and lands
amidst a gang of European counterfeiters. One
false note, and her new destination
is deadly indeed.

Odds on Miss Seeton
Miss Seeton in diamonds and furs at the roulette table?
It's all a clever disguise for the high-rolling spinster . . . but
the game of money and murder is all too real.

Miss Seeton, By Appointment
Miss Seeton is off to Buckingham Palace on a secret
mission—but to foil a jewel heist, she must risk losing the
Queen's head . . . and her own neck!

Advantage, Miss Seeton
Miss Seeton's summer outing to a tennis match serves up more than expected when Britain's up-and-coming female tennis star is hounded by mysterious death threats.

Miss Seeton at the Helm
Miss Seeton takes a whirlwind cruise to the Mediterranean—bound for disaster. A murder on board leads the seafaring sleuth into some very stormy waters.

Miss Seeton Cracks the Case
It's highway robbery for the innocent passengers of a motor coach tour. When Miss Seeton sketches the roadside bandits, she becomes a moving target herself.

Miss Seeton Paints the Town
The Best Kept Village Competition inspires Miss Seeton's most unusual artwork—a burning cottage—and clears the smoke of suspicion in a series of local fires.

Hands Up, Miss Seeton
The gentle Miss Seeton? A thief? A preposterous notion—until she's accused of helping a pickpocket . . . and stumbles into a nest of crime.

Miss Seeton by Moonlight
Scotland Yard borrows one of Miss Seeton's paintings to bait an art thief . . . when suddenly *a second* thief strikes.

Miss Seeton Rocks the Cradle
It takes all of Miss Seeton's best instincts—maternal and otherwise—to solve a crime that's hardly child's play.

Miss Seeton Goes to Bat
Miss Seeton's in on the action when a cricket game leads to mayhem in the village of Plummergen . . . and gives her a shot at smashing Britain's most baffling burglary ring.

Miss Seeton Plants Suspicion
Miss Seeton was tending her garden when a local youth was arrested for murder. Now she has to find out who's really at the root of the crime.

About the Author

The Miss Seeton series was created by Heron Carvic; and continued after his death first by Peter Martin writing as Hampton Charles, and later by Sarah J. Mason under the pseudonym Hamilton Crane.

Heron Carvic was an actor and writer, most recognizable today for his voice portrayal of the character Gandalf in the first BBC Radio broadcast version of *The Hobbit*, and appearances in several television productions, including early series of *The Avengers* and *Dr Who*.

Born Geoffrey Richard William Harris in 1913, he held several early jobs including as a interior designer and florist, before developing a successful dramatic career and his public persona of Heron Carvic. He only started writing the Miss Seeton novels in the 1960s, after using her in a short story.

Heron Carvic died in a car accident in Kent in 1980.

Hamilton Crane is the pseudonym used by Sarah J. Mason when writing 15 sequels and one prequel to the Miss Seeton series. She has also written detective fiction under her own name, but should not be confused with the Sarah Mason (no middle initial) who writes a rather different kind of book.

After half a century in Hertfordshire (if we ignore four years in Scotland and one in New Zealand), Sarah J. Mason now lives in Somerset—within easy reach of the beautiful city of Wells, and just far enough from Glastonbury to avoid the annual traffic jams.

Note from the Publisher

While he was alive, series creator Heron Carvic had tremendous fun imagining Emily Seeton and the supporting cast of characters.

In an enjoyable 1977 essay Carvic recalled how, after having first used her in three short stories, "Miss Seeton upped and demanded a book"—and that if "she wanted to satirize detective novels in general and elderly lady detectives in particular, he would let her have her head ..."

You can now **read one of those first Miss Seeton short stories** and **Heron Carvic's essay in full**, as well as receive updates on further releases in the series, by signing up at farragobooks.com/miss-seeton-signup